MYSTERY
OF
THE DEAD
POLICE

Philip MacDonald

MYSTERY
OF
THE DEAD
POLICE

Vintage Books

A Division of Random House

New York

First Vintage Books Edition, January 1985
Copyright 1933 by Philip MacDonald

Copyright renewed 1961 by Philip MacDonald. All rights
reserved under International and Pan-American
Copyright Conventions. Published in the United States by
Random House, Inc., New York. Originally published
by Doubleday and Company in 1933. Published by
arrangement with Doubleday & Company, Inc.

Library of Congress Cataloging in Publication Data
MacDonald, Philip.
Mystery of the dead police.
Reprint. Originally published: [Garden City, N.Y.]:
Doubleday, 1933.
I. Title.
PR6025.A2218M9 1985   823'.912   84-50302
ISBN 0-394-72670-7

Manufactured in the United States of America

Chapter I
RAID

IN 1900 the population of the small town of Farnley in Surrey was eight thousand and ninety-four. In 1910 this figure had increased by two hundred. In 1920, owing to certain depletions in the male population, it had sunk to eight thousand and sixty. But in 1930 it had increased out of all knowledge—the official figure being no less than fourteen thousand, seven hundred and thirty-eight.

This sudden giant stride was due to the idea, shyly enough inaugurated in the three years immediately following 1918 but boldly swelling with each succeeding year, that because a man must work in the grey and dangerous jungle of London it does not follow that he must eat his evening meal there and sleep there and spend there his Saturday afternoons and Sabbaths.

In 1920 Farnley was to the eye much as it had been in 1870. But in 193— one could not, except from the air, see any of the 1870 Farnley (which, after all, was only a few buildings removed from the 1770 Farnley) without first nosing one's way through an uneven but dense belt of the new Farnley. All round the old Farnley, in a continuous and ever-widening and uneven belt, there had sprung up new living boxes, until the town as a whole was like a horse's tooth in that one could tell its age by the rings. Outermost ring—green tiles, white plaster, severe formalistic line, 1932: next ring—red tiles, ye olde half-timberinge and Colonial porch, 1929: next ring—parti-coloured tiling, red brick, white paint and pergolas, 1925–27: innermost ring—grey slate, fretwork porticos, and peeling green paint combined with yellowing white Georgian simplicity, the old Farnley itself.

In 1925 there had been a cinematograph show every Monday and Friday evening in the Assembly Rooms—price of tickets threepence to a shilling, children half price, no dogs or babies in arms admitted, smoking strictly disallowed, and money back upon those frequent occasions when, the film having broken halfway through Reel Two, the operator was unable to join it before a quarter to eleven. Today in Farn-

5

ley there is not only the colossal Pantheon Picturedrome—
all Ionic pillars and organ solo, seating capacity fifteen hundred—but there are also, scattered about here and there
among the various rings of villadom, no fewer than three
other cinematograph theatres, all fitted with the latest sound
equipment and, although not so large and lururious as the
Pantheon, of great comfort and efficiency.

In 1925 that section of the Surrey constabulary which
policed the small town had its headquarters in the cottage
of the sergeant in charge—Number Four Sunflower Lane.
Today there stands in the very centre of the old High
Street—where had once stood the shy, shabby, and altogether gentlemanly little house of Vice Admiral (retired) Sir
Roger Wetherby, R.I.P.—an imposing and aggressively post-
war Germanic erection of bright red brick over whose bronze
and gun-proof glass door hangs a blue lamp upon each side
of which appears in letters of white the word Police.

There are now, instead of four, no fewer than twelve
policemen to deal with Farnley as it should be dealt with.
There is also, resident in Farnley, an inspector, although
his duties are not solely confined to Farnley. The twelve
are made up of two sergeants, three senior constables, and
seven ordinary constables. They direct the traffic in Farnley; they patrol the straight, narrow streets of the old Farnley and the broad circular streets of the new Farnley; they
pass small boys along, flash bull's-eye lanterns into shop
doorways; occasionally, if they are feeling cross, make
rude remarks to the occupants of the cars that still persist
in lining Shotters Hill upon dark nights; arrest tramps, direct Americans to the old church, and generally do all the
hundred and one things of which the country town policeman's duties are composed.

Upon the night of the 12th of May, 193— there were six
men on the premises of Farnley's grand new police station.
Two of these may immediately be discounted, they being
prisoners in the small line of new cells at the back of the
station. The other four were all in the Charge Room, which
led immediately, through the door of bronze and gun-proof
glass, onto the old High Street. Seated upon a high stool
behind the high desk was Sergeant Thomas Guilfoil, comfortably paunched, sandy-tonsured, and, to ease his bull-like
throat growing weekly too tight for last year's tunic, par-
tially unbuttoned. Upon one of the benches which lined
the yellow-washed walls sat, in a row, like three enormous
but painfully clean urchins, Constables Farrow, Clintock,

and Brown. Normally there would only have been one of those three upon night duty, but of late weeks there had come in the country immediately surrounding Farnley an alarming succession of motor bandit raids. The chief constable of the county had promised added protection to garage proprietors and other sufferers. That he was endeavouring to keep his word was shown by the extra night-duty men on call and the fact that of these one was a qualified car driver. The police car, ready for instant use, stood at this moment in the covered alleyway behind the cells.

Among themselves Farrow, Clintock, and Brown whispered and giggled, seeming more than ever urchin-like. The round clock upon the wall immediately over the bent head of Sergeant Guilfoil chimed twelve times. With the last chime there mingled the shrill and angry pealing of the bell of the telephone which stood at the sergeant's right hand. The giant urchins ceased their play, turned three suddenly adult faces towards the high desk. Guilfoil lifted the receiver and spoke into the mouthpiece.

"Police station," he said. "Sergeant in charge speaking. . . . Speak up! I can't 'ear you. . . ."

The three men upon the bench heard an excited cackling from the receiver. They could not catch words, but they saw from the sudden tensity of Guilfoil's attitude and the raising of his sandy eyebrows that here was something beyond the usual.

". . . 'Ow many?" said Guilfoil urgently. ". . . All right. . . . Do your best. . . . I'll send 'elp by car."

He slammed the receiver back onto its hook. He looked at Constable Farrow. "Car!" he said. "Round the front— quick!"

Farrow, a young and heavy-seeming giant who yet moved quickly like a cat, was gone, snatching his helmet from the bench beside him. The door of the interior of the station swung violently with the speed of his going.

Guilfoil looked at the other two men, now on their feet. He spoke to the senior. "Brown, you're in charge. Get in the car, go like 'ell to Sir John Morton's. Know it?"

Brown nodded. "Yes," he said. "Big house two miles out on the Frenton Road."

From outside, muffled by the thick walls, came the sudden roar of a car's engine.

"That's Farrow," said Guilfoil. "Move now! And better take these." He jerked open a drawer in the right-hand side of the desk and from it pulled two service Webleys.

"Coo!" said Constable Clintock.

Brown went up to the desk and took the revolvers.

"One for you," said Guilfoil, "one for Farrow. Clintock 'ere 'asn't passed 'is test."

From the street outside came three blaring notes from a hooter. Farrow was ready.

Guilfoil looked at the stolid Brown. "Go careful,' he said. "Message was from Sir John's butler. 'E says there's armed raiders in the 'ouse. 'E thinks they've got someone. They've got a car outside. Use your own judgment and be off! This might mean . . ."

What it might mean was never destined to reach Brown's ears. Followed by the gaping Clintock, he was gone. The door to the street slammed behind them. Sergeant Guilfoil sat back in his chair. From his sleeve he pulled a handkerchief and mopped at a flushed face. To his ears came the screeching whine of the car going off up the High Street in second gear.

"Blow me *tight!*" said Sergeant Guilfoil. For things were happening in Farnley. He was not certain whether or not he liked them to happen, but he was entirely certain that no fault could be found with his handling of the situation. The very least possible time had elapsed between his receiving the message and the setting off of the car. He was glad that it was Brown's turn for duty. A good man, Brown —next on the list for sergeant. A good, steady man. Sergeant Guilfoil breathed hard and, twisting his fatness round in his high chair, looked at the clock. His fingers fumbled at his tunic pocket and took from it a yellow packet. With an air faintly surreptitious he lit a cigarette. He was rattled —he admitted to himself that he was rattled—and there's nothing like a draw to quiet a chap down.

2

The turning into the drive of Fairlawns is more than right-angled and very awkward, but Farrow could drive. The police car, which had been doing its very best sixty-five along the straight macadamed surface of the Frenton Road, slackened at the right moment, was changed down miraculously just before the turning, and, swinging right with a velocity which shot Clintock from one side of the back seat to the other, swept into and up the long winding drive.

There was no other car before the house. There were no

lights in any of the many windows. The moon looked placidly down upon the placid and ugly and dignified house. No
sound except the muffled throbbing of the police-car engine
disturbed the silver quietness. Brown, standing at the foot
of the steps which led up to the porticoed and pillared
front door, put up a hand to his head. The fingers of the
hand tilted his helmet forward and scratched at his clipped
back hair.

"Rum!" said Brown. "Damn rum . . . !" He turned to
Farrow. "Tom, you slip round the back. Keep your eyes
skinned. Clint, you stop 'ere."

He marched up the six shallow steps and shone the light
of a torch this way and that about the massive door. To
the right-hand side of it, halfway up, was a bell push. Upon
this he set the end of a square thumb and pressed. From
somewhere within the house came a steady, muffled pealing.

For a long time nothing happened. With stolid persistence
Brown kept his thumb upon the bell push. The muffled pealing of the bell went on becoming, at least to the ears of the
listeners, a permanent part of the night.

And then a beam of yellow light shone suddenly from a
window near the roof and above the portico. There came
the sound of an impatient rattling of this window and then,
as it opened, a sleepy and angry voice which made hoarse
demands of the night.

Brown took his thumb from the bell push and went down
the steps two at a time and stood upon the flags of the
terrace. He looked up at the open window, from which he
could see there leant a head and shoulders.

The hoarse demands were being repeated, yet more
angrily.

"Never you mind!" said Brown with placid authority.
"Police 'ere. Just you come down."

The window was slammed with a force which threatened
to break its glass. After a minute's interval the light went
out. After another minute or two there came sounds from
behind the front door—the screeching rattle of bolts being
withdrawn, the chinking rattle of a chain being dropped.
Brown went up the steps again. As he reached the last
the door opened and a light in the roof of the portico
burst into life. He found himself looking at a small and
square and bald-headed person from beneath whose dark,
enshrouding dressing gown protruded some inches of striped
pyjamas, more of bony ankle, and a pair of heelless slippers.

Brown stuck to the time-honoured formula: "Now, then," he said. "What's all this?"

The door opener gibbered. What, Brown made him out to say, was all what? Why, he went on more coherently, did the police want to come creating disturbances at gentlemen's houses in the middle of the night? When he told Sir John, Sir John, Brown gathered, would be indignant, and righteously so. And when Sir John was indignant—which was very rarely, Sir John being a perfect gentleman—things got uncomfortable for those that deserved to have things made uncomfortable for them.

Brown unhooked his right thumb from his belt. His right hand went with a queer uncertain little gesture to the pocket in which there lumpily reposed the heavy service revolver. He felt, increasingly with every moment, that the legs of Farnley's police force had been pulled. He managed at last to cut across the flow of outraged eloquence.

" 'Oo are you?" he said. And was immediately informed with shrill indignation that he was talking to Henry Bates and that Henry Bates was Sir John Morton's butler. And no mushroom growth, either. Henry Bates, it appeared, had been with Sir John Morton not for ten weeks but for ten years. And during those ten years Henry Bates could not remember a more outrageous performance than tonight's. If the police thought . . . And so on and so on.

"That's as may be," said Brown heavily. "But I've got my duty. A telephone call was received at the police station at one minute after twelve *pur*portin' to come from Sir John Morton's butler and *re*portin' that this house was in the 'ands of criminals. We'll just take a look round." Ponderous and unsmiling and with a certainty of demeanour which was by no means reflected in his inner mind, he pushed aside Mr. Henry Bates and entered the hall of Fairlawns.

3

It was a quarter to one when Farrow brought the car to a halt before the police-station door. Clintock and Brown got out. Farrow backed the car towards the alleyway at the side of the station. Brown went up the two steps and pushed open the heavy door and went in, followed by Clintock.

"Look 'ere, Sergeant," Brown began, "somebody's bin . . ." His voice died away in mid-sentence. He turned with a grin to Clintock at his elbow. Clintock whistled, and a broad smile threatened to cut in half his round, red, infantile face.

"Blimey!" he said, whispering. "Good job 'twas us and not inspector."

For Sergeant Guilfoil was asleep. He was still in his high chair at his high desk, but his head had fallen forward and now—his right cheek pillowed on his blotting pad, his arms out of sight beneath the desk—he slumbered in great peace.

Brown winked at Clintock. The wink said: Watch me give him a shock. He went, heavy-footed, towards the desk. He stood in front of it and rapped on it with imperious knuckles. Clintock tiptoed up to stand at his left shoulder.

"Sleeps heavy," said Clintock, the smile still broad upon his face.

"Does that!" said Brown. His voice was puzzled. "I wonder if . . . *Good Goddlemighty!*"

He took a sharp pace back from the desk. The colour had suddenly fled from his usually red cheeks. He slowly raised his right arm so that the index finger of its hand was pointing straight at Guilfoil's head.

"Look!" said Brown. "Look!"

Clintock, moved to sudden aghast action at something in the voice, came round and stood at Brown's shoulder. From here he could see what he had not seen before—Sergeant Guilfoil's forehead—and in the middle of Sergeant Guilfoil's forehead was a neat round black hole as big, perhaps, as a half-crown.

Sergeant Guilfoil, when at last the two men were sufficiently freed from horrified astonishment to go to him, was found to be very dead.

Chapter II

EXTRACT FROM A DIARY

13th May, 193—

It worked, it worked, it worked! Of course I knew it would, because the plan was perfect. But, on the other hand, I was afraid that it mightn't; that something or other, some one of the thousand things that might have gone wrong, could crop up and spoil everything. But no! Telephone call from the box at the station at midnight; walk the three hundred yards from the station yard to the corner of High Street; wait in the shadow to watch the car go off and out of sight; stroll up to the station and walk in; tell the one at the desk my little story about being stranded for the night; wait till he's in just the right position, and then out with Martha—and plonk!—there you are! Martha made hardly any noise at all; no more noise than if somebody had dropped a wet cloth onto the floor. That Reeve-Armstrong's the best silencer yet.

There it was, all as smooth as butter! I'd rehearsed it in my mind often enough, God knows. But never did it go off quite as smoothly as the real thing last night.

Well, that's one. And thank the Lord I managed it on the date!

Chapter III
LOVING CUPS

POLICE CONSTABLE X.L. 8543 Henry Beecham was new to Mayfair. This was the first night duty he had done since his transfer, a week ago, from J.B. Division. J. B., as you may or may not know, looks after the larger and rougher half of London's more easterly end. Life in J.B., or in that part of its orbit in which Henry Beecham had operated, had been far from a bed of roses; night duty, especially, being both eventful and dangerous. So persistently eventful and so frequently dangerous that—it's one pleasing factor —it had been the rule that policemen went always, between the hours of nine p.m. and eight a.m., in indissoluble couples.

Henry Beecham was not sure whether he was going to like the change. At first he had been certain, but that had been for a week of day duty. Now, at two-thirty in the morning of the 9th of June, he strode silently and slowly along Bruton Street, which formed the western limit of his beat, and took stock of his situation. By the time he had reached the corner of the quaint little backwater of Fothergill Street, he had come to a definite conclusion. He did *not* like the change. Nothing ever happened in Mayfair. When once a feller had seen all the pretty ladies and all the big cars and moved along a couple of street hawkers, he was finished. And as for this night duty, with no one to talk to and nothing to do, it was, Henry Beecham decided, the

ruddy limit. He turned into Fothergill Street and paused
at the corner underneath the lamp to look at his watch
for the fourth time in an hour. He found, as he had gloomily suspected, that time was going slowly. He went on up
Fothergill Street, a despondent droop to his fine shoulders,
the corners of his young mouth turned dismally down, and
a blank feeling of utter boredom weighing like a wet gray
blanket upon his soul. Nothing *happened* round this part of
London. Nothing ever had, nothing ever did, and nothing
ever would! Heartily he wished himself back in J.B. Mis-
erably he pondered the fact that it would be impossible
to get back to J.B. They didn't want policemen round this
part of London; all they needed was a lot of messenger
boys. Or, if they must have policemen, they certainly didn't
want policemen like Harry Beecham—Harry Beecham who
had taken Carlo Piccatti out of his own house on the night
he had stabbed Frank Gintaro; Harry Beecham who knew
half the Polini gang by sight and wasn't afraid to say so;
Harry Beecham who had for three years running been light-
heavy champion of the Metropolitan Police. Harry Beecham
who . . .

And then, turning out of Fothergill Street into the little
alleyway called Clarendon Passage, he found that things
could, after all, happen in Mayfair. He collided at the moment of turning the corner with a figure which leaned
casually against the wall of Clarendon Passage immediately
underneath the lamp which stood out on a wrought-iron
bracket from the top of the wall.

"Here!" said Harry Beecham; and then drew back and
stared and added: "Beg your pardon, sir!"

The figure drew away from the wall and stood upright,
revealing itself as a titanic young man resplendent in evening clothes. From the top of his Nordic and flaxen head
to the soles of his gleaming shoes was no wrong note. The
set of the tie, the purity of the shirt and waistcoat, the
bloom of the white carnation snug in the buttonhole of the
left lapel, the hang of the gold chain descending in a gracious curve from beneath the waistcoat to the right-hand
trouser pocket—all these things told more of seven o'clock
upon the previous evening than somewhere near three upon
this morning. And yet, despite this orderly beauty, Henry
Beecham, staring out from beneath the peak of his helmet,
detected a certain wildness about this giant stranger. It was
not in the pose, which was as easy and certain as the
clothes. It was not in the fact that the stranger wore no

hat or coat, for was this not Mayfair and was the night
not a warm and pleasant night? It was purely a matter of
eyes. The eyes of the stranger, set far back beneath the
overhung brows of the fighter—as, indeed, were the eyes
of Henry Beecham himself—were definitely bloodshot round
their blueness; more, there was in the blue a queer light
of some other colour—a wild troublesome light. . . .

"Nice night, sir," said Henry Beecham, and took a step
to his right and made as if to pass on down Clarendon
Passage.

He did not pass down Clarendon Passage because he
found that, as he stepped to his right, so the stranger stepped
to his left, blocking the way. Henry Beecham became aware
that this was indeed a big man. Henry Beecham himself
stood six feet and one inch in his boots, but he found himself topped by an inch and more. Henry Beecham was
wide and thick and weighed thirteen hard stone, but he
saw facing him now fourteen and more which were wider
and thicker and, it seemed, in as fine condition.

"It is," said the stranger in a deep and resonant voice,
"indeed a pleasant night. But don't go, officer, don't go!"

There was a moment's pause before Henry Beecham answered. He was, he told himself, new to Mayfair. He was
also new to the ways of nobs. Had a similar situation arisen
on any of his old beats, he would have known how to deal
with it, but here he was uncertain.

"Yes, sir," he said at last, swallowing the "Now, then;
now, then!" which had very nearly passed his lips. "But
if you'll excuse me, sir . . ." He made once more to pass.

But the stranger did not move. Instead, he clasped his
hands before him, with a mock girlish gesture at which
Henry Beecham could scarce forbear to smile, and spoke
immediately in a voice which took any thought of smiling
right out of Henry Beecham's head, for it was a voice
which showed all too plainly that the law was in process
of having its leg pulled.

"Please, officer, please!" said the stranger. "Do not leave
me! I have been awaiting you! Time has seemed long—so
long!"

"Now look 'ere!" said Henry Beecham gruffly. "Now look
'ere! You take my advice, sir, and go home. You know
what you'll do if you hang around here like this, you'll
catch a chill. You get along, sir, and let me get along with
my dooty."

The stranger unclasped his hands and held them palms

torward before his face, as if to shut out some dread sight. From behind them his voice came muffled and broken.

"Ah, no!" he said. "Ah, no! Please, *please* don't speak to me like that!"

"That's enough o' this!" said Henry Beecham. *"Quite* enough!"

He took a step to his left, put his right hand to the stranger's shoulder, and started to push by between him and the wall.

The stranger did not move. The shoulder beneath Henry Beecham's fingers was solid and hard. Henry Beecham stopped, but not because of resistance. He stopped because, as he had put his left foot forward, it had struck something which lay in the shadows at the foot of the wall; something heavy and hard and hollow. He dropped his hand from the stranger's shoulder and switched on the lantern at his belt and twisted it until its ray shone downwards upon the thing at his feet. It lay at the foot of the wall, just where the stranger had been leaning. It must have been, in fact, behind or between his feet as he leant.

Henry Beecham drew in his breath in a little hiss and then expelled it in a sharp yet low-toned whistle. He bent sharply and picked up from the ground a policeman's helmet.

" 'Ere!" he said. "What's this?"

The stranger dropped his hands from his face and thrust them into his pockets. When he spoke, all trace of banter had gone from his voice, and Henry Beecham, looking at him by the light of the wall lamp which now bathed the whole of his face, noticed anew the wildness of the blue eyes.

"That?" said the stranger, looking down at the helmet which now swung by its chin strap from Henry Beecham's fingers. "That? That's mine. It's a sort of a hat."

"Yours?" said Henry Beecham in a voice which he meant to be intimidatingly official, but which succeeded only in being entirely astonished. "What *is* all this?"

"Your bewilderment," said the stranger, "is quite natural. It is also, if I may say so, not without pathos. I can see that I must explain matters to you. I live near here, just round the corner, in fact. Tonight it struck me—as I may say it has been striking me quite frequently of late—that the best thing I could do was to throw a party. Accordingly I threw one. It is still in process. Earlier in the evening, officer, a slight—er—accident led to there being, quite suddenly, a rather serious shortage of drinking vessels at my party. It then occurred to me that we must apply to this party the old principle of the loving cup. The party being rather a special party and taking kindly to this suggestion, it occurred to me to put to the vote the question of what vessels would be the most bizarre and, shall we say, exciting. Several suggestions were made, officer, some of which I will not mention. But it was left to me—I say this in all modesty—to give birth to the idea which met with instantaneous acclamation."

Henry Beecham interrupted. "I don't know what all there 'ere is," he said with some incoherence. He held the helmet up and thrust it almost into the face of the stranger. "What *I* want to know is this: what are you a-doin' of with *this?*"

"But, officer," said the stranger, taking half a step backwards and surveying Henry Beecham with his blond head upon one side, "that is what I have been doing my poor best to explain to you for the last three or four minutes."

"It's my belief," said Henry Beecham sternly, "that you've been drinking."

"Your belief is correct," said the stranger, courteously. "I *have* been drinking. I have been drinking steadily and with increasing fervour for the last fortnight. I trust, however, that I can be said to carry my liquor with decency." He paused a moment, to add at last, with a certain briskness in his tone: "Now, then, we can't hang about here all night. I've waited long enough for you. Suppose we get to business."

"You've been drinking!" said Henry Beecham, clinging to the one spar of sanity in this sea of the inexplicable. "That's what you've been doing! And what's all this about you waitin' for me?"

"I was waiting for you, officer," said the stranger, "because I promised my guests that there should be two loving cups. I have collected one. You hold it in your hand at the moment. I want another and that, at the moment, is on your head. Are you going to give it to me quietly like a nice little constable or have I got to take it? For your own sake, officer, I hope that you'll be more courteous in acceding to my request than was your colleague."

"I'll tell you," said Henry Beecham, "what you're a-goin' to do—you're goin' to come along with me."

The stranger took his hands from his pockets. "And so," he said, "you refuse to give me your hat?"

"There's been enough o' this," said Henry Beecham. "Now, are you comin' along quiet or have I . . ."

"Pity!" said the stranger and with a sudden and lithe swiftness shot out his left hand. It caught the chin strap of the helmet which Henry Beecham held in his hand and pulled. Henry Beecham, taken by surprise, came with it. The stranger's right fist, travelling in a highly expert arc of some fourteen inches, crashed against the point of Henry Beecham's chin.

Henry Beecham had not been light-heavy champion of the Metropolitan Police for three years without receiving many blows; but never before, in the ring or in any of those dangerous purlieus of J.B. Division, where policemen must hunt in couples, had he received a blow like this. All the stranger's fourteen and a half stone were behind it, and the stranger's fist, at the moment of impact, twisted with an extra squeeze of explosive force. A sheet of flame went up inside Henry Beecham's head, and a curious sound came from his lips.

"Gluk!" said Henry Beecham and, his knees crumpling, fell forward.

The stranger caught him, set him carefully down against the wall beneath the lamp, slipped off his helmet, and, swinging this and its fellow trophy by their straps, turned back into Fothergill Street. There would have floated back to Henry Beecham's hearing, had that sense been working, the notes of the song that the stranger sang as he went.

2

Ten minutes later Henry Beecham came back to realization of life. His head had fallen forward onto his knees. He opened his eyes and groaned and tried to lift his head. A stab of pain shot through it. He felt very sick. He rested a moment and then tried again and at last got himself sitting upright. His head sang. Inside it gnomes were beating with a myriad of hammers upon a thousand anvils. Black and red and yellow specks danced before his eyes. In a moment he put up tentative fingers and gently felt the point of his chin where was now a hard and rapidly enlarging lump. To test his aching jaws he spoke.

"Coo!" he said in a thick and muffled voice. "What a clip!"

For a moment he could not remember where he was, or who the dealer of the clip. Then memory came back in a sudden and breath-taking wave. His head felt cold and he remembered the reason for its coldness. He, Henry Beecham, must go back to the station; the station where, as yet, he knew none intimately, and tell how he had been robbed of his helmet by a gentleman who wanted to drink out of it. He groaned again. The groan, this time, was caused as much by mental as by physical anguish. It was with great joy that he remembered the other helmet. He was not, after all, alone in this extraordinary situation.

Beneath him the flags of the pavement struck hard and cold. With difficulty, for his head was still swimming and his cordinations were uncertain, he got to his feet. The effort brought on a wave of nausea, this time a wave which would not be denied. When he raised his head it was to be aware, with a sudden shock which did a good deal to clear his perceptions but nothing to conquer his feeling of weakness, that there had been a witness of his illness. Just inside the mouth of the passage and between him and the lamp stood, in its own shadow, the figure of a man. A man of medium height and medium build and neat yet undistinguished clothing. A man who wore a light-coloured dust coat and a black felt hat pulled down over his eyes so that it seemed to the watery and uncertain vision of Henry Beecham that the voice which spoke to him from beneath the hat came not from a face but from a blankness. It was a pleasant enough but entirely undistinguished voice, its tone neither high nor low, its accents neither coarse nor polished.

"Feeling queer?" said the voice unnecessarily.

"Ah!" said Henry Beecham. And then, with a sudden desire to justify himself: "Been assaulted."

"Dear, dear!" said the voice. "Much hurt?"

The fingers of Henry Beecham's right hand went once more up to his chin where, with extreme tenderness, they felt about. He shook his head. The man in the dust coat seemed to be looking for something on the ground. His head was bent, and by its movements Henry Beecham could tell that its eyes were sending glances this way and that among the shadows at the foot of the wall.

"Where's your helmet?" said the nondescript voice.

The sick heart of Henry Beecham sank yet lower into his stomach. It came to him with a flash of foresight that this would not be the last time he would hear that question. He mumbled something in his throat and bent forward in simulated search. The movement brought the blood to his head with a sudden rush, and a dark mist began to shape itself before his eyes. He straightened quickly and took a totter-

ing half-pace backwards. His broad back slapped against the
wall. A groan, half stifled but nevertheless audible, burst
from his lips. He felt very ill.

"Mystery!" said the man in the dust coat. His voice was
faintly muffled. He was stooping lower still now and had
gone farther into the darkness of the passage.

Henry Beecham closed his eyes, leaning his head back
against the wall. He wanted desperately to be sick again
and was determined not to be.

"Here!" came the voice dimly to his singing ears. "What's
this?"

Henry Beecham opened his eyes with an effort. He decided that he must no longer lean against the wall, and,
thrusting at it with his hands, levered himself upright. He
found that the man in the dust coat was standing close to
him, upright again. In his hand, held out towards Henry
Beecham, was something white which fluttered in the soft
breeze.

"What?" said Henry Beecham, stupidly. "What's what?"

"It's a handkerchief," said the man in the dust coat. His
voice seemed to drop into the silence and make holes in it
which immediately closed themselves up. "Silk." The voice
faded as he held the thing towards the light and bent low
over it. Still Henry Beecham could not see the face. He did
not worry over this, but wished passionately to be left alone.

"Initials and all in the corner," said the man in the dust
coat. "C.V. Nice quality stuff. Heavy silk." He suddenly
stretched the thing out to its full length, disclosing it as the
largest of handkerchiefs. He held it by its corners and let it
fold itself diagonally. "Big enough for a scarf," he said.

A sudden idea flashed into Henry Beecham's mind. Handkerchief. Silk. Man's size. Clean! There had been the edge
of a silk handkerchief peeping nattily out of the wild giant's
outer breast pocket. . . . Henry Beecham lurched forward
unsteadily.

"Here!" he said thickly. "Give us that!"

"Certainly," said the man in the dust coat, on a sudden
high headnote. But what he gave Henry Beecham first was a
blow between the eyes.

It was strong enough and shrewd enough and, although
the merest caress compared to the blow which had reduced
Henry Beecham to what he was at this moment, it was the
beginning of the end. He staggered back, off his balance.
The back of his skull cracked dully against the bricks of
the wall. He made a queer little noise in his throat, and

his body sagged. He made an effort to straighten himself, but before he could something soft came about his throat—something soft and cruel which tightened and tightened. . . .

When they found him he had been dead for more than an hour. His face was of a queer, deep blue colour, and between his clenched teeth there protruded obscenely the tip of a swollen tongue. About his neck, and almost imbedded in the flesh, was knotted tightly a white silk handkerchief.

Chapter IV
EXTRACT FROM A DIARY

9th June, 193—

A gift! A gift from the gods! It may have interfered with my tidy programme, but I couldn't very well refuse it, handed to me as it was on a dish with a little label bearing the words: "Help yourself." To think that if I hadn't gone to that music hall and hadn't started talking to that very pleasant naval man I shouldn't have gone back and had a drink in his rooms and I shouldn't have been walking down Fothergill Street at a quarter to three! After all, it isn't often that you find one helmetless and half senseless in the heart of the West End of London. To my unknown assistant I offer many thanks. If that was his handkerchief I'm afraid he may get into trouble, but I can't help that. He shouldn't go about knocking them half silly.

Today is the first day I've been unable to find anything at all about the one at Farnley in any of the papers. Perhaps this means that they've given it up as a bad job. Or perhaps, poor fools, they think that they're onto something at last and are accordingly keeping quiet. Probably, though, it isn't they who have kept it out of the news but the editors. It was a seven days' wonder and then it died. Yesterday only two papers had little tiny paragraphs about it. Today—nothing. I wonder how soon it will be before it crops up again. Not long! They'll be getting the idea soon.

When I sat down I meant to put in a full account of last night's gift, but I'm too tired. Very comfortable quarters here. Seems a pity that the programme will necessitate my moving so soon. However, I musn't grumble.

Chapter V
CAN DO

THE telephone beside Jane's bed rang shrill. She stirred and opened her eyes and blinked happily at the broad bar of sunlight which pushed its way through the gap between the yellow curtains. She sat up. A tenuous shoulder strap slipped down over one rounded ivory arm. She shook her head, tossing away from her forehead the short and lovely mane of jet. She stretched out an arm for the telephone and plucked the instrument from its base and set it to her ear. When she said, "Hello!" there was colour in her cheeks, and beneath the fine black brows her blue eyes were smiling. Before the telephone had poured into her left ear more than half a dozen short sentences, her cheeks were waxen, the blue eyes were clouded with fear and bewilderment and the soft curve of her lips was strained into a thin line downbent at its corners.

The telephone went on talking.

"But—but it's *impossible!*" Jane's voice showed as plainly as did her face what emotions beset her.

The telephone spoke at length.

"What shall we *do?*" said Jane. "I—what about—what do they call it?—bail?"

The telephone answered.

"Oh!" said Jane bleakly. "Oh, I see!" And then, in answer to the telephone's last cackle: "Yes. I could be round in half an hour. . . . Oh! . . . All right! . . . This afternoon, then, at five."

She put the instrument back upon its hooks. She sat bolt upright in the large bed. The blue eyes stared straight before her, seeing nothing of the charming room. The sunlight still flooded in through the chink in the yellow curtains, but its cheer found no echo in the white young face so suddenly lined, nor in the still small body.

Jane stirred. Once more her hands went out to the table by her bed, and from it took a little clock. The hands stood at one minute to ten.

At twenty-five minutes past noon Jane was walking east-

21

wards down Capulet Street. She had just come out of the
Green Park. The day was magnificent. The sun which had
been shining at six o'clock still shone. The park, in this second day of sunshine after three weeks of incessant rain,
had been green indeed—green and gold and blue. The streets
were full of the gay colours of summer frocks worn today
without fear. There had been, even, two men in straw
hats and the inevitable old Colonial in white duck. Despite
the heat, the air was light and heady; it was like a white
and sparkling wine; like the air of New York in spring.

The day, in short, would have delighted the real Jane
Frensham. But this young woman who now walked with me-
chanical gait, with set face whose skilful colouring could
not have concealed from one who knew her that beneath it
was a deadly pallor—this young woman was not the real
Jane Frensham. This was a terrified and miserable and bewildered husk of the real Jane Frensham.

She walked on. Every now and then the head of a passer-
by would turn to send a glance after her. If the glance
came from a woman it was because of Jane's clothes, which
were admirable; if from a man, it was because of Jane's
face and body and carriage. But fewer men's heads turned
this morning than would have upon an ordinary morning.

Jane came to the end of Capulet Street. Before her was
the wide ominibus-congested river of Victoria Street. At the
corner stood a newsboy. Unusually for one of his trade, he
shouted while stationary. The yellow placard held before
his legs shrieked in letters four inches high and nearly as
thick:

POLICEMAN MURDERED

His voice shouted hoarsely:

" 'Orrible crime in Mayfair! Strangled constable! 'Orrible
crime in Mayfair. P'leece constable murdered!"

He was selling his papers fast. Jane meant to walk by, but
her legs halted and her hands fumbled at her bag and produced a penny. When the sheet, still wet from the press,
was in her hand, her legs began to function again. She
turned and walked on. She had not gone more than a hundred yards before a queer feeling seized her. Her head
began to swim, and something went wrong with her sight.
Her knees felt weak and her back as if it had no bone in it.

Through her clouded mind there shot, with a stab of horror, the thought that she was going to "make a scene!"

This must not be. She got herself to the inner limit of the pavement and, turning, pretended that she was looking into a shop window. The fact that it was the window of a firm of sanitary engineers did not reveal itself to her. Her eyes were tight shut. Behind their screwed-up lids she fought with her mind for control of her weakening body. When she opened her eyes again her sight at least was all right. She turned and walked, very slowly, onwards. She knew that if she could get another fifty yards she would be opposite the discreetly handsome door of the Restaurant Savarin and that within the Restaurant Savarin was sanctuary. She achieved the fifty yards. The gold-braided blue bulk of the commissionaire drew itself to attention. The gold-braided blue arm swung open the door at the head of the two shallow marble steps which led up to it.

Jane managed the steps; how, she has never been able to understand. She also managed—a fact which she has quite forgotten—to give a gracious good-morning to the smiling, cap-touching George.

The cocktail lounge of the Savarin lies immediately within the doorway—a fact for which Jane thanked God. She sank into the first of those gilt basketwork armchairs which look so uncomfortable but which are, in fact, the reverse. A wave of relief swept over her, sending much-needed blood back to her head. She felt better. She closed her eyes and relaxed.

At this hour, twenty-five minutes to one, the lounge was almost empty. There was, in fact, only one other person in it—a man who sat to face the doorway at the table next to Jane's. He saw Jane, but Jane did not see him. Jane was not in a condition to take notice of anything save her own sensations. The man, laying aside the paper which he had been reading, stared at her, not covertly, but with frank interest. He had noted the slump with which she had let herself fall into her chair. He now noted certain signs which made it apparent that the charming colour was not the work of God. He leaned forward over his table and pressed the button of the bell attached to its leg.

A white-jacketed waiter came hurrying, reached out for the glass upon the table, and then, seeing that this was still half full, dropped his hand.

"Not me," said the man who had rung; with his head he made a gesture towards Jane.

Jane became aware that someone was standing over her. She opened her eyes and found this to be a waiter; mercifully, a waiter whom she knew. He was looking down at her with an inquiring tilt of the head. In his brown and Latin eyes was an expression blent of solicitude and wonder.

Jane, with an effort, managed a smile and a greeting and an order. Giulio hurried away, to return bearing a tray upon which was a tall glass that was yellow and tinkled.

Jane drank. Giulio hovered, solicitous, about her. Jane set down the glass and smiled at Giulio. Jane said that she felt better. She had, she said, felt faint. It must, she said, have been the sun. She was, she said, very grateful to Giulio, whom she now paid and tipped with a lavishness almost wanton.

At the next table its occupant buried himself in his paper. From behind it presently his hand came out and touched the bell again. In a moment Giulio was at his side and was given an order.

Jane, sipping at her brandy and soda, glanced at her fellow customer. She could see, beneath his table, a pair of elegant and grey-clad legs, brilliantly polished and marvellously hued brown shoes, socks of pale, corn coloured silk covering well-shaped but entirely masculine ankles. Above the table she could see nothing save the headlines of the noon edition of the *Evening Gazette*.

SHOCKING MURDER IN MAYFAIR
POLICEMAN STRANGLED
BARONET MOTORIST ARRESTED

"Oh!" said Jane in a little half-choked gasp. Horror had come back to her. She felt as if cold water had been poured down her spine. But her worst enemies—had she had any, which is doubtful—could not have said that she lacked courage. The weakness of a few moments ago had passed. She was herself again, and in her veins there glowed pleasantly the warmth of the spirit she had drunk. Her face flamed with anger at herself as she realized that the small half-strangled "Oh!" had been audible to the man behind the paper. He lowered the paper so that his face was visible. Jane found herself staring across the few feet of intervening space into a pair of eyes which regarded her with a cool level gaze of entirely impersonal interest. She knew herself to be blushing and hated herself for it. For a moment she returned the stare and then, finding that the eyes did not waver, dropped the gaze of her own. She was angrily conscious of something queer about the eyes and equally angrily determined not to bother her head with what it might be.

Her anger did her good. Tightly clenched in her left hand she found her own rolled-up paper. Setting her teeth, she opened it and began to read. Hers was the midday edition of the *Comet*, marked "Special Five-thirty Edition." She read:

POLICEMAN KILLED
WELL-KNOWN BARONET ARRESTED ON MURDER CHARGE
STUNNED BY BLOW THEN STRANGLED WITH HANDKERCHIEF
SIR C. VAYLE CHARGED
STORY OF STOLEN HELMETS

An appalling discovery was made in the early hours of this morning in the heart of Mayfair. While on his inspection of the beats under his control in Mayfair, Sergeant Hobson of X.L. Division of the Metropolitan Police this morning made a horrible discovery. In the mouth of Clarendon Passage, which leads down to Shepherd's Market, Sergeant Hobson found the dead body of Constable Henry Beecham. Constable Beecham had obviously died of strangulation. About his neck was tightly knotted a large white silk handkerchief. His face showed signs of the rough handling to which he must have been submitted before being strangled. C.I.D. officers were rushed to the spot and, following investigations, proceeded at six o'clock to No. 13 Fothergill Street, the residence of Sir Christopher ("Sudden") Vayle, the celebrated motor-racing driver.

ALL-NIGHT PARTY

Despite the hour, the C.I.D. officers found that a party was in full swing in Sir Christopher's house. Following interrogation, Sir Christopher accompanied the detectives to Vine Street Police Station where, after making a statement, he was detained.

FORMALLY ARRESTED

Later in the morning a notice was issued to the press
from Scotland Yard stating that a warrant had been
taken out and executed against Christopher Llewellyn
De'Ath Vayle, fourth baronet, and that Sir Christopher had been arrested upon a charge of murder.

It is understood that the prisoner will be removed
from Vine Street to Wandsworth Prison during the day.
The inquest upon the body of Constable Beecham will
be held next Monday.

STOLE HELMETS FOR LOVING CUPS

The *Comet* understands that the helmet of Constable
Beecham was missing when the body was found and,
further, that this morning another constable upon a
near-by beat was forced to report the loss of his helmet.
The two missing helmets, it is understood, were found
by the C.I.D. officers in Sir Christopher Vayle's house,
where, lined with saucepans from which the handles
had been torn, they were being used as drinking vessels.

No official statement has been issued with regard to
this, but our special correspondent states that the other
constable whose helmet was stolen was taken to Vine
Street early this morning to identify Sir Christopher
Vayle as the man who had assaulted him and stolen
his helmet.

And so on went the *Comet*. In the centre of the page,
inset in a black-edged "box" and different type, was a con-
densed biography of the arrested man. It was headed:

"SUDDEN" VAYLE

Born in 1896, Sir Christopher Vayle was educated at
St. James's School. On the outbreak of the war he went
to Sandhurst. In 1915 he was commissioned to the
Royal Artillery, with whom he served in various
branches on three fronts. He was decorated with the
M.C. and bar, the D.S.O., and the *Légion d'Honneur*.
Badly wounded in 1918, his life was despaired of and
he was not in possession of his full strength until late
in 1920. In 1921 his father died and he succeeded to the

baronetcy and the whole of the immense Vayle fortunes, which are derived from the Vayle and other steel works. In 1924 he took up motor racing as a hobby. By 1927 he had become one of the world's foremost racing drivers both on road and track. By 1930 he was known to the English-speaking world—affectionately, for his popularity has been astounding—as "Sudden" Vayle. The nickname of "Sudden" derives from his school days when his third name of De'Ath was made a joke of by his schoolfellows. Among notable motoring feats he has performed are the following: won the French Grand Prix twice; won the Ulster Trophy twice, and has three times held the Brooklands Lapping Record. Sir Christopher Vayle is also a noted cricketer, having played for his county and for the Gentlemen. He is also a noted amateur boxer. For the past two years rumour has linked his name with that of Lady Ross-Nairn, better known by her stage name of Leda Fitzroy. It was rumoured that Lady Ross-Nairn, who divorced Lord Ross-Nairn in 1928, was to marry Sir Christopher, but three months ago the engagement of Sir Christopher to Miss Jane Frensham, daughter of Lieut. General Sir Hector Frensham, the chief commissioner of police, was announced. The marriage was to have taken place next month, but a fortnight ago an announcement was made in the press to the effect that the engagement was broken off. Since then, rumour has been busy again with the names of Sir Christopher and Lady Ross-Nairn.

Against her will Jane, having read all the rest of the page, read this. As she read, her teeth bit hard upon her lower lip. Suddenly, forgetful of where she was and of the man who had stared, she savagely crunched the paper into a hard ball and flung it from her. Dropping into her lap, her hands interlocked their long fingers. The force with which they held each other was told by the sudden and almost incredible whitening of the knuckles.

From behind her came the sound of a heavy door swinging open. It was cool here in the lounge, and the sudden blast of hot air coming in from the sun-baked street startled her to realization of her surroundings. Past her table walked the huge commissionaire called George. His splendid cap was carried in his white-gloved hand, and his bald pate glittered nobly. In two long but decorous strides he was at the

table of the man who had stared and was bending over it
with a deferential urgency.

"Sir!" boomed George.

The man put down his paper. For a moment before he
looked up at George his eyes rested again upon Jane. Then
they sent their glance, smiling now, up to George's face.
Jane watched. She was avid of anything which might serve,
although only for a second, to take her mind even partly off
horror. She listened to George. He spoke in what passed with
him for a confidential whisper, but it boomed round the
soft gayness of the lounge like muffled thunder.

"I warned you, sir," George was saying. "You can't say as
I didn't warn you!"

The man at the table stood up. Since he was no longer
looking at her, Jane looked at him. Standing, he was revealed
as a man of slightly over medium height, but looking shorter
than he was by reason of an almost excessive breadth of
shoulder. He was, despite the paradox, of a lean solidity;
he was also, undeniably, of an elegance whose very casual-
ness was part of its subtle but undoubtedly high artistry.
He had a clean-shaven, square face seeming at one look
pleasant enough but utterly unremarkable, at another still
pleasant but somehow unforgettable. The sort of face, Jane
told herself, still fighting furiously for distraction for her
mind, which you would either think you would be bound
to remember and then find that you couldn't, or feel sure
that you wouldn't remember and then find that without effort
you had.

When he spoke, it was in a voice as characterful or
characterless as his face—a voice neither low-pitched nor
high. His words came curiously; each word was spoken
distinctly and quickly, but each sentence gave the impression
that it was drawled, the pauses between the words seeming to correct the quickness of the words themselves. He
seemed a favoured and well-known customer. Jane, who
used the Savarin a lot, wondered how it was that she had
never seen him and then thought immediately that perhaps
she had, only had forgotten. She listened to the conversation. It became plain to her that the trouble was a motorcar.

"You can do it once, sir," said George. "You can do it a
dozen times, but, as I've said to you often and often, they'll
get you in the end. There's a new man on this beat and
he's a bit too O.T. for my liking. There he is and there he'll
stay till such time as you come out. He's taking partic'lars of
the car now! Best thing you can do, Mr. Revel, is to come

out and let 'im write some more in his book and then drive
the car round the back."

The man called Revel smiled. "And put five guineas into
Lieutenant General Sir Hector Frensham's pocket?"

Jane sat up with a little jerk, then immediately subsided.
She had never been able to remember that her father's name
was a household word.

"I never incur fines, George," said the man called Revel.
"All this will cost me is a drink for you, a telephone call,
and ten shillings and six-pence."

George shook his bald dome of a head. "I tell you, sir,
'e'll stand there till you *do* come out. You won't get out of
it this time, sir."

"Can do," said the man called Revel. *"Ecoutez!"*

He crossed to a corner table beside the door, where there
stood a telephone. He picked up the telephone and asked
for a number. George, twisting his cap in his hands, watched
with a puzzled half-smile upon his red moon of a face.
Jane found herself half-turned in her chair to watch the man
at the telephone. Their eyes met again. She turned away with
a movement which she intended to be casual but which, she
felt, was gauche in its briskness. She pretended a study of a
small engagement book plucked from her bag. She realized
with a flash of interest what it was that had struck her first
about this man's eyes. Something odd there had been, and
until now she had not been able to place it. It was not that
they were extraordinary in themselves, but that they were as
near to being black as eyes ever come. And one does not
often, thought Jane, find such eyes in the head of a man
whose hair is as blond as—as—Christopher's. . . .

She caught at her breath. Horror flooded back upon her.
She fought it. She came out of a black whirling maelstrom
of despair to hear the voice of the man at the telephone.

"That Starr's Garage, . . . Put me on to Mr. Morton, please.
. . . Is that Mr. Morton speaking? . . . This is Revel . . .
Morton, my car's outside Savarin's. . . . There's a bobby by it.
He wants me for obstruction. Get your breakdown lorry
round for it. Tell the fellows to tinker round a bit and jack
up the front wheels and tow her off. I'll fetch her after lunch.
All right? Thanks."

Chapter VI
FOOTNOTE

It is curious to think that if Jane Frensham had not heard the actual conversation between George, the commissionaire, and Nicholas Revel and one end of the telephonic conversation between Nicholas Revel and the manager of Starr's Garage, the history of England during this decade might have proved entirely different.

For if Jane had not been, for some reason which she has never been able to fathom, sufficiently interested, despite her misery, in Nicholas Revel and his ingenuity, she would never have allowed Nicholas Revel to give her lunch upon that day. And Nicholas Revel, being what he is, would not have troubled himself to try again, along more orthodox channels, for Miss Frensham's acquaintance.

And if he had not had Miss Frensham's acquaintance and friendship, and if he had not put Miss Frensham under the deepest obligation to him, he would never have received from Sir Hector Frensham, chief commissioner of police, the attention which, in due course, he did receive.

And if Nicholas Revel had not spent an hour with Sir Hector Frensham on the afternoon of the ninth of August in this same year, the government would almost certainly have fallen, at a time very evil for the country, and London would have been under martial law—or something very much like it—with results which can only be conjectured.

Chapter VII
PRESS BUTTON A

Nicholas Revel hung up the receiver. He turned to the now broadly grinning George and slipped a coin into George's vast palm.

"Thank you, sir," said George and, still smiling, went out to await with unholy joy the forthcoming discomfiture of the law.

Nicholas Revel went back to his table and his half-finished

drink. Jane stood up and walked across the lounge and down
the stairs in its far corner. She was making for the private
telephone booth outside the basement bar. Fear and horror
still held her, but with them now was mixed a great anger
with herself. It was time, Jane thought that Jane did something. High time.

What she did was to telephone. She telephoned first to
Scotland Yard. From her father's secretary she learned a
Paris telephone number at which it was possible that she
might get her father. She booked this call and spent the time
which must elapse before it came through in telephoning
first to certain relatives and second to three friends. The
relatives were, as she had really known they would be,
sympathetic but entirely unhelpful. Of the three friends,
two were unavailable and one by the end of the conversation a friend no longer.

And then, baking in the little oven of the booth, she got
Paris. Luck, which she had thought to have deserted her, returned. She caught her father. Their talk was short and to
the point. Sir Hector, who had, before he went, stated truth-
fully that he *must* be in Paris for at least a week, concluded
the conversation by stating that he would be in London as
fast as train and 'plane could carry him.

"Bless you!" said Jane.

She put the receiver back on its hook and leaned for a
moment against the wall of the booth. She felt weak again,
but now with the bitter weakness of fatigue which follows
hard work well done. She had, she thanked God, as she
went slowly up the stairs to the lounge, at least *done* something. The thought of her father buoyed her. True, the few
hours which must elapse before his return stretched before
her like days; but even days, she told herself, do pass.
She came to the top of the stairs. The lounge was now fill-
ing up, but still the man that George had called Revel sat at
his table. He seemed absorbed in his paper, and Jane let herself glance at him. The table at which she had been sitting
was still empty. She had left on it paper and gloves. She
went back to it and sat. She was conscious of lassitude. She
supposed that she must lunch somewhere. Since she was here,
perhaps here? Or should she go home? Or perhaps drop in
on Betty? Or perhaps . . .

She became conscious, with a shock small but none the
less sharp, that the man Revel had left his table and now
stood at hers, bending a little as if to speak to her. Before

the surprise of his mere presence had died away there came
with his words a greater.

"Miss Frensham," he said, "will you lunch with me?"

Jane saw that he was smiling—an attractive smile; his
teeth were very white, and his black eyes, with the smile,
narrowed until they were almost shut. She did not speak.
She has said that she tried, but that astonishment for the
moment took away her voice.

"What about a cocktail?" said Nicholas Revel and sat
himself down to face her. His hand pressed the bell push
upon the table leg.

Jane, as she has confessed, goggled.

"I . . ." she began. "What . . ."

Giulio came hurrying.

"Dry Martini?" said Nicholas Revel. "Bronx? Sidecar?
White Lady? . . . . Try a White Lady. . . . Yes, a White Lady's
just the thing for this morning. Giulio, two large White
Ladies—not too much lemon, and make it snappy."

Giulio, beaming, but with a hint of astonishment behind
the beam, hurried away.

Jane's emotions were chaotic. Astonishment was succeeded
by anger, anger by bewilderment, and all three by a sudden
and overpowering desire to giggle. And if there was one
luxury which she never permitted herself it was giggling. She
took command of herself and tried again. She raised her
eyebrows and was frigid.

"I am afraid," she said, "that I cannot understand . . ."

She was interrupted.

"Of course you can't!" said Nicholas with heartiness.
"Of course you can't! I shouldn't try. Not for a minute.
What about food now? I'd suggest a little smoked salmon,
one of Mario's chicken salads and a sorbet—the whole washed
down with a bottle of '21 Liebfraumilch. You may not believe it, but they've still got '21 Liebfraumilch here. The only
place in London. The only place, quite possibly, in the world."

Giulio came with two glasses which frothed and were
very cold.

"I look towards you," said Nicholas Revel, "and I bows."

Jane, to her own astonishment, found herself drinking.

"That's better!" said Nicholas Revel approvingly. "Much
better! Try a smile!"

2

Jane finished her smoked salmon. "Now," she said, *"I'm* going to say something. You may not know it."

"Oh, but I do! I haven't let you get a word in! Until now the time hasn't been ripe. Shoot!" Nicholas Revel raised his glass and drank.

Jane smiled. It was a brief smile, and she took it off the moment she found it on. That she should find herself eating with this man was extraordinary enough. That she should find herself smiling at him without reserve, as if he were the old friend his demeanour so falsely suggested, was more extraordinary still. Perhaps, thought Jane, a little *too* extraordinary. She strove to wipe all feeling from her face.

"Questions," she said. "Who are you?"

"First name Nicholas."

"And the second?"

Once more the black eyes almost disappeared in his smile. "You know that. You heard George use it."

"How did you know *my* name?" Jane's voice held a touch of asperity.

"Easy! When you first came in you were nearly out. You looked at the front page of my paper, which was plastered with Vayle. That made you worse. You pulled yourself together when you found me looking at you, and you read your own paper. More Vayle. You crunched up the paper and chucked it away from you—not a usual thing for a girl to do in public. The front page of the paper—equalling Vayle—was moving you, not pleasantly. You were connected with Vayle in some way. You were lucky enough not to be the Fitzroy but you were some woman connected with Vayle. Jane Frensham had been engaged to Vayle. I mentioned your father's name to George. You jumped."

"Oh!" said Jane. "Oh . . . I see!" She frowned. "What's your idea exactly?"

"Idea?"

"Don't be silly! If you want it rougher: what's your game? What are you doing?"

Once more Nicholas smiled, but this time only with his eyes. "I am in process," he said, "of putting you under the deepest of obligations."

"Really!" said Jane, repressing, "The hell you are!"

"Yes, really!"

"Why?" said Jane.

"What's your idea in bringing that up?"

"Meaning that you won't tell me?"

"Not at this stage."

"Oh!" said Jane and reflected that her ration of "oh" for one day must very nearly have been exceeded. "I suppose you will next refuse to tell me what this obligation is that I'm going to be under?"

Nicholas Revel shook his blond neat head. "Oh, no! I propose to relieve you, by tomorrow morning at the latest, of your main worry in life."

"Which is?" said Jane.

"Please!" His voice was plaintive. "If there was no charge of murder against Vayle but only a mild matter of slugging policemen when he was tight and pinching their helmets, you wouldn't be wandering about London in a half-swoon any more, would you?"

For a moment Jane glared. Then, with a sudden change of expression, said simply: "No, I shouldn't."

Her voice shook with mingled fear and excitement. She put her elbows on the table and cupped her chin in her hands and leaned nearer to her strange host.

"What do you mean?" she said. "Please tell me what you mean. Please!"

"Exactly what I implied. I'll get that murder charge washed out altogether."

"*Oh!*" said Jane. And then, with a demon of doubt creeping into her mind and voice: "But you. . . . But how. . . . But what?"

"Can do!" said Nicholas Revel.

3

They had coffee in the lounge.

"I still don't understand," said Jane.

Nicholas smiled at her. "Of course you don't. Why should you? Sure you've got these questions right?"

Jane nodded.

"What are they?"

"Don't bully!" said Jane. "What has Christopher said? What time did he leave the policeman? What time did he get back to his house? What was he wearing exactly? Did he go straight back to the house after leaving the policeman? Which way did he go? Has he said anything about remembering losing his handkerchief? Were there two helmets?

How did he carry them? If there was only one how did he carry it . . . ? Correct?"

"Yes." Nicholas looked at the watch upon his wrist. "It's now half-past two. We'll go round and get the car. . . ."

"Suppose," said Jane, "I was to report that car business?" There was a mock solemnity in her voice and a sparkle in her eyes which paid handsome tribute to the confidence which this stranger, without remotest attempt at explanation of himself, his status, or his intentions, had inspired.

"I don't understand," said Nicholas. "What car business?"

Jane stared, then smiled. "Oh, I see! You're like that!"

"I'm not," said Nicholas Revel, "like anything."

There was a small silence. The black eyes met the blue.

"No," said Jane slowly after a moment. "I don't think you are."

Nicholas got to his feet. "Come on!" he said.

They went. George held the door open for them. He saluted. About the corners of his mouth twitched the beginnings of a smile.

4

"What a lovely car!" said Jane outside Starr's Garage at twenty minutes to three. And: "It *is* a lovely car!" said Jane outside her father's house at fifteen minutes past five. "It's a left-hand drive—what is it?"

They stood together on the curb. Nicholas slammed the near-side door of the long-bonneted grey coupé. "French," he said. "Brillon-Meyer. Not too bad. Fast." He put a hand to his hat. " I suppose I'd . . ."

"Oh," said Jane with a trace of hesitation, "won't you come in?"

Nicholas dropped his hand from his hat. "Yes," he said.

Jane had forgotten her key. The imposing door of Number Fourteen Gordon Place was opened to them by an imposing manservant. They passed from blazing sunlight into cool dimness.

"Any messages, Porter?" said Jane.

"A message from Mr. Scott, madam. He telephoned from Scotland House to say that Sir Hector would be arriving at Croydon at six-thirty. I have given orders for the car to meet him."

"Thank you," said Jane.

She smiled, and across the faintly cadaverous solemnity of Porter's face there flitted the ghost of an answering smile. Porter was pleased. He had seen Miss Jane when she had left the house that morning. He had read the papers. He had not expected to see Miss Jane so quickly back to something so near her normal self. As he held open the door of the library—the second door on the right side of the square hall—he wondered who the gentleman might be; a well-dressed gentleman and very easy in his manner.

He wondered still more when, ten minutes later entering the library with a tray upon which were glasses and decanters, he caught the end of one of the gentleman's sentences.

". . . All you've got to do," the gentleman was saying, "is to forget all about it."

"You mean," said Jane when Porter had gone, "that I'm to forget that I met you?"

Nicholas added soda water to the whisky in his glass. "No, not that! Anything but that, lady! You've got to forget that we've had any discussion whatsoever about l'affaire Vayle. I'm not interested."

"How on earth," said Jane after a little silence which she had found oddly uncomfortable, "am I to explain you?"

"Godolphins."

"What?" Jane opened her eyes.

"Godolphins. Great friends of mine."

"But I don't know anybody called Godolphin."

"You've forgotten," said Nicholas, "that's all!"

"I don't believe there are any people called Godolphin."

"Yes," said Nicholas. "Oh, yes. Vesta Godolphin was at school with you. I was in the army with her brother. Not Claude. The other one—Lancelot. Odd, your meeting Vesta this morning after all these years."

"Yes," said Jane and laughed. "Very odd. She's got terribly fat."

Nicholas sat himself down upon the arm of a saddle-bag chair. He seemed very much at home. A well-dressed gentleman and very easy in his manner.

"It's not the contour I mind," he said. "It's the spots." Jane made a wry mouth. "I didn't notice them."

"No," said Nicholas and drank. "You couldn't. . . . Once more, now, are you perfectly certain that you got the answers to my questions without giving yourself away?"

Jane nodded. "Dead certain."

"I'm quite sure you managed Vayle all right. It's the fellow at the Yard that worries me—your father's secretary."

"He needn't," said Jane firmly. She smiled a little half-smile. "I was very nice to George Scott."

"I see. The poor devil had only half his mind on what you were talking about?"

"Something of the sort," Jane admitted.

Nicholas finished his drink. He stood up and set down his glass. "Must go," he said. "Lot to do."

"But what?" said Jane in a different voice. She felt with the imminence of his departure a sudden sense of flatness —a feeling which, she feared, heralded the complete return of sanity and consequently of horror. After all who was this man and what? And how could he . . . ?

His voice cut across her thoughts. "Don't worry," it said. He moved towards the door.

"Stop!" said Jane on a sudden high note. "How do I know . . . When do I see you again? . . . How can I get hold of you? . . . Where . . . ?"

Nicholas came back. He stood very close to her. She wondered, for a moment whose emotions she could not analyze, whether he were going to touch her. He did not touch her. She nerved herself to meet the gaze of the curious eyes. She had expected them to be grave, and it was with a shock that she found them half-closed in a smile.

"Don't worry," said Nicholas. *"Auf wiedersehen* and *a rivederci."*

Jane was left staring at a closed door. She was aware that manners demanded either that she should ring for a servant to show out her guest or go herself, but she did neither. Presently there came to her ears the sound of the front door closing and then, a moment or two later, the whirring hum of the big car as it drove away.

Chapter VIII
AFTER THE FACT

HAD you chanced to pass Number Fourteen Gordon Place at a minute or so past six when Nicholas Revel came out and got into the big car and drove off in the direction of Oxford Street, it is highly probable that you would have said, had the question been raised, that you would know this man again.

Had you chanced to be, an hour and a half later, in the

saloon bar of the Bull and Trumpet in Notting Dale, it is safe to say that, unless you were a friend or a close acquaintance of Nicholas Revel, you would not have recognized him in the man standing at the corner of the bar.

And yet nothing concrete about him was changed except his clothes. And even then, those which he wore now were by the same tailor and very much in the same admirable style as the clothes of the Savarin and Gordon Place. But where the grey suit had been new (though not too new) and of a lightness which could only be affected by a person of means and considerable leisure, the brown suit of Notting Dale was of a heavy and utilitarian material; was so worn as to be, in places, almost threadbare and was by many other indications plainly of considerable age. There were other changes, too: in place of the smart grey hat and irreproachable linen were now a battered though rakish affair of worn black felt and a white shirt whose scrupulous cleanliness only served the more to show up the fraying of its cuffs and the neat but obvious darn below the edge of its collar; the light-weight unwrinkled shoes of Gordon Place had been replaced by battered and heavy brogues; the gold cigarette case of the Savarin by a crumpled yellow packet.

For Nicholas Revel was thorough. He was now, most thoroughly, a gentleman, albeit uncomplaining, more than a little down on his luck.

That he was known to the Bull and Trumpet was patent. Not only did several members of its motley clientele nod to him, but Bessie, in such intervals as she had from serving, chatted with him pleasantly and even confidentially across the bar, her excessively golden head very close to the brim of the desperate black hat.

It was not until he was halfway through his second tankard of bitter that Nicholas Revel—to the Bull and Trumpet, Captain Phelps—so much as approached the object of his visit. He set down the tankard, picked up the paper which Bessie had set down for him on the bar, and glanced at the Stop Press for the winner of the four-thirty at Sandown Park.

"Polonius, eh!" he said, looking at Bessie over the top of the paper. "Anything on?" Captain Phelps was a racing man.

Bessie shook the golden head. "No such luck. Good price?"

Captain Phelps nodded. "Fifteens. . . . Good *Lord!*"

"What's up?" said Bessie. "Forgotten something?"

"Remembered something," said Captain Phelps. "Where's Joe?"

"Joe?" said Bessie. "Which Joe?"

"Big fellow," said Captain Phelps. "Fellow I play skittles with. Think he's a taxi driver."

"Aow," said Bessie. "Joe Palmer. No—ought to be in any minute. Why?"

"Last time I was in here I tipped him Polonius. If he went on then he got a real long price."

Behind Captain Phelps the swing doors opened with a crash.

"Talk of the devil!" said Bessie.

Captain Phelps turned to confront a tall and burly man who, despite the heat, wore atop of his clothes the oil-stained remnant of what had once been a trench coat. Between the collar of this and the peak of a down-drawn check cap looked out a blurred but genial face which proclaimed its owner as having had to do—and largely—with the ring.

"Evening, Joe," said Captain Phelps.

"Wotto to you, sir!" said Mr. Palmer with heartiness.

"Just talking about you," said Captain Phelps.

"Go on!" said Mr. Palmer.

"Fact," said Captain Phelps.

A very close observer might have noticed behind the smile in Mr. Palmer's small but genial eyes a faint trace of bewilderment. But he would have had need to be a very close observer.

Captain Phelps winked at Bessie. "Pretending to forget."

Bessie flashed teeth. "Mean, I call it!"

"Polonius," said Captain Phelps. "Fifteen to one. Did you do as I told you or did you not?"

"Kor ruddy swop me!" said Mr. Palmer readily. "Come 'ome, did 'e?"

Captain handed over his paper.

Mr. Palmer remarked with astonishment that he was perverted.

"Per-*lease!*" said Bessie with outraged dignity.

"Sorry!" said Mr. Palmer, for a moment crestfallen. And then a wide smile split the blurred countenance. "Chavin, Captain?" said Mr. Palmer.

Starting celebration at the bar and including the forgiving Bessie in the first round of it, Captain Phelps and

Mr. Joseph Palmer were soon at a small table in the far corner. They did not appear to be whispering, and yet, had you sat yourself down at the next table to them, when you would have been a bare eighteen inches from their backs, you would not have caught a single word that they said, though these words were many—at first and lastly from the lips of Captain Phelps; for a long middle period from the lips of Mr. Palmer.

2

Sir Hector Frensham stood before the fern-filled fireplace in the drawing room of Number Fourteen Gordon Place and tried not to look at his daughter. He found this difficult because his daughter was in distress and there existed between him and his daughter that very perfect friendship which should be the inevitable relation between parent and child but which, so irretrievably foolish are most parents, is so far from inevitable as to be a rarity. Sir Hector fidgeted. He pulled out a cigarette case and opened it; shut it again although it was full; walked across the room to a table upon which stood, by the side of a decanter-and-glass-laden tray, a cigar box. As he walked he might have been mistaken, from the back, for a man of thirty. He was tall and erect and slim; an enthusiastic woman journalist had once compared him, a little hysterically but not unhappily, to the "blade of his own sword." Only the handsome whiteness of the close-cropped but plentiful hair could have given to a stranger any indication of the age that he would see in the face when the man turned. And then, looking at the face, the stranger would probably have made a mistake of ten years. For at the most Hector Frensham looked in the middle fifties, whereas a week before this night he and Jane had celebrated his sixty-fifth birthday.

He opened the box and took a cigar and cut it. Behind him, her small slimness almost lost in the depths of a huge chair, Jane crouched. Her face was covered with her hands. She was taut and very still. Behind the covering hands her white teeth bit painfully at her nether lip.

For the first hour after her father's home-coming she had been still under what she could only call the spell of the strange man with whom she had so strangely spent the afternoon. During the second hour, when she and Hector Frensham had talked with calm sanity of Christopher Vayle, and Jane's love for Christopher Vayle, and the present circumstance of Christopher Vayle and how it was that so soon as he was in trouble Jane had been very sorry indeed that a childish misunderstanding had led her to break off her engagement to Christopher Vayle, Jane had felt confidence in her stranger oozing with every moment. At the end of this second hour it had gone almost completely. She saw the whole episode now for the madness that it was. The man was either knave or fool, perhaps both. No, not fool. Definitely not fool. Therefore knave? Perhaps only charlatan? But whatever he was, necessarily in this matter a man of straw, for what possibly could he do? Added to her returned misery, somehow doubled in intensity by its temporary absence, Jane felt great contempt for herself. During dinner neither she nor Hector Frensham had so much as mentioned the matter which was clouding their world, but after dinner, alone again, they had inevitably come back to it. Hector Frensham being, as has been said, Jane Frensham's best friend, did not seek to offer facile consolatory hope. Jane, coming nearer and nearer to what she felt must be an unbearable crisis of despair, was several times upon the brink of telling her father of her foolishness of the afternoon. But each time she reached this brink something, perhaps only the promise she had given but probably something more, sealed her mouth.

Hector Frensham, the unlighted cigar between his fingers, turned and came back slowly across the big room. Jane dropped her hands from her face and pulled herself upright with a small and, to Hector Frensham, infinitely pathetic squaring of white shoulders. She looked up at her father, and he saw that the blue eyes were dry, but saw also that they glittered with a hard fierce light which hurt him more than any tears would have done. He threw the cigar into the grate. He sat himself upon the arm of the big chair and slipped his arm about his daughter. Against the arm he could feel that the whole of her body was shaking. His grasp tightened.

They sat in silence.

3

By midnight the dance floor of the Café Berlin had shrunk to a space, so encroached upon was it by those extra tables which were perpetually being set up for latecomers, very little larger than that of a tablecloth. Upon it fifty or sixty couples endeavoured to dance.

Ferdie Kruhn dragged the last saccharine wails of "Moonlight and Lilies" from his Sixteen Lieutenants. There was much applause, but as this had been an encore to the nth, no more music; only much bowing and satanic smile from Ferdie. The dance floor emptied. The dancers squeezed their bodies back to their tables.

Down the broad staircase which led up to the cocktail bar, foyer, and steep stairs to the level of Piccadilly came, heralded by a sudden hush, a Very Important Person, having upon his arm a lady of quiet but very considerable beauty. He was met at the foot of the stairs by a maître d'hôtel trained by custom to exhibit towards the Very Important Person a manner only slightly different from that which he exhibited to all his patrons. He led impressive way to a table in a far corner, and gradually murmur seeped into the hush; swelled by rapid stages to the old full-throated babel.

At a table for four at the edge of the dance floor a woman said, addressing equally the two men flanking her and the woman facing her:

"I don't care—I think he's sweet!"

"I didn't think," said a voice in her ear, "that you'd seen me."

She turned. *"Nick!"* she cried. *"Dar*-ling!" She was a very pretty woman.

Nicholas Revel looked down at her. He was smiling. He was completely but quietly resplendent.

Ferdie Kruhn and his Sixteen Lieutenants burst into the opening noises of "Let Me Kiss You and Die." The woman upon the far side of the table got to her feet, and one of the two men followed. They lost themselves in the maelstrom of dancers.

Nicholas slid into the man's chair. For a long moment the woman at the head of the table looked at him, smiling; then, with a start remembering convention, turned to her other companion.

"I don't think," she said, "that you two know each other. ... Mr. Revel—Captain Um-ha."

Nicholas smiled and nodded. Captain Um-ha smiled. The hostess poured champagne into a glass and passed this to Nicholas, who drank. Captain Um-ha, making civil sounds in his throat as unitelligible as his name had been upon his hostess's lips, excused himself and was gone.

The woman sighed with relief. "Nick," she said, "I'm very angry with you!" She did not look at all angry. She was a very pretty woman.

"Impossible!" said Nicholas.

She shook her head. "It isn't impossible—it's a fact. Why didn't you come to my party last night, you low thing? Don't your promises *ever* mean anything?"

"Rarely," said Nicholas.

"You're a beast."

"Possibly," said Nicholas. "But you're mistaken—in this instance."

The pretty woman, staring in astonishment, was, if possible, prettier than ever.

"I don't understand," she said. Her brown eyes were puzzled.

"It's so easy. I *was* at your party. I enjoyed your party very much. It was one of the better parties——"

She interrupted. "But, Nick . . ."

The puzzled look in the brown eyes faded as they met a long and steady stare from the black eyes.

"I see," she said.

"I enjoyed your party very much," said Nicholas. "And I'm very glad to have seen you tonight because I feel I owe you an apology."

White shoulders lifted in a shrug. "Whatever for? I'm sure you behaved quite well—as well as you always do."

"I thought," said Nicholas, "that perhaps I overstayed myself a thought."

"If you did, my dear, I didn't notice it."

"Nice of you to say so. Extraordinary thing, until I happened to look at my watch just after I'd left the house I'd no idea it was so late. Had you?"

Again the white shoulders were raised. "I don't know."

"It was half-past two," said Nicholas.

"Now I come to think of it," said the woman, "I did know the time. I remember looking at the clock just as you went."

The music stopped on the last note of "Let Me Kiss You and Die." There was a rippling crash of clapping. The Sixteen Lieutenants and their leader plunged straightway into the opening salvos of "Shotgun Wedding."

"Dance?" said Nicholas Revel.

4

A shaft of moonlight came through the small barred window high on the wall. It cut a silver swathe across the centre of the wall. It did not touch the narrow bed against the inner wall.

From somewhere without came three deep booming chimes from a big clock. The hollow echoes of the last chime died tremblingly away, and again thick cold silence came down like grey fog.

In the cell something stirred. There was a harsh rustling of tossed blankets, then a metallic creaking as the bed came under a sudden redistribution of great weight.

Christopher Vayle sat upon the edge of this unaccustomed couch. The stone floor struck chill to his naked feet. He propped his elbows upon his knees and dropped his chin into cupped hands. He stared at the bright narrow path made by moonlight with eyes which saw anything but what was before them now.

5

It was at eleven-thirty the same morning that Sir Hector Frensham telephoned to his house from Scotland Yard. Porter, answering upon the hall instrument, was shocked. There was no precedent for Sir Hector's voice to come immediately atop of a ring. Always it had been either Mr. Scott or one of Mr. Scott's subordinates who established connection between Sir Hector and his household.

This sudden impact of Sir Hector's voice was trying, thought Porter, to the nerves. He felt his austere efficiency oozing from him, for Sir Hector's voice had in it an excited urgency which Porter had never heard before, and its words were coming so fast that Porter was forced to ask, awkwardly enough, for repetition.

And then—more highly unprecedented yet—Sir Hector Frensham called down round curses upon the dignified head of Emmanuel Porter, who gasped and, as the oaths requested him, pulled himself together.

He gathered that Sir Hector Frensham wished to speak with his daughter, and that urgently. Porter set down the receiver and ran, to return a minute later and gaspingly state, "Miss Jane's maid says Miss Jane's sleeping. Miss Jane has passed a very restless night, sir, and the maid says that she persuaded Miss Jane this morning to take a mild sleeping draught. Miss Jane left very strict orders that, if she did get to sleep, she should not be waked. Should I tell the maid to waken her to speak to you, sir?"

"No," said the telephone in Sir Hector's everyday voice. "No. Leave word that when she does wake, Miss Jane is to ring me up."

"Yes, sir," said Porter and heard with great relief the click of the receiver at the other end being replaced.

6

It was at two-thirty that afternoon that a closed police car, with blinds drawn over the tonneau windows, pulled into Scotland Yard from the Embankment. There descended from it a large plain-clothes man and, following him, a brown-suited, hatless, blond-headed figure which made the escort seem, despite his height and burliness, a man of only a little over middle size and punily built. These two hurried through the doorway opposite which the car had halted.

A quarter of an hour later a taxi drove into Scotland Yard from the Whitehall side. It had no occupant other than the driver, who was halted at the entrance by the constable on duty and not allowed to proceed until there had been some little discussion and at last the production of a paper from the taxi driver's inner pocket. Under the guidance of the policeman the driver parked his cab and eventually was ushered into the building.

Some ten minutes after this a long grey coupé was halted at the Embankment entrance. Its driver, who seemed also its fortunate owner, produced a paper which he showed to the constable on the gate, parked the car in the recess halfway down upon the right-hand side, and, showing the paper to another constable, was directed to the same doorway through which the taxi driver had disappeared.

From three o'clock until ten minutes past Nicholas Revel sat in the armchair in the room of Superintendent Connor and smoked cigarettes with its owner. At ten minutes past three a message came for Superintendent Connor, and he led Nicholas down stone stairs along a corridor at their foot and into a room at the end of the corridor.

The door swung to behind Nicholas and his companion. Nicholas looked about him. He was in a bare place with yellow-distempered walls. There was no furniture. Around the walls, three feet from the floor, ran a continuous bench.

Seated at varying intervals upon this bench—or rather upon two sides of its square—were six men, all of a size far above the average. All were hatless. All were fair complexioned.

Superintendent Connor whispered something into the left ear of Mr. Nicholas Revel who, taking a step forward, pointed unhesitatingly to that one of the six who sat on the angle of the bench—a man larger by far than his fellows; a man with the blondness of a viking who wore brown clothes as much better than those of his companions as his body was larger than theirs; the man, in short, who had come out of the police car at two-thirty.

"Thanks," said Superintendent Connor and took Mr. Revel away and back to his room.

"There wasn't a doubt," said Nicholas Revel. "Pick him out anywhere. Wonder you bothered to have a parade."

Superintendent Connor lifted broad shoulders. He murmured something about routine. He gave Mr. Revel another cigarette and thanked Mr. Revel cordially.

Mr. Revel said he must be getting along. He also said:

"Suppose you haven't found my taxi driver yet? Not that it'll matter much now if you don't."

The corners of Superintendent Connor's mouth twitched into a half-smile.

"We found him all right," he said quietly.

Mr. Revel opened his eyes very wide. "Quick work!" he said with something of awe in his tone.

Once more Superintendent Connor shrugged. "Don't know about that, sir. Ordinary matter of business. If you want to know the fellow's name, it's Palmer. Joseph Palmer. He was on night duty so he slept all day yesterday—that's why he hadn't been to us before. We found him just as he was off to the local station. He was in that room downstairs only five minutes ago. He had no more hesitation in picking out Vayle than you had."

"Good!" said Nicholas. "Strikes me it's lucky for Vayle we happened to see him."

"It's more than lucky!" The superintendent's tone was sombre.

He shook hands with Mr. Revel and thanked him again and bade him an *au revoir*.

"Eh?" said Nicholas Revel. "What's that?"

The superintendent smiled. "I'm afraid, sir, that you haven't heard the end of this. There'll be a charge against Sir Christopher Vayle." There was in his tone every time he mentioned the name of Vayle a certain bitterness. "Assaulting officers of the law."

"Oh-ah. . . ." said Nicholas Revel. "Quite."

7

At seven o'clock that evening Sir Hector Frensham and his daughter drank sherry in the library of Number Fourteen Gordon Place.

Sir Hector Frensham looked at his daughter and was glad. Jane was so radiant that barely could he feel rancour against Christopher Vayle, the primary cause of much misery to Jane and the aid—however unconscious—to the murderer of what seemed by all accounts to have been one of the most promising young men in the uniformed ranks of the force.

"Darling!" said Jane. "It's too marvellous!" And then added, for perhaps the tenth time: "You're sure *nothing* can go wrong now?"

Sir Hector smiled at her. "Don't be a damned little fool! How *could* anything go wrong? These two witnesses have very definite statements. They have picked Vayle out at an identification parade; and all their times agree, and, moreover, have been checked. We didn't tell 'em that, of course, but they have. No, nipper, there's nothing more for you to worry your head about. Unless you object to Master Vayle getting what he deserves for . . ."

"Don't!" said Jane, for a moment unsmiling.

She got to her feet and went to her father's side and hooked an arm through his.

"Come on!" she said.

"All right," said Sir Hector.

"And the subject's barred for tonight."

"All right," said Sir Hector again and took his daughter out to dine and see the latest thing in imported musical comedies.

After the theatre they supped. They got back to Number Fourteen Gordon Place at a few minutes to one. They went to the library. Jane slipped off her cloak and lit a cigarette and curled herself into one of the big chairs.

"Drink?" said her father.

Jane shook her head. "Not for me."

"I'll have one, though," said the chief commissioner of police. But didn't; for through the door there came to their ears the sudden shrill blaring of the telephone.

"Damn!" said Sir Hector and looked at his daughter.

"What on *earth* . . . ?" said Jane.

Sir Hector crossed the room with his long cavalryman's stride. He went out leaving the door wide behind him. He took the receiver off its hook and set it to his ear.

"I want," said the telephone, "to speak to Sir Hector Frensham. . . . Scotland Yard here. Very urgent. . . . Oh, is that you, sir? Connor here. Bad news, sir. . . . Report's just come in that the constable on duty outside the Slovene Legation has been found dead."

"Good God!" said the chief commissioner of police.

"Bad business, sir! I've seen Inspector Harris who found him. He says the man was slit straight up the stomach. Like a Jack the Ripper job. We don't know yet, but Harris says he reckons the man's been dead about an hour when he found him. Thought I'd better let you . . ."

"Yes, yes. Quite right, Connor," said Connor's chief. "I'll come over."

Chapter IX

EXTRACT FROM A DIARY

11th June, 193—

Was too tired last night to write, so left it over until today. Was so excited after successfully dealing with Number Three that I couldn't get to sleep, dead beat though I was. Got back here at one-fifteen, had a nightcap, went straight to bed but *couldn't* drop off. Read *Lavengro* until my eyes were too tired to read any more of the small type; put out the light; tossed about for an hour; put on the light again; read for an hour, and so on and so on. At half-past seven this morning in desperation got up, had a very hot bath, took five aspirins, drank a pot of tea, left order that I wasn't to be disturbed, and tried again—result marvellous. Slept like a dead man from eight-thirty until three in the afternoon.

It is now half-past nine. I've had a damn good dinner. There's nobody else in the writing room, and I'm sitting down with this book, a cigar, and what's left of my coffee.

I seem to be deliberately putting off getting down to brass tacks about last night. Suppose I'm sort of savouring success. The only thing I don't like about the campaign to date is the *easiness* of it. That seems to be a grumble; I suppose a poor sod like me must have something to moan about!

God! It worked like perfect machinery which has just been

oiled. Not a thing went wrong. I knew when I left here just after eleven that it would; but that didn't stop me either from being careful (I *must* be careful) or from being surprised that it went as smoothly as it did.

It's just struck me that there is something wanting. . . . Now I've remedied the defect. I've been upstairs and got the little leather case which holds those two photographs of Elsie. I've opened that and stuck it up in front of me. In front of it I've put the long blue envelope. Now I *am* going to get a hundred per cent. satisfaction out of this silly business of writing it all down.

The old bozo who's got the room opposite mine has just come in. He pulled his whiskers and grunted good-evening. I grunted back at him. He's settled down now by the fire with a paper. I wish he'd stop rustling the damned thing. I know what he's reading. He's reading the front page. And all over the front page is the history of Number Three. What a stir-up it's given London. They've got the idea now; they're wondering where they're going from here. Funny to think that there's only one person that could tell 'em and that's me! Wonder what the old B.F. by the fire there would think if he could see what I'm writing. Good mind to get up and go across to him and ask him whether he's aware that he's talking to the man that any one or all of Them would give their great, flat feet to find.

I've finished the coffee. I've finished the cigar. I've had a good look and a good healthy grin at Elsie's photograph. I've tipped the stuff out of the blue envelope and had a good look at it and bunged it back and sealed it up again. I feel two hundred and fifty per cent.—if not more.

Just remembered that I was going to put down here a full account of Number Three. It was lovely the way it worked out. It was damn silly how easy it was. And the knife was satisfactory. All the same, I don't think I'll use that way again. Don't know why, but it seems more dangerous somehow—I mean from the point of view of getting nabbed.

Here goes for the account, anyhow. Some day, after I'm dead, I suppose someone will get hold of this book. It ought to make interesting reading.

I left here just after eleven. It's a big enough place and there's enough in and out from the restaurant to make it quite impossible for anyone to mark your comings and goings. Over my dinner jacket I'd got a dark, light-weight overcoat. I'd got a black felt soft hat. In the left-hand pocket of the coat I'd got a dark muffler and a pair of old dogskin gloves. In the right-hand pocket of the coat I'd got the knife, in two parts—the blade which I bought a week ago at a small ironmonger's in Camberwell, the handle which I bought on the same day in Notting Hill, and cut to fit three days ago in the middle of Richmond Park. The blade is the blade of what they call a French chef's knife. It was sharp when I bought it. It was a damned sight sharper when I used it. I tried it out (with gloves on) after dinner, about an hour before I started. The point was really a point, and the edge—well, it sliced a single hair I pulled out of my head. I believe you could have shaved with it. A good bit of steel.

I walked through Mayfair into Park Lane. I took a bus at Park Lane to the Marble Arch. I got off there and walked along beside the park, past Lancaster Gate, as far as Notting Hill Metropolitan Station. I took an inner circle train (third-class ticket) and went in a half-full smoker to High Street. I got out at High Street and took a bus back to Knightsbridge. At twelve o'clock I was walking down Fortescue Street behind Harrow Square. I passed the Slovene Legation at about three minutes past twelve. It's the house on the corner of the Square and Fortescue Street.

He was there—just as he had been when I marked him a week ago. I knew he would be, but I was pleased to see him all the same. I couldn't do anything first time because I could hear somebody else, on the same pavement as I was, about twenty yards behind me. I walked straight by and into the square and once almost round it. Not quite round it, because I didn't go back up Fortescue Street. I went instead down Fortescue Mews and came out in Palethorpe Terrace, turned left and left again into Fortescue Street once more.

Oh, it was great! This time the street was empty. I walked straight up it on the left-hand pavement. There was nobody behind me. There was nobody in front of me—except Number Three. When I'd still got about fifty yards to go I stopped, fumbled in my pockets, took out the knife, slotted it into the handle, and put it back in my pocket. I took out a cigarette and stuck it in my mouth. I walked on. I had the knife, in my right hand, in my pocket. Still nobody behind me, still nobody in front of me—except Number Three. I was very hot, but I didn't grudge the overcoat. A jacket pocket would have been big enough for the knife. I remember thinking it was a good thing the night wasn't so hot that it would make an overcoat look silly. I'd seen plenty of men in light overcoats already.

I got up to him. He was standing there, just in the shadow of the first pillar of the portico. He'd got his hands behind his back in that lordly, damn-you, bloody silly way they have. I went straight up to him. I had the unlighted cigarette in my left hand. I said, "Good-evening. I wonder whether you could oblige me with a match?" He looked at me. I didn't mind. He could have looked at me under a thousand arc lights if he'd wanted. I knew he'd never be able to tell anything.

It was easy, easy, *easy!*

He said: "I think so, sir." Very slimy and civil he was. He began to fumble in his pockets. He brought out a box of matches. I came close to him. He struck one. Both his hands were up. I brought my right hand out of the pocket with the knife in it. My God, it was easy!

I liked the cigarette trick, so I took the matchbox away from him as he lay by the railings.

Still there was nobody in Fortescue Street. I was absolutely calm. I put my left hand into my pocket and pulled out the black woollen scarf and wrapped it round the knife so that not a drop of mess could get onto my clothes. I then put the bundle back into my right-hand pocket and walked quietly on. He hadn't made a sound. I walked through the squares to Victoria and round the station, down Wilton Road to St. George's Square and then the river. I smoked a cigarette leaning on the parapet of the Embankment. I was a gentleman, going home from a party, looking at the moon on the water.

How pretty!

Somewhere in the Thames sludge is the knife—and a pair of gloves.

Chapter X
DIES IRÆ

IT WAS, you will remember, on the 13th of May that Sergeant Guilfoil of the Surrey Constabulary was found dead in Farnley police station, the cause of death being a head wound from a pistol shot. The affair was a five days' wonder. POLICE SERGEANT SHOT, said the *Daily Telegraph*. POLICE-MAN MURDERED, announced the *Times*. ARMED RAIDERS SLAUGHTER POLICE SERGEANT, cried the *Dispatch*. MURDER

IN POLICE STATION, yelled the *Morning Standard*, SHOT TO
DEATH AT POST.

On the 14th of May it was announced that the police held
an important clue and that an arrest was expected. On the
15th of May the press noted that no arrest had been made
and that the police were reticent. On the 16th of May Fleet
Street girded up its loins for a wholesale attack upon the
police and their methods. There was much rubbing of hands
and smacking of lips in Fleet Street because this season until
now had been a particularly dull season. But the attack was
not to come—at least not then. For on the night of the
16th of May, Hans Ericssen, the Norse-blooded but inter-
nationally financed multimillionaire, blew out his brains in
the royal suite of a London hotel. . . .

However, in the early hours of the 9th of June the dead
body of Police Constable Henry Beecham was found in the
mouth of Clarendon Passage, Mayfair. The press, as you
have seen, made much of this sensation. Not only had a
policeman on duty been murdered, but it appeared that the
murderer was that widely known and universally popular
personality, Sir Christopher Llewellyn De'Ath Vayle, fourth
baronet. On the evening of the 10th of June, however, an
official communiqué was issued from Scotland Yard to the
effect that owing to fresh evidence the murder charge against
Sir Christopher Vayle had been dropped, Sir Christopher
being retained in custody on a charge of assaulting the
police.

On the morning of the 11th of June Superintendent Connor
of the C.I.D., surveying a colleague over a pile of newspapers, remarked gloomily that the lid of hell had undoubtedly come off, for like one hound the press, baulked of a
continuance of the Vayle sensation, flung itself upon the
bones of the two dead policemen. What had been done about
Sergeant Guilfoil? What was going to be done about Constable Beecham? Where was the important clue? What had it
led to? What was the country coming to? If the guardians of
the peace were not safe themselves, peace was a hollow
word. How could the law remain majestic when the police
could not even apprehend the authors of deadly crimes
against themselves? What was wrong with Scotland Yard?

And so on and so on. And so on.

But this, which the police and public took in their blissful
ignorance as a storm, was to prove itself within two hours
of a middle morning to be the merest breeze. For the noon
editions of the papers on the 11th of June contained the news,

reluctantly enough given by the authorities, that upon the preceding night there had been found, in Fortescue Street—where he was on the special duty of guarding the property and person of a foreign ambassador—the dead and lacerated body of Police Constable Thomas Franklin. . . .

2

On the night of the 17th of June, at five minutes past eleven, Cathleen Storey of Number Eight Platt's Villas, Fulham, found, in a huddled untidy heap at the foot of his own front steps, the body of Edward Storey. Edward Storey was her husband. He was also, although only thirty-seven years of age, the most fancied candidate for the next vacant inspectorship of A.X. Division of the Metropolitan Police. Sergeant Storey had been killed by a blow which had broken the last two joints of his spinal vertebræ. It was obvious to the experts who saw his body later that the blow had been dealt by a sandbag. Sergeant Storey had come off duty at eight o'clock. His wife had expected him home by nine at the latest. By ten o'clock she had become a little anxious; but only a little, for policemen's wives are not easily made anxious by unpunctuality. So many things, Cathleen Storey told herself, have a way happening. Poor Cathleen! Until, only vaguely uneasy, she went out of the door to look up the high-walled lane and found what was left of Edward Storey with her feet, she was a plump and pretty wife—a benevolent and loving and even-tempered mother. At ten o'clock upon the next morning—the morning of the 18th of June—she was a stricken, twitching hag; she lay alternately moaning and shrieking upon the bed, to which she had to be held by two stalwart nurses.

At ten-thirty o'clock upon that morning, Sir Hector Frensham stepped into his car in Scotland Yard. He was haggard and unshaven. He had not been home since eleven a.m. upon the previous day.

At ten-forty that morning Nicholas Revel asked his telephone for the number of Miss Jane Frensham. He was told was told that Miss Frensham had just gone out.

At ten-forty-five upon that morning there appeared in his vast room upon the fourth floor of Otterworth House, Lord Otterworth himself. He addressed a meeting, convened by himself, of all the seven of his editors.

At eleven o'clock upon that morning Mr. Eustace Fauntwelp of 18 The Grove, Acacia Avenue, Balham, S.E., took pen and paper and addressed the editor of the *Morning Standard*. "Dear sir," began Mr. Fauntwell, "Is it not time that drastic measures were taken to revitalize what the sad events of the past weeks have shown to be an effete and worthless police force . . . ?"

At eleven-thirty o'clock upon that morning the mother and father of Thomas Franklin, late Number X.L. 2146 of the Metropolitan Police, watched the long box which contained all that there was now of Thomas Franklin being lowered into a hole in the ground.

At noon upon that day his senior private secretary brought in to the Home Secretary the green foolscap pages upon which were typed the parliamentary questions for the day. "My God!" said the Home Secretary, and studied the many pages. There were more than three times the usual number, and ninety per cent. were upon one topic. "Will you please tell Colonel Eckersleigh," said the Home Secretary, "that I am unavoidably prevented from attending the House today. I should be obliged if he would take questions."

At one p.m. upon that day there appeared upon the streets —a quarter of an hour earlier than usual—a special late extra seven-thirty edition of the *Evening Express*. In place of headlines, paragraphs, and photographs the front page bore only, staring out from its white background with the effect of a blow, a gigantic letter X.

At one-thirty p.m. upon that day Sir Hector Frensham sat at the head of a long table. Upon each side of the table were ranged eight men. The seventeen had been there already for the better part of an hour. They would be there, it seemed, for more than another hour. At three p.m. (English summer time) upon that day, the news editor of the New York *Comet* spoke roughly to two of his sub-editors. "For crying out loud!" said the editor. "Has this Rosenbluhm dame *bought* the front page? Take her off! And don't ask me what's to take her place. You boys are dead! There's a place called England. There's a place called London. D'you know what they're doing in London? They're croaking cops—hundreds of 'em! Get to it!"

At ten o'clock that night Police Constable Percy Batey bade good-night to Police Constable Frederich Rogers who had just relieved him. From round the corner there came to their ears the receding footsteps of the sergeant and the other two reliefs that he was posting. "Well," said P.C. Batey, "Night-night, Fred." "Cheerio!" said P.C. Rogers. "Mind you

REVELRY BY DAY 55

watch for the Bogey Man," said P.C. Batey, and P.C. Rogers laughed. "That's all right," he said. "I got me fingers crossed!"

At eleven-thirty that night two men, strangers to each other, talked at the cocktail bar of the Alsace Hotel. The first to speak was a man who held strong—and he prided himself—original views upon the topic that obsessed London. "It's all very well," he said, "but it must be their own damn fault! Must be! And if it *is* their own fault, well, I say it serves them right. Red tape! That's what's at the bottom of this—red tape!" "I can't agree with you, sir," said the second man. "I can't agree with you! I've travelled a very great deal, and I think the English police one of the very finest forces in the world. Good-night, sir." The second man turned on his heel and went from the bar. He wore dinner clothes but no hat or topcoat. He was at present living at the Alsace. He took a lift up to the third floor and went along the softly carpeted corridor to his room. He locked himself into his room. He sat down at the writing table in the corner by the window and took from a locked leather case upon the table top a thick black book, also locked. He unlocked the book and spread it upon the table with careful, almost loving fingers. He began to write in the book. He smiled to himself.

Chapter XI

REVELRY BY DAY

CHRISTOPHER LLEWELLYN DE'ATH VAYLE, having been once remanded, was brought before Mr. Malpas, at Heron Street, on the twenty-third of June. It was hot outside the courtroom. It was much hotter inside the courtroom, which was so densely crowded as to lead Jane Frensham to tell herself that at last she knew the phrase "packed to suffocation" for something more than reporter's license. Behind her, while Mr. Malpas dealt rapidly and justly with a riveter who had empurpled the left eye of his wife, two women fainted and were removed.

"Phoo!" said Jane to herself. "It's *hot!*" For a moment her head felt queer and something happened to her eyes. The dusty windows, the dingy yellow oak, the banks of staring faces, the dais and Mr. Malpas and his clerk and the dock and the witness stand—all these, for one dread instant, swayed and became blurred at their edges and leaned towards one another with a misty trembling. Jane screwed her eyes tight shut and behind her white forehead took herself to task. She opened her eyes slowly and sighed relief. The world was steady.

"Phoo!" said Jane again. And then, *"Oh!"*

She had seen, standing in a momentarily doorless doorway at the far corner of the courtroom, the grey-clad, blond-headed figure of Mr. Nicholas Revel. She had not seen Mr. Nicholas Revel since the evening of the 9th of June. Upon the 10th she had heard his name from her father as that of the surely heaven-sent witness who was certain to free Christopher from the charge of murder, but she had not mentioned to her father that she had met and talked to and eaten with Mr. Nicholas Revel. Several times she had been on the verge of taking Hector Frensham into her confidence; but each time she had refrained. Although the two murders which had followed that of Henry Beecham had implied more strongly than any proof that Christopher Vayle could not have been the killer of Henry Beecham, Jane was not sure—not at all sure—what the official outlook would have to be if the evidence which officially cleared Christopher were proved, even now, to be entirely false. Although she knew Hector Frensham as no one else alive knew him, she was yet not certain as to whether he would accept such staggering information purely as a private person. But whether he did or not, it would worry him, and he had (Jane sighed) enough worry, God knew! And besides, every time she felt that she could not bear to keep this astonishing secret a secret any longer, Jane remembered that she had made a promise to Christopher's strange saviour. Every day since the withdrawal of the murder charge she had expected to see Nicholas Revel or to hear Nicholas Revel's voice on the telephone. But every day she had been—yes, *disappointed* was the word. She had looked him up in the telephone book and had not found him. There was not a single Revel with one L. There was not even a Revell who had N for an initial. She had gone so far, later in the week, as to telephone to the Savarin and, speaking in a voice which she fondly imagined disguised, endeavour to extract an address from George. But George either did not know or would not tell. Starr's Garage, approached in the same manner a few days later, definitely knew but definitely would not tell. They didn't, they said very properly, give clients' addresses unless authorized to do so by such clients. And Jane had had to be content. She had, of course, thought of obtaining his address from the slavish Scott, but prudence had restrained her. Scott was too near Sir Hector. Besides, any inquiry at Scotland Yard was, *in posse* if not *in esse,* a breach of faith. And now here he was, and she was wondering why he had come.

It did not take her long to find out. The riveter dismissed with a fine and a caution, Mr. Malpas gave a twitch to his chair and a quick shuffle to his papers and leaned back, fingertips together. Below him the clerk spoke to the uniformed usher, who shouted. Almost before the echoes of the bellow had died away, Christopher Llewellyn De'-Ath, fourth baronet, made his first appearance in any dock. Jane, looking at him with a sudden thrill of pleasure not unmixed—despite the ignominy of his position—with pride, became conscious that the femininity of all kinds which surrounded her was fluttered. She did not blame it. Christopher, pale though he was and soberly clad—almost too soberly, Jane thought—was so absolutely *right.* And there was no denying the distinction of his features or the grandeur of his great body. For the first time Jane found herself in undivided sympathy with the resolution, entirely his own, which had led Christopher to refuse to accept freedom on bail while awaiting this trial.

The packed room was hushed. So thick and dense was the silence that Jane was conscious of the blood pounding in her ears. She kept her eyes straight before her. She could see, without turning her head, both Christopher and the magistrate. They seemed, curiously but doubtless properly enough, the only unmoved persons in the place—Christopher pale and grave and steady-eyed, Malpas leather-faced and shrewd and wise and utterly matter-of-fact.

The charge was read—a long, unpunctuated rumbling of which Jane did not bother to catch a word. In reply to another but shorter drone:

"Guilty," said Christopher Vayle with decision.

Malpas looked down at the man in the dock with a quick bird-like twist of his head. "Represented?"

"No," said Christopher Vayle.

Malpas raised heavy lids from small bright brown eyes. "Why not?"

"I've pleaded guilty to the charge. I did not consider it necessary to be represented."

"H'm!" Malpas grunted.

Three witnesses were then called. The first, Police Constable Patrick Dorney of X.L. Division, stated that at about a quarter past two in the early morning of the 9th of June he was approached by a man whom he had no trouble in identifying as the prisoner. Prisoner had talked a great deal of nonsense. P.C. Patrick Dorney had told prisoner to move on. That was all that P.C. Dorney remembered until some minutes later he came to himself, with a jaw which he had at first feared was broken, and discovered that his helmet had been stolen. Questioned by the magistrate, P.C. Patrick Dorney stated that, amongst the nonsense which prisoner had talked, there had certainly been mention of helmets, prisoner having made some remark about wanting them to make cups out of or some such.

"Was he drunk?" snapped Malpas.

P.C. Patrick Dorney hesitated.

"Was—he—drunk?"

"Not apparently," said P.C. Dorney, and was allowed to stand down.

"Call Nicholas Revel."

Mr. Nicholas Revel, so tastefully and coolly clad in the lightest of grey suits and the freshest of blue linen, presented a picture on the witness stand so easy and unruffled that he seemed to bring with him a much needed drop in the temperature. In answer to questions, Mr. Revel gave an address in Knightsbridge, admitted to being of independent means, and stated that upon the night of the 8th of June he had attended a party at the house of a friend. The party had been held at a house in Clarges Street. He had left at two-thirty upon the next morning and taken a taxi. In Fothergill Street, opposite the mouth of Clarendon Passage but upon the other side of the street, the driver had been compelled to stop the taxi and see to his engine. Mr. Revel, looking out of the window, had noticed a man, whom he identified as the prisoner, come out of the mouth of Clarendon Passage and, turning right, walk briskly away. His attention had been attracted by the size of the prisoner and the fact that he was in full evening dress with no hat or topcoat. He had noticed, with no little astonishment, that the prisoner appeared to be carrying two policeman's helmets. A little later, just before the taxi moved off, Mr. Revel had seen a helmetless policeman, walking unsteadily, come out of the mouth of Clarendon Passage and look this way and that along Fothergill Street. He had been in two minds as to whether he would ask the policeman if he needed assistance, but decided that, as the policeman must have seen the taxi and had not asked for assistance, he did not need any. The taxi driver, having completed his tinkering, had then got back into the cab and they had driven off.

Mr. Revel descended from the witness stand and made unruffled way to a seat in the row behind the press table.

The next witness was Mr. Joseph Palmer, owner and driver of taxicab GH 4838, hackney license number BK 41872. Mr. Joseph Palmer corroborated, with a wealth of detail and some humour, the evidence of the gentleman who had been his fare upon the morning of the 9th of June. Mr. Joseph Palmer, released, made exit from the courtroom.

Malpas leaned folded arms upon his table and looked full at the man in the dock.

"Anything to say?" said Malpas.

"Yes," said Christopher Vayle. His voice was steady and under perfect control, but it was toneless, flat and dead.

"Say it," said Malpas.

"The first witness was wrong. He implied that I was not drunk. I was drunk. I'd been drunk for about ten days. This is not offered as an excuse. It's a statement. I think it makes a bad job worse."

"H'm!" Malpas grunted.

Silence.

"Realize you're lucky?" said Malpas.

"Yes," said Christopher Vayle. "And if this is what you're driving at, I do realize, fully, that I was the indirect cause of Beecham's death. If I hadn't hit him he wouldn't . . ." He paused for a moment. Jane, watching with anguished eyes, saw the tip of his tongue come out and drag itself across his dry lips.

"If I hadn't hit him," said Christopher again, the toneless voice a little louder than it had been, "he would very likely have been able to defend himself against the man that killed him. He might even have arrested him. If he had arrested him . . ."

Malpas grunted again. "Quite. Might not have been these other cases. Quite. . . . Well, young man, I'm going to give you . . ." And here came the well-known Malpasian pause before judgment. "I'm going to fine you two hundred pounds *with* fourteen days' hard labour, or I'm going to fine you five hundred pounds."

"I'll take the two hundred and the fortnight," said Christopher Vayle, whose annual income was thirty thousand pounds.

"Next case," said Malpas.

The silence into which the two voices—one flat and toneless and deep, the other sharp and high-pitched and definite —had been dropping words like pebbles into a well was annihilated. Two or three gasps became a low murmur of many voices. The low murmur became a hum, the hum a babel. There came the sound of a gavel upon wood and, to Jane's ears as she tried to get through the door-seeking crowd faster than they would let her, shouted words about clearing the court.

She gave up struggling. She went with the crowd. Her eyes were heavy with tears which smarted in them but which she would not allow to fall.

2

In front of Jane the shuffling crowd suddenly thinned. She felt hot sunlight in her face. The glare stung her already smarting eyes and for a moment she closed them.

When she opened them again it was to find herself in a narrow street, almost alley, which she did not know at all. Actually it ran along the side of the court buildings, joining two main thoroughfares. Drawn up at the curb immediately opposite the doorway outside which she stood was a long grey coupé. Jane blinked once more. She felt a touch on her arm and jumped.

"Oh!" said Jane.

She looked at Nicholas Revel. He stood at her shoulder, hat in hand. He smiled.

"What you want is a drink," said Nicholas Revel. "Perhaps two."

His fingers closed on her elbow, and Jane found herself crossing the pavement towards the car. She sank into the comfort of the seat next to the driver's. A small sigh escaped her.

"Nice!" said Jane. "Thank you."

The grey car bored sinuous way out into the Charing Cross Road, swung left, and, darting this way and that among inferior fellows, pursued rapid and effortless but erratic course.

Jane opened eyes now dry to the white and gold and green of the gardens bordering the Mall.

"Oh!" said Jane.

"Why?" said her driver.

"So quick," said Jane. "Where are we going?"

"I told you," said Nicholas Revel. "To get a drink. Perhaps two."

They had two in the cool, dim lounge of the Hyde Park Hotel.

"Feeling better?" said Nicholas.

Jane smiled at him. "Much! You know, it isn't fair!"

"What's not?"

"My always being all swimey when I meet you."

"Always?" said Nicholas and smiled.

"Well . . ." began Jane, and found herself actually blushing. "Yes, it is only twice, isn't it?" she said primly.

Nicholas Revel put back his head and laughed.

"I don't *think*," said Jane, "that I like you very much."

"Don't worry about that—you will."

Jane tried to repress a smile but failed. "But I certainly owe you a great many thanks."

And now she gazed at her companion with serious, widened eyes whose blue beauty was reward in itself.

"Don't care for thanks," said Nicholas. "Obligations are my line."

"Yes?" said Jane and looked puzzled.

Her companion put down his glass and got to his feet. "Come on!" he said.

"Where to?"

"Lunch—luncheon, if you like it better."

"But I can't," said Jane and seemed to mean what she said.

"Obligation," said Nicholas.

"But I really can't!" Jane looked at her watch. "In half an hour I'm lunching in Grosvenor Place. I simply can't put it off."

Nicholas sat down again. "Who with?"

"Betty Gore-Smith. D'you know the Gore-Smiths?"

"No," said Nicholas. "Have another drink?"

Jane shook her head. "If you did know the Gore-Smiths you'd realize that I *can't* put them off. I—I'm awfully sorry!"

"Why worry?" Nicholas beckoned a waiter, who came and was given an order.

Nicholas got to his feet. "Forgive me," he said. "Back in a minute."

He was back in four. He sat down and drank the cocktail which the waiter had brought. He paid the waiter and put change into his pocket and looked at Jane.

"Right?" he said. And then, as they came down the steps and crossed the pavement to the car: "I'll drop you."

"Thank you," said Jane, darting a sideways glance at his profile, which told her nothing.

The car, instead of going straight up Knightsbridge, swung left into the park.

"Quicker, really," said the driver.

"Perhaps it is," said Jane.

But the car, when it reached Hyde Park Corner, did not halt for the right turn out of the park. It swung left, leaving the Corner behind.

"What on *earth* are you doing?" said Jane.

"Going back to Emperor's Gate, thence to Richmond."

"Richmond!" Jane's voice sounded strange even in her own ears.

"Yes. Lunch by the river."

"Oh!" said Jane. "Indeed! If you insist upon being so—so ridiculous, I suppose I shall have to wait until we're held up, then I can get out."

"Why do that? The Gore-Smiths are off."

"The . . ." began Jane and fell silent. She twisted round in her seat and stared at Nicholas Revel. "You don't mean . . . ?"

"Yes. You aren't well. Porter rang up Mrs. Gore-Smith. Although you felt seedy this morning you had intended to go to lunch. You got up late and dressed. After that you felt so bad you went to bed again."

Jane was silent. She twisted round again in her seat and sat staring out through the windscreen straight ahead of her. Nicholas was silent, too. Jane spoke first, but not until Hammersmith Bridge lay behind them.

"Porter?" began Jane. Her voice sounded as if she were speaking to herself. It also sounded puzzled.

"Yes, madam," said Porter's voice at her side.

"Oh!" said Jane, and jumped. For the second time in her acquaintance with this man she became conscious of the number of "oh's" which went to the making of her conversation. She turned her head, her eyes wide. She saw that the driver was indeed Nicholas Revel and not Emmanuel Porter.

"I trust, madam," said Porter's voice, coming out of the mouth of Nicholas Revel, "that I have not done irretrievable wrong. I regret that my facility for vocal imitation should have startled you, madam."

Suddenly Jane began to laugh.

"*That's* the stuff!" said Nicholas Revel.

3

They lunched in a tall, many-windowed room looking out over the river. Outside the sun poured down over trees and water, touching the world with a Midasian yet wholly benevolent finger. They had coffee upon a veranda at the foot of which a small green lawn ran down to the towpath. Jane felt the sun hot upon her, but from somewhere a small breeze came to turn what might have been uncomfortable heat to a benison of warmth. She stared out over the gold-flecked bronze of the water while her second cup of coffee, unheeded, grew cold.

"Penny," said the voice of her host.

Jane started. "I—I was thinking. I don't know that I could tell you what about. I mean, even if I wanted to."

"Quite," said Nicholas and looked at the two inches of ash upon his cigar. "A fortnight's not too bad, though."

"A fortnight? What *are* you talking about?"

"Seven days, one week," said Nicholas. "One fortnight, fourteen days—hard or otherwise."

"Oh!" said Jane.

Nicholas Revel became aware that blue eyes were staring at him. He turned his head and met their gaze with his own. Upon Jane's face was a look of puzzled wonder, upon the face at which she looked no expression which could be read.

"You know, I just *can't* make you out!" said Jane.

"Flattering," said Nicholas. "Have a drink?"

Jane shook her head. She went on staring. She brought into her eyes that detached and scientifically inquiring look which she had never known to fail in reducing man to abject matter.

But it did nothing to this man. Suddenly Jane was conscious that she could no longer meet the unreadable look of the unlikely black eyes. She dropped her gaze and felt a wave of colour sweep up hotly to the top of her poll. In her mind she raged against herself.

"And weather like this makes it easier," said the casual voice of Nicholas Revel.

"Makes what easier?"

"Fourteen days' wait."

"It's not difficult!" Jane's voice was sharp with anger.

"Oh! Glad to hear it. I've been wondering what you could see in——"

"Stop!" said Jane. "You're going to make a mistake."

"As how?"

Jane drew a deep breath. "P'r'aps I was wrong. I thought you were going to say something about—about Christopher."

"I was. You think I'd better not?"

"Was it something unpleasant?"

Broad, grey-clad shoulders were lifted in a small shrug.

Jane's eyes, from beneath their fine-drawn arches of black, flashed sudden blue fire.

"Don't say it!" said Jane. "What was it?"

Nicholas smiled. "I won't. What the devil did the boob want to take the fourteen days *for?* Why not pay the full fine? If it had been five thousand quid it wouldn't 've hurt *him!*"

"You wouldn't understand," said Jane haughtily.

"Nobody with any sense could."

"*Anyone* could!" said Jane. "Except knaves or fools."

The smile of Nicholas Revel became a grin.

"You mustn't be rude," he said. "Obligation. Heavy obligation."

For a moment Jane glared in silent fury. The grin at which she glared did nothing but widen. She gave up anger.

"I just *can't* make you out!" she said helplessly.

"Positively all deception!"

"But surely, surely," began poor Jane, "you can see—that Christopher is blaming himself. . . ."

"I can *see* it, all right. But I can't understand it."

"And yet you can—can take all that trouble and tell all these frightfully dangerous lies—dangerous to yourself, I mean—just to help a man you've never met and say you can't understand."

"I did nothing of the sort," said Nicholas with decision.

Jane stared in astonishment.

"D'you mean to tell me," she said, "that you *did* see Christopher that night?"

"Of course not!" The voice of Nicholas was impatient.

"Well, what d'you mean by . . ."

"I mean that I didn't do anything to help a man I'd never seen. That would have been purely quixotic. I'm never that."

"I see," said Jane, and looked away. "Not quixotic, only chivalrous."

"Chivalrous my foot!" said Nicholas with emphasis. "You were in trouble. By getting you out of trouble I've put you under an obligation."

Jane lifted her eyes only to drop them almost instantly.

"You keep on talking about obligations," she said.

"Naturally."

Silence. Nicholas smoked placidly. Jane played with her coffee spoon.

"What does it mean?" said Jane desperately. "Does it mean that there's something that you want me to do for you?"

"Perhaps," said Nicholas Revel.

Jane lifted her head, braving herself to meet the unreadable stare of the black eyes. But they were not looking at her.

"What is it?" she said.

"Let's leave that now," said Nicholas, still looking out over the river. "Tell me, I suppose your father's having a toughish time?"

"Daddy? Why, whatever's he got to . . . I don't know. . . . What *are* you talking about?"

"Complete change of subject every Tuesday and Friday. I was asking how this police pogrom was affecting Sir Hector Frensham."

"Oh," said Jane. "I see." But she didn't sound as if she saw. Her voice, paradoxically, was both relieved and disappointed. As she went on, however, it grew ténder and sad. "Poor dear! Toughish isn't the word for the time he's having. I'm very worried about him. Very worried indeed. D'you know, since the last of these dreadful murders he's only been home two nights. And then I'm certain he didn't sleep. Not properly, anyhow. You see, he feels not only the things that everybody else feels—I mean horror and bewilderment and—and—well, that sort of what-*are*-we-coming-to feeling; but he's got a sort of really personal feeling, too. I think to him it's rather as if he were a man who'd been put in charge of a lot of children and wasn't looking after them properly. And then, of course, the inevitable criticisms, although he doesn't let them interfere with him, are beginning to get on his nerves. I'm afraid, awfully afraid, that he's beginning to believe that half the things the newspapers say about him and Scotland Yard must have some truth in them. You see, although anybody that knows anything about the police knows how wonderful they really are, I suppose it's very difficult for laymen to realize just how difficult it is to stop this awful X business. I'm afraid I'm not saying what I mean very well, but it's all such a——"

"I know exactly what you mean," said Nicholas. "You mean that people are so used to thinking in catch phrases like 'the authorities must step in,' and 'this must stop; let the police see to it,' that they've got into the habit of thinking they really mean something when they say 'em."

"Yes," said Jane eagerly. "That's exactly what Daddy was saying the other day. He'd been looking at some of the letters to the papers. He was rabid about them. And really very funny, bless him, in spite of his worry. But it *is* the most extraordinary thing that's ever happened, isn't it? I mean even to me it does seem almost—well, incredible that this can go on."

"Don't see that," said Nichols Revel. "Don't see that at all. Why shouldn't it go on? What's to stop it? It'd be different if X was a gang."

Jane stared in wonder. "It *is* funny the way you keep saying exactly the same things as Daddy. He's sure X is singular, though some of his best men are certain it's a gang."

"What do they think it's a gang of?"

Jane shrugged. "I don't know. He hasn't told me. Something like Bolshevists, I suppose. After all, it'd be a good move for any sort of anarchists, wouldn't it?—I mean for anyone who's trying to destroy order. . . ."

"It isn't a gang," said Nicholas. "If it was, all this would soon be over, if not already. The minute there's more than one mind on this sort of job there's the danger—or chance if you like it better—that someone, somehow, somewhere will start blabbing; for money; for fear; for any one of a hundred reasons."

"You sound very sure it's one man," Jane said.

"I am."

"How can you be sure?"

"How can your father be?"

"He may know something that I don't," said Jane. "He doesn't tell me everything."

"He doesn't *know* anything," said Nicholas Revel. "He can't. If he did, something would have been done. In this sort of affair, to know something is to do something. I'm not saying it necessarily ought to be, but it has to be."

Jane stared out across the river. The corners of her mouth dropped, and the lines of a frown drew her brows together.

"You sound as if you thought that it might go on a long time yet." A little shiver shook her.

"I do."

"But—but it *can't!*" said Jane.

"What's to stop it? Not the police."

Jane turned her head and stared. Her eyes sparkled suddenly, and a faint flush of extra colour came into her cheeks.

"And why not?" she said.

"Because they're going about it the wrong way."

"Indeed!" said Jane. "And how do *you* know what way they're going about it? You've read the papers, haven't you?

"Yes," said Nicholas.

Jane beat upon the table with a small fist. "Then you must know that you can't know anything. For days it's been explained in the papers that the police plans obviously can't be made public."

"Oh, quite!"

"Then how dare you," said Jane with dangerous quietness, "how dare you sit there, looking so—so *damned* superior, and say that you know what the police are doing and that it's no good?"

Nicholas looked at her with an expression of great solemnity behind which there lurked, infuriatingly, a hidden smile.

"Any man of imagination is in a position to say what I've said. One can't help knowing roughly how the police work. One knows what's happened to them and that it's unprecedented. Mix well, stir, and leave to simmer."

"Very weak!" said Jane with a scornful curl to her upper lip.

"Weak it is," agreed her host. "That's why I say that without luck they'll never get X. I tell you what: I'll have a bet with you. I'll give you two to one that I'll write down in five minutes a summary containing at least seventy-five per cent. of the *extra* steps—d'you follow me?—that the police have taken since X began to strut his stuff. Two to one in anything you like."

"Done!" said Jane. The frown still faintly creased her white forehead, but she laughed—a puzzled little sound. "You're not unpopular with yourself!"

"What's the bet in?"

"I'll let you know. But Daddy may not tell me if you're right."

"He will," said Nicholas and rose and walked away.

Jane looked out again over the river. She defeated an inclination in herself to turn and look at her host as he walked back towards the veranda steps.

He was back within two minutes. In his hand was a

small block of scribbling paper. He sat down to face her and took a thin gold pencil from his pocket.

"Wait!" said Jane and glanced at the watch on her wrist. "Ready? Go!"

She watched while unhurriedly he wrote. The pencil slipped over the paper, hardly pausing at all. It covered one sheet and then half of another.

Nicholas Revel sat back in his chair. The gold pencil went back into his pocket. Jane looked at her watch to find that four minutes had gone by.

"Finished?" she said.

He nodded.

Jane held out her hand. "May I see?"

He shook his head. From a side pocket of the grey coat he produced an envelope.

"I borrowed this as well," he said. He folded the two sheets upon which he had written and put them in the envelope and sealed it. "When you are ready, give that to your father. Don't look at it before."

Jane looked at him, her eyes full of suspicion.

"I mean it," he said. "It's all there."

"Seventy-five per cent?" said Jane slowly.

He shrugged. "Possibly more. Certainly not less. What's the bet in?"

"I've told you," Jane said. "I'll let you know."

She picked up the envelope and looked at it reflectively.

"Trust," said Nicholas.

"It's extremely rude to seal envelopes," said Jane with severity. "Tell me something."

"With pleasure. If it's not a rude answer."

Jane still looked down at the envelope. "If you're so clever," she said acidly, "why don't you tell me to tell my father what he ought to do instead of just telling him what he's done?"

Nicholas smiled.

An angry Jane loathed herself for liking the smile while what she wished to do was to wipe it off with something hard and heavy.

"Couldn't be bothered," said Nicholas Revel.

"*Oh!*" said Jane. And then: "Just for that you shall."

"You'd like me to?"

Jane nodded.

"I'll write it," said Nicholas and once more took out his pencil.

This time he covered one page. He felt in his pocket and produced another envelope.

"Lucky I brought two," he said and put the sheet into it and sealed it. "Show your father that *after* the other."

"If I don't forget both of them," said Jane loftily, and looked at her watch. "Are you going to take me home or have I got to find a train?"

"No hurry," said Nicholas. "He won't be home yet."

Chapter XII
COPYRIGHT RESERVED

MISS ALICIA ROOKSBY came out of the mouth of Hampstead Tube Station onto the sunlit precipitous street. To her right hand clung Master Philip Dunscombe, to her left Miss Patricia Dunscombe. Miss Rooksby halted on the pavement. She was looking for a taxi. It was early-closing day and the street was not full. She felt a sudden tug at her right hand and there came an excited squeal from the six-year-old Philip.

"Horse!" said Philip. "Horse!"

Miss Rooksby, aware of a sedate tramping of hoofs, followed the direction of the boy's outflung arm and saw, passing them upon the other side of the road, a mounted policeman astride a well-built grey who carried himself with an air.

"Haven't you seen enough horses for today?" said Miss Rooksby, for the three had just returned from Olympia.

"No!" said Philip stoutly.

"Well, I have," said Miss Rooksby and laughed and hailed a taxi, which presently bore the three of them up the hill and out of this story.

The grey horse's name was Prince. His rider was Constable Thomas Nutting. The pair were, as could be told by their demeanour, unaggressively pleased with their appearance.

They had ground for their pleasure. Prince's coat, had he been of any other colour, would have reflected sunshine like soft silk; as it was, his whiteness dazzled. The leather of bridle, reins, and saddle shone with the soft, rich glow of well-soaped leather. The steel of bit and curb chain and stirrups glowed with that dark light which only burnished steel can give, and what light the sun could spare from these things touched with sparkling glory the boots and buttons and cap peak of Prince's rider.

Thomas Nutting sat his horse well. Under his cap, blue eyes twinkled in a square-chinned, clean-shaven face whose skin was tanned to a clear mahogany brown. He was a well-built person, and his uniform both fitted and became him.

Prince, claimed by his master to be the fastest walker in the force, climbed the steep hill towards the pond and the Heath which lay around and beyond it. Thomas Nutting, his body erect yet giving easily to the smooth movement beneath him, would have liked to whistle or even to sing. He felt it hard that, being on duty, he could do neither. A moment later he felt, being something of a philosopher, that such minor hardships only served to enhance the general excellence of life. At the top of the hill, just as the pond came into sight, a lorry was endeavouring to back with the obvious intention of turning. As is usual with lorries, the driver, while backing, was completely unable to see the road to one side of him, and coming fast towards it from the Heath was a large, two-seater car.

Prince felt a slight pressure upon his flanks. His smooth walk changed smoothly to a smooth trot. The lorry driver caught sight of Thomas Nutting and, seeing the warning hand upheld, ceased backing. The two-seater, which had pulled up with a shrieking of brakes, was waved forward by the same hand which had stopped the lorry. It came slowly between the tail of the lorry and Thomas Nutting and his mount, now motionless as a statue at the extreme edge of the road. Driving the two-seater was a woman, beside her an elderly man. In the rumble seat of the two-seater was a blue-bonneted nurse. She was a very pretty girl. She looked appreciatively at the picture made by Prince and his rider. Thomas Nutting, who had something of an eye, looked her full in the face as the car crept past. She flushed, ducked her head, and then raised it again to smile. Thomas Nutting's right eye closed in a wink. The two-seater accelerated and was gone. The lorry driver completed his evolutions and took his charge thundering off across the Heath. Prince walked on. Thomas Nutting reflected momentarily and with pleasure upon the prettiness of the nurse. These reflections did not last long. They were very properly ousted by reflections upon the person and personality of

Miss Lilian Crofts, who was so shortly to be Mrs. Nutting. You could say what you like, but Lilian had 'em all beaten a mile.

Prince of his own accord turned and crossed the road and, mounting a low bank, was on a narrow track leading to a thinly wooded part of the Heath. Thomas Nutting leaned forward and patted the arched and beautifully muscled neck. A wide smile creased his brown face, showing white, strong teeth. The old horse knew what was what! Do the same thing with him three days running and he would do it of his own accord ever after. The trees came nearer and nearer. Feeling the slightest extra pressure upon his mouth, Prince halted. Thomas Nutting raised himself in his stirrups and looked back at the road, first to his right and then to his left. He also sent glances all round that part of the Heath in which he now was. He saw nothing. He took these precautions because he was now off his beat; more, he was about to filch, if luck was with him and she had been able to get to the meeting place, five minutes—perhaps more—with Lilian.

Prince walked on with sedate grace. His shoes made a soft thudding upon the sun-baked earth of the narrow winding path.

They came into the shade of the trees. The path continued as a slightly wider ride through the wood. Thomas Nutting looked at the watch upon his wrist. Five minutes to get to the tree from here would make it six o'clock. Lil had said six to six-fifteen. When she said that sort of thing she generally meant six; that was the sort she was —no nonsense.

There was nobody about. Very softly Thomas Nutting began to whistle. He was a notable whistler, and his fluted, double-tongued rendering of "Marching Through Georgia" would have been pleasant to hear.

It was gratefully cool in the wood. The sun came through the green tracery in irregular splashes of warm gold. The path was covered with softly mouldering leaves upon which Prince's shoes made a pleasant thudding shuffle. And all around them birds chittered sleepily, their notes mingling with the bright clinking of Prince's tackle.

Thomas Nutting dropped his reins onto Prince's neck. Life was good but could be made even better by tobacco. And there was no one about.

Prince walked on. Thomas Nutting had a cigarette in

his mouth and a box of matches in his hand when he saw something which made him drop both irretrievably.

Prince, feeling a leg pressure and a sudden snatch, most unusual, upon the off side of his mouth, pivoted to his right and bounded forward.

"Whoa!" said Thomas Nutting and kicked feet out of the irons and dropped his arms upon Prince's neck and slid to the ground.

Before him, not more than three yards from where he stood, was a giant oak which marked the juncture of the path he had been riding along with one which cut across it at right angles. And at the base of this there lay in a distorted sprawl the body of a man in the silver-buttoned broadcloth of the Metropolitan Police Force. His legs were oddly twisted and the left arm was flung out palm upwards. The right arm was close to his body. The chin pointed up to the sky. The sun coming through the branches of the oak painted the body with an irregular golden lattice. The head was bare, but a few feet away from it lay its helmet.

After one motionless instant Thomas Nutting covered the three yards in as many strides. He dropped on his knees by the body and bent over it, his hands fumbling feverishly at its tunic.

The body moved. The right arm, which had been close to the side, came up in a short and viciously powerful sweep. Momentarily the sun glittered on something which was held in the hand.

The mouth of Thomas Nutting opened, and there came from it a queer sound, half grunt, half sigh. His eyes widened in a stare like that of an astonished child, and then his whole face puckered like the face of an injured child. He clapped both hands to his stomach and coughed and pitched forward. As he fell, the body, with a quick twist, rolled clear.

2

At a quarter to seven that evening Constable Minchin of F.T. Division rang up the Hampstead police station from a police box just off his beat. He reported that he had been informed by a motorist that a riderless white horse which appeared to be a police horse had been seen loose upon the Heath. The motorist had endeavoured to catch the horse but, although he had been close to it on several occasions, had been unable to do so, as had various other persons making the same endeavour. Constable Minchin had the motorist's name and address—J. Salaman, 116 Pope's Road, Hendon.

The sergeant in charge sent two men up to the Heath immediately. A hour later they reported by telephone that they had found and caught the horse, which most certainly was a police horse and belonged, as the speaker knew for a fact, to Constable Nutting.

They had made inquiries of all passers-by but could find no one who had seen Nutting, although he had been known to have ridden up towards the Heath at some time just after five.

3

At a quarter to eight that evening George Francis Watkins, an A.A. Scout, was bicycling homewards along the main Filminster-Brackenham Road, twenty-three miles from London, when he was hailed by the driver of a blue touring car bearing the A.A. badge. The man who was driving the car was its only occupant. He wore a light-coloured dust coat and a brown felt hat. He very civilly asked Scout Watkins the way to Finsmere Pond, that famous beauty spot between Brackenham and Merrowmere. Scout Watkins gave the information and was thanked. The car drove off. Scout Watkins mounted his bicycle and continued his ride in the opposite direction.

It is curious to think that had Scout Watkins been able to see beneath the dust coat he would no doubt have been astonished by the sight of the blue broadcloth and bright buttons of the Metropolitan Police Force.

4

Sir Hector Frensham and his daughter sat to face each other at the dining table of Number Fourteen Gordon Place. Every now and then Jane stole covert and anxious glances at her father's face. When he looked at her she smiled gaily enough. When he did not look at her the smile was absent. Hector Frensham, during these past weeks, had begun to look his age and perhaps more—Hector Frensham, who once had been the youngest sixty-five that could be imagined! And besides the new lines and the dark half-circles under the eyes and the absence of their usual smile from the eyes even when the mouth underneath them was pretending to smile, there was, Jane saw tonight with an added pang, actually a droop to the square shoulders. Throughout the meal she kept up a stream of inconsequent talk, but when they drank coffee and smoked and Porter was gone from the room she fell silent.

Hector Frensham pierced a cigar. When it was alight he looked at his daughter through a blue cloud. He smiled— a real smile this time, compounded of affection and admiration. Jane looked at her best tonight.

"What have you been doing with yourself all day?" he said.

"Nothing much," said Jane. "Funny you should ask me, because I was just going to tell you. I went out to lunch. I went on the river. Then I came home."

"River and the Gore-Smiths? That doesn't seem to fit."

Jane was glad of the cloud of cigar smoke; she felt herself colouring.

"I didn't lunch with the Gore-Smiths," she said.

"Oh!" said Hector Frensham and waved away the smoke and looked more closely at his daughter. "New man?"

"Yes," said Jane.

"Do I know him?"

"Yes," said Jane. "At least I think you do. . . . He's the man who came and gave evidence about seeing Christopher."

"Good Lord!" said Hector Frensham. "No, I didn't see him—Connor saw him. What's he like?"

"I don't know," said Jane slowly. "He's attractive. He made me very angry at lunch."

She frowned at recollection. Slowly the frown changed to a smile, and she laughed a little.

"What did he do?" said Hector Frensham idly.

From a small evening bag of black moiré Jane produced the two sealed envelopes.

"There!" she said. "How can I know which one to give you first when he hasn't . . . Oh, but he has!"

On one of the envelopes in a corner was a large figure 2.

"What's this?" said Hector Frensham. "A joke?"

"I don't know." Jane slid the unmarked envelope deftly down the length of the table. "Open it in a minute when I've told you what's supposed to be inside. What made me so cross at lunch was that we were talking about—about —X. . . ."

"Ah!" said Hector Frensham, with bitterness. "I don't suppose yours was the only conversation on that topic."

Jane looked at him with compassion. "I'm sorry, dear, you know I don't . . ."

"Don't be a silly young ass!" said her father. "Go on! What was this row?"

Jane explained.

Hector Frensham weighed the envelope in his hand. He looked at it with a curious twist of his mouth. Once he took it in both hands, and it seemed for a moment to Jane, watching, that he was going to tear it into shreds, unopened. But his fingers instead ripped open the envelope. Jane found, with a little shock, that she had been holding her breath.

Hector Frensham unfolded the two sheets of cheap paper. Jane watched his face. She did not know what emotions she was prepared to see, but she found that the quick stare of astonishment was not surprising.

Hector Frensham read on. He came to the end. He lifted his head and looked at his daughter.

"Extraordinary thing," he said.

"Is it . . ." stammered Jane. "Has he . . . ?"

"Yes. You've lost your bet, old thing. Here, give me the other envelope."

Jane got up and came round the table and perched herself upon the arm of her father's chair. She gave him the second envelope. She reached out a hand and took the two sheets from her father's fingers.

"What's in this one?" said Hector Frensham, tapping the envelope numbered 2.

"That's what *ought* to be done."

"Oh!" said Hector Frensham.

He opened the second envelope and read.

"Good Lord!" he said. "What is this man?"

"I don't know," said Jane, who had finished her reading.

"He's got ideas," said Hector Frensham.

Jane waved the two sheets which had been in envelope the first.

"Is this all?" she asked.

"All what?"

"All you've done?"

"Not quite. But you told me the bet was seventy-five per cent. There's about eighty-five there."

"And what ought you to do?" Jane reached out for the second sheet. But Hector Frensham folded this and put it into an inner pocket.

"Sorry!" he said.

"Mean!" said Jane.

5

At half-past ten that evening Inspector Mordaunt, in charge of the search party of F.T. Division sent out by orders from headquarters to scour the Heath for signs of Thomas Nutting, began to wonder whether or not he should call off the search for the night.

At twenty minutes past ten he decided to do so. But at twenty-one minutes past ten one of the search party—Police Sergeant Robert Forbes—doubling back in answer to the whistling of his inspector, tripped over something which lay beneath a big oak tree at the junction of two rides in a small wood.

At ten-forty Chief Detective Inspector Marraday of Scotland Yard, having given certain routine orders, telephoned to Number Fourteen Gordon Place.

Jane, hearing the telephone, fled downstairs from the drawing room. She had just coaxed Hector Frensham to an early bed.

"My father is out," said Jane in answer to the telephone's inquiry. "I don't know where I can find him. Can you tell me how urgent it is?"

"Urgent's not the word, Miss Frensham," said Marraday, who had met Jane. "There's nothing Sir Hector can *do*. It's only that we've strict orders to . . ."

"I know, I know," said Jane. "I'll try to find him, Mr. Marraday. But if I can't I'll leave a note for him so that he'll know at once in the morning."

Jane went slowly upstairs. After considerable thought she wrote the note. This she gave to Porter to be delivered with early tea.

6

At a quarter to one in the early hours of the next day Mr. Dudley Garten walked down Norfolk Street to the Embankment. Mr. Dudley Garten was upon the regular staff of the *Evening Clarion* which, as all the world must know, is the younger brother of the *Morning Herald*. Mr. Dudley Garten (known to Fleet Street, as also to Scotland Yard, as the Horsefly) was what is known upon the cinematograph screen and in novels as a crime reporter. He was a short spare little man with untidy clothes, a brusque and unpleasing manner, a genuine love of his unpleasing vocation, no respect for anyone in the world or out of it, and horn-rimmed spectacles. The first two fingers of each of his hands, and a great part of the back of these hands, were stained a violent yellow brown with nicotine.

He had had an exasperating day, which is the same thing as saying, about him, that he had had nothing to do. He was as late as this because he had attended a beer party given by a man who disliked him intensely and who had not asked him to the party.

He crossed the road to the Embankment side and walked along towards Westminster. It was a fine night and hot. Glancing every now and then over the parapet, he could see the Thames as a dark sluggish stream glittering every here and there with reflections of the Embankment lights. Over him and over London the sky arched in a dark blue, star-studded vault. A thin moon cut the velvet like a yellow sickle. Disregarding the few twisted huddled forms upon the benches, Mr. Garten felt himself alone in London. Just past the mouth of Northumberland Avenue he halted. He had not smoked for ten minutes. He dug in pockets with the yellow-stained fingers and brought out a yellow packet. He lit a cigarette and leaned upon the parapet and looked at the river and smoked.

London was very quiet—like a gigantic sleeping animal, thought Mr. Garten in small Clarendon type. He got to the end of the cigarette and spat and watched the oily water. Childlike, he waited for the hiss of fire extinguished, but he did not hear it because of another sound which suddenly obtruded—heavy and fast and erratic footsteps.

They were coming in the same direction as he had himself and were presently accompanied by the sound of a man's voice. The voice at first seemed to Mr. Garten's sharp and pointed ears to be singing in a strange tongue. Then, as the walker came nearer, Mr. Garten realized that it was no song that he heard, but fluent and Latin and chanted imprecation.

Mr. Garten turned idly about and rested his back instead of his elbows against the stone parapet. He saw a man pass him—a tall, lithe person with something feline about his determined but slightly irregular gait. Mr. Garten who was standing immediately beneath one of the Embankment lamps received an impression of well-cut dark clothes, a pale but olive-skinned face, and a black felt hat pulled low down over one eye. Had it not been for the thin streak of black hair, downbent at each corner, which adorned the long upper lip, Mr. Garten would have been reminded of

Mr. Michael Arlen's Cavalier of the Streets.

Opposite Mr. Garten the walker became aware that he was no longer alone. His incantations ceased abruptly. He shot a sideways glance at the standing man and walked on, faster than before.

Mr. Garten chuckled to himself. He knew what was in the mind, at this moment, of the man who had just passed him—the thought that he, Dudley Garten, might be X. Mr Garten knew this because that was what every solitary man in London must think of every other solitary man after the hour of eleven-thirty p.m. . . .

Mr. Garten started as if he had been stung. He thrust himself away from the parapet and hurried in the wake of the stranger. He had lived more than long enough to know that one never knew and that the moments when one was cursing oneself for a fool in following a hunch were often the immediate forerunners of moments of triumph.

And, sure enough, within two minutes and fifteen seconds Mr. Garten, if he had been able to spare a hand, would have been thumping himself upon the back. He drew up to within some five yards of his quarry and was content to keep this interval. He was wearing shoes which had rubber heels and he made no noise. With satisfaction he heard the chant begin again. The sound floated back to him clearly upon the hot breathless air. Mr. Garten puzzled over the language; that it was Latin was obvious, but he was not enough of a linguist to know whether it was Italian, Spanish, or Portuguese.

Suddenly Mr. Garten halted and withdrew himself, watchful, to the curb. His quarry had come to a stand—opposite to the tall figure of a policeman who stood, thumbs hooked into his belt, with his back to the parapet.

Mr. Garten's heart began to beat a great deal faster than was its wont. He saw that the policeman, faced with the dark and now silent figure, had taken his hands from his belt. Mr. Garten could see that this policeman would not now be taken unawares. He heard the policeman's voice but could not catch the words which it made. Very quietly he drew closer and heard the policeman speak again.

"*Wot* did you say?" said the policeman.

"I ask," said the voice of the stranger, mouthing its English with difficulty. "I ask wezzer you have ze—ze—match."

The policeman stood immovable. "No, I 'aven't," he said shortly. "And wot d'you want a match for?"

A stream of his own language came from the stranger's mouth.

"Wot's the good of that to me?" said the policeman and took half a step closer to his questioner.

Mr. Garten saw white teeth suddenly flash in the olive-skinned face. Because he could not see the stranger's eyes he could not tell whether this was smile or snarl. Mr. Garten found some difficulty in breathing. Automatically the yellow fingers of his right hand went to his pencil pocket while those of his left closed themselves upon the notebook in his jacket pocket.

The stranger's right hand went to a pocket, too. It went very quickly and came away holding something dark and hard from which the feeble rays of the nearest lamp drew a dull gleam.

Mr. Garten caught his breath. He did not know it, but both his hands acted. The notebook and the pencil came out of their hiding places. But all Mr. Garten was conscious of was that he was shaking with excitement and that his mouth was dry.

"*Ar!*" said the policeman. "*Would* you?"

He leaped forward in a movement astonishingly lithe and quick for a man of his bulk and clothes. His left arm swung and there came from the stranger a sharp cry. To Mr. Garten's eyes it seemed that the policeman's fist had struck at the hand upholding the dark something which must have been a pistol. There was a whirling dark glitter in the air, a clink of metal upon the stone as something hit the parapet—and then a sharp splash.

"Oh, God! Oh, God!" said Mr. Garten—not in fear but in fervent thanksgiving. Here was NEWS! Now the swart stranger seemed helpless in the grasp of English law. But English law was taking no chances. There shrilled out through the still night the harsh, high-pitched scream of a police whistle.

Mr. Garten thought it time to disclose himself. He bustled up. He did not have to pretend to be out of breath. He offered his help. He was told, grimly, but in tones trembling with triumph, to stand by. He possessed his burning ego in such patience as he could muster.

At first the captive poured forth a torrent of words in his own language, but shaking reduced him at last to silence. His captor turned to the avid Garten.

"See wot 'e did?" said the policeman. "See wot 'e did?

Pulled a gun on me, 'e did! If I 'adn't been quick . . ."
He let sinister silence finish his sentence.

"I thought it was a gun," said Mr. Garten. "I was too
far away to see."

"It went over the side," said the policeman, and once
more blew upon his whistle.

"I belong to the press, officer," began Mr. Garten.

Chapter XIII
EXTRACT FROM A DIARY

23rd June, 193—

Very tired but must record the successful episode of
Hampstead Heath. Have tied another knot in the ribbon.
Seems funny to think that *something* made me keep that
bit of ribbon. Funnier still to think of what Elsie would say
if she could see it. With that memory of hers she would
know at once that it was hers; would probably even know
where it came from. There are five knots now. If I didn't want
to keep it (there's lots more room) I'd send it to Scotland
Yard under plain cover and let them puzzle their brains
over that. I've thought of doing that quite often lately, but I
think it gives more satisfaction as it is.

*And I must be careful not to do anything likely—any-
thing possible—to give them any line, however far-fetched,
on me.*

Damn! Underlining that I've gone through the paper and
spoiled the next page! Never mind, it's another reminder.
I've got to be pretty strict with myself or I shall go writing
letters to them. I wish I could get that idea out of my
head. It's begun to keep me awake. What a kick I should
get out of that!

But I must not do it!

Damn! Through onto the next page again.

Had to break off just now. My hand was shaking so that I
found I couldn't write. As I can't talk to anyone about things,
this book's got to ease my mind, and if I get into such a
state that I can't write I shall burst. I'm quite steady now,
so here goes for a note about this evening.

When I first had the idea, about four days ago, of getting
a mounted one I threw it away as being too dangerous; but
the very danger of it made it more attractive. And then,

when I drove up to the Heath the other day for a breath of air and saw one on a grey horse and noticed him ride on to the Heath I began to see my way. I went up the next day without the car. He was there at the same time. I noticed that when he went on to the Heath he looked all round to see that no one was watching him. I followed him through a wood and saw him meet a girl. I guessed he did it every day. I was right, I was right, I was right! Seems to be a habit with me these days. Seems as if every idea I get is the right one. A nice comfortable feeling! But I must not let it get the better of me. After I'd seen him meet the girl I came home and thought it out. I worked it like this: although the papers won't tell what They're doing, They must be doing *something.* And one thing they certainly must have done is to tell each one separately that he's got to be very careful how he lets strange men approach him. That's a difficulty more easily got over with a man on foot than with a man on horseback, and for a bit I thought a mounted one was too difficult a nut to crack after all. And then I suddenly had the idea. I got that driving past the Albert Hall when there were a lot of people going in for some ball or other. Fancy dress. I saw two or three get out of a car.

That shows you what fools they are, doesn't it? It certainly showed me that there wasn't any general prohibition on letting out the uniform. After all, why should there be? I've only just had the idea myself, so it stands to reason that, slow-witted as they are, they won't have got it yet. Anyhow, I went along to Noel Gabriel's the next day and had no difficulty in getting the full rig. Didn't give my name, of course. I paid in advance. I found out that they let out lots of these for fancy-dress balls—which was the excuse I gave, of course. My first idea was to get rid of the uniform after I'd finished with it, but on second thoughts I decided to send it back by post, which is what I said in the shop I'd do. If they ever think of this way of getting hold of one of them it'll be so much later than this that Gabriel's will never be able to sort me out. Especially if everything about the transaction was in order. That's how I reasoned, and it seems pretty good to me. The Corinthian Club's Fancy Dress Dance was held at Finsmere Pond Hotel tonight, so what I did—look how careful I am to block every hole!—was to motor down that way and change my clothes in a lonely part of the Heath about two miles away from the pond. If I was spotted on the way down I was going to the dance. If I wasn't, well, it's a pleasant drive, and no harm done. In the morning I shall make the uniform up into a parcel and take it over to Lewisham and post it from a branch post office. If I choose a busy branch they won't notice me. If they do, it won't matter.

Clever, eh? And I shan't give them another chance. By the time they think of this dodge, if they ever do, I shall be onto a new one—trust me!

It worked just like butter! While any one of them might be chary about going to see what was the matter with an ordinary civilian body, they'd be bound to rush at one of their own bodies. That's how I worked it out and that's how it worked out. Clever, eh?

The only risk I ran was that some other person seeing me lying down would come along before the mounted one. But I'd a hunch that they wouldn't, and they didn't.

(Now I come to think about it, perhaps it *was* too risky. Be careful, boy! Be very, very careful.)

Oh, it was beautiful, the way it worked! Until I heard him coming I was just an ordinary one standing about—although in rather an unusual place. The moment I heard him coming I was a dead one. The minute he saw me he was off that white horse like a flash.

Then I got him. It went in slish! It was a better knife than the one I used in Fortescue Street.

I've just looked back in the book to the entry I made about the Fortescue Street one, and I find that I said I wasn't going to use a knife any more. I still think perhaps I'd better not any more. But I couldn't see another way of getting that one. And it's far and away the most satisfactory. It's—I can't find words enough to describe it. I wish I could write better.

Now for a rest. I really begin to feel that the excitement of all this—and I can't say how exciting it is—is getting on my nerves a bit. I think a nice quiet week's golf at the sea is what's wanted now. I'll think up some place tomorrow and go to it.

Been having some lovely discussions about X with people all over the shop. The theories that are being given are simply sheer delight. Let me laugh a bit! How do I laugh on paper? Ha-ha is a bit silly. Ho-ho sounds sillier still. What about Ha-ho? Let's try it, anyway.

HAHO! HAHO! HAHO! HAHO! HAHO! HAHO! HAHO! HAHO! HAHO! HAHO! HAHO! HAHO! HAHO! HAHO!

I feel better now. That's not very good, though. I must think up another way. It's a funny noise to imitate in writing, anyway.

Well, I've just looked at the ribbon again. That's five knots. I think I'll put Elsie's photograph under my pillow tonight and put the ribbon on top of it. She might feel that wherever she is—you never know. And I wonder where that great yellow-moustached swine is now. Gosh! I wish I could find him. I'll never forget the way he looked with his red face and yellow hair peeping out from the top of *my* bedclothes. Like some . . .

Here, I must stop this—my hand's started to shake again. Well, night-night, diary. I'll go and have one with you before I go to bed. Back into your case, now.

Chapter XIV

BIGWIGS ON THE GREEN

"OH, DEAR!" said the Prime Minister and ran his hands through his shock of grey hair. "Sturgess!"

"Sir?" said the Prime Minister's private secretary.

"Get hold of Knollys on the telephone. As quick as you can."

"I don't think he's in town, sir."

"I don't care if he's in Hades! Get him on the telephone!"

"Yes, sir," said Sturgess, and was gone.

The Prime Minister walked up and down the room, finally coming to a halt by the window and looking out over the pleasant garden of Number Ten.

The door opened.

"The newspapers, Mr. Campbell," said the efficient Miss Dobb.

"What!" The Prime Minister spun round. He glared across the long room at Miss Dobb. "Take 'em away!" he said.

Miss Dobb hesitated.

"Take 'em away!" said the Prime Minister.

"Very well, Mr. Campbell." Miss Dobb removed the papers and herself, closing the door after her with a careful soundlessness.

Sturgess came in. "I was wrong," he said. "He's in town. He's on the wire now. He was asleep, sir."

"Tell him I want to see him at once."

"He seems . . ." began Sturgess hesitantly.

"Tell him I want to see him!" said the Prime Minister and went back to his window. He looked out over the garden, but he did not see the garden.

Forty minutes later there came to him the rolling and, for once, untidy corpulence of Spenser Knollys, Secretary of State for War in the present government, and the stormiest petrel in many other positions in many other governments.

Knollys dropped into a chair. He puffed and blew and waved away the cigarette case which the Prime Minister held out to him, and began to fill himself a pipe.

"Well?" said the Prime Minister.

"Bloody ill!" said Spenser Knollys. "How else d'you expect me to be? Dragged out of bed in the middle of the night! If you can't run your bloody government, why the hell don't you retire? What's the trouble?"

The Prime Minister—used to his war minister's conversation—stared in astonishment at the question only.

"Do you mean to tell me that you haven't heard?" he said slowly.

"Haven't heard what?" Knollys puffed irritably at his pipe. "You aren't going to tell me Langton's found out about the guardee?"

"I do not understand," said the Prime Minister with cold disfavour. "I should not have brought you here at this hour of day for backstairs gossip. . . . I was referring to—ah—the matter of—ah—X."

"Oh, my God!" said Knollys. "The poor devil on Hampstead Heath. . . ."

"No, no, no! Last night a policeman arrested a man on the Embankment. He stated, and was supported by a witness, that this man drew a pistol from his pocket and threatened him. The man was a foreigner—could hardly speak a word of English. The Otterworth papers this morning are full of the capture of the mysterious criminal." The Prime Minister's feelings seemed to be too much for him. Abruptly he ceased speaking and began once more to pace the room between desk and window.

Knollys sat up. "Judgin' by your agitation they've got the wrong man."

"Yes, yes," said the Prime Minister. "Else why should I have sent for you? *But*—it is Barberoni's nephew!"

All the breath came out of Knollys in a long whistle. For a moment a little of the colour seemed to leave his round cheeks, and then, suddenly and disconcertingly, he put back his head and laughed—a bellowing sound.

"Be quiet!" said the Prime Minister.

Knollys mopped his eyes. "Tell me all!"

The Prime Minister came back to the desk and sat sideways upon the edge of it and played with a heavy ebony ruler.

"Yesterday," he said, "young Barberoni was, I understand, most unexpectedly defeated in the lawn tennis championship games at Wimbledon."

"Saw him," said Knollys. "Astonishin'! It wasn't that Barberoni played badly, it was that young Culloch was inspired. Best single I ever saw. D'you know, that last set went to sixteen-fourteen! And nearly every game went to deuce and 'vantage five or six times! Never seen anything like it in the whole of my life. I was goin' to stay and see some of the women, but after that all the others seemed . . ."

"Please!" said the Prime Minister. "The defeat seems to have agitated the young man out of all proportion. . . ."

"Damned serious thing!" said Knollys.

"Please! According to his own account, given early this morning through an interpreter . . ."

"Don't he speak English at all?"

"What little he does appears to have deserted him in the stress of the moment."

"Stress is good!" said Knollys. "If they thought he was X he'll have had a nasty night."

"Good heavens, Knollys! You don't suggest . . ."

"You know I'd suggest anything! Go on!"

"Let me see. . . . Ah, yes! Young Barberoni's statement. He admitted that after this unexpected defeat yesterday he went away by himself and, ah—consumed a good deal too much alcohol. He gave an accurate account of where he had been up until, I think, somewhere about half-past eleven. After that his memory seems to have gone. He says he walked about for a long time. It is certainly a fact that somewhere between half-past twelve and one he was on the Embankment. He asked a policeman for a match. The policeman, very properly under the existing—ah—unfortunate circumstances, was suspicious. Moreover, he did not understand the young man very well. Barberoni, it appears, plunged his hand into a side pocket and brought it out carrying some new-fangled type of cigarette case which is the exact simulacrum of an automatic pistol. . . ."

The Prime Minister was forced to break off. He gazed with

disfavour upon his Secretary of State for War, who was once more laughing a laugh which would have shaken rafters.

"Sorry!" said Knollys at last. "Sorry! But you can't help seeing that it's got a funny side to it!"

"I cannot extract any humour whatsoever from the situation," said the Prime Minister coldly. "No humour whatsoever! To continue: the policeman—and I feel one must exonerate him under the circumstances—finding himself apparently threatened with a firearm, acted promptly and decisively. He sprang at Barberoni and struck the thing from his grasp. Unfortunately it sailed through the air and, glancing off the parapet, fell into the river. Barberoni was arrested and taken to William Street police station and detained. He was so upset by his disappointment of the afternoon, his—ah—libations of the evening, and his—to him—completely inexplicable treatment at the hands of the police that it became impossible for him to make himself understood. It was not until early this morning, when an interpreter was provided, that he was able to make it understood who he was."

The Prime Minister paused for a moment, to go on, with a tinge of bitterness in his tone: "I was telephoned for this morning at the somewhat early hour of seven-thirty. It was Langton." He referred to the Home Secretary. "Frensham had been speaking to him. And so, Knollys, had the Ambassador. . . ."

"From all plagues, maniacs, dictators, and nephews, good Lord deliver us!" said Knollys. "Altogether it's not so nice-looking, is it?"

"A pretty kettle of fish indeed!" said the Prime Minister. "If Barberoni gets to hear . . ."

"*If!*" said Knollys. "You mean if he's not heard already. Don't be so damn silly!" He blew clouds of rank-smelling smoke at the ceiling. "And he's only been wanting some excuse to cut up rough! Yes, it's a devil . . . ! Y'know this is Langton's pigeon."

"My dear fellow!" said the Prime Minister resignedly. "You know as well as I do what Langton is."

"Better!" said Knollys. "Much better! Some have portfolios thrust upon 'em. Though why, God knows—and He won't split! . . . I suppose what all this is leading up to is that you want *me* to go over to Paris and see Barberoni."

"Precisely," said the Prime Minister, his tone showing relief. "Precisely. You are the only one who . . ."

"Blah, blah, blah!" said Spenser Knollys rudely. "All right.

I'll have a bang at it. I'll fly over this afternoon. Good job he's there and not in Rome."

"In a way, yes," said the Prime Minister. "In another, no. . . . Knollys!"

"Yes?"

"What are we going to do? I don't mean about Barberoni, I mean in regard to this dreadful state of affairs in London— these terrible murders!"

Spenser Knollys lifted his shoulders.

"I feel, I really do feel, that strong measures will have to be taken," said the Prime Minister, rising and beginning once more to pace the room.

"Undoubtedly!"

"You agree, then?" The Prime Minister turned on his heel and looked down with astonishment at his sprawling, ungainly colleague.

"Yes, yes. Rather. Every time. Strong measures must be taken. Before they can be, though, there are two rather awkward questions to answer, Campbell. What strong measures and whom by? You know, sometimes you make me sick!"

"Knollys!"

"I say sometimes you make me sick! You talk like a letter to the editor of the *Morning Muckheap! Strong measures must be taken!* In a minute you'll say that somebody or other's got to 'step in'! You're drugging yourself with words, man. For God's sake pull yourself together!"

"Knollys!"

"It isn't a bit of good bleating my name! I'll take everything back and write you a letter of apology you can frame and hang in the hall if you'll only answer one of my two questions: *what* strong measures are going to be taken and *who's* goin' to take 'em?"

"These—ah—terrible crimes are undermining the prestige of the law," said the Prime Minister.

"You don't say!" said Knollys.

The Prime Minister paid no heed. "And, therefore, I think we should be justified in . . ."

"Don't!" Knollys screamed.

The Prime Minister recoiled in alarm. "Don't what?"

"Say anything about strong measures! Confine yourself to telling me what they're going to be!"

The Prime Minister flushed a dark and unbecoming red. "Really!" he said stiffly. "If you cannot conduct yourself in a manner more . . ."

"Sorry!" said Knollys. "Go on!"

"Very well," said the Prime Minister. "The meas—ah—steps which I was going to put forward for consideration were—and this is your province, Knollys—that we should call upon the military arm to assist the civil arm. You are as well aware as I of the fact that Frensham would like to double his duty posts—and has, in fact, done so in a few places—but that he cannot do this generally for lack of men. What would be simpler really than to double or even treble his man power by the use of the military?"

The Prime Minister halted and looked down at his colleague. Spenser Knollys lay back in his chair; his pipe was out and his eyes were closed. The Prime Minister waited, knowing his man.

Knollys opened his eyes. "No!" He shook his head. "No, it won't do, Campbell. It won't do at all. It'd be fatal!"

"Oh!" said the Prime Minister, crestfallen.

"Not a bit of good," said Knollys. "I'll tell you why: in your own phrase, these murders are undermining the prestige of the law. You're right. But how much more would it be undermining the prestige of the law if you called out the army to help the bobbies to protect themselves? See what I'm driving at?"

"Yes," said the Prime Minister. "Yes. A point of view. Certainly a point of view."

"It's a damned sight more than a point of view! It's the truth! You can't say to London: 'Look here, you've been bamboozled for years into thinking policemen can look after you. I'm sorry, but they're so far from being able to do that that they can't even look after themselves, so I think we'll have to spend a bit more money and get the army to help 'em!' It won't do, Campbell!"

"No," said the Prime Minister after a silence. "Perhaps it won't. But for the love of heaven, Knollys, what *are* we going to do? What steps *can* we take?"

The Secretary of State for War looked at his leader with eyes momentarily wide. There had been an unusual and refreshingly human note in the ministerial voice.

"Good God!" said Spenser Knollys to himself. "I believe it's alive after all!" Aloud he said: "I don't know; and that's a fact."

"Have you given your mind to the problem?"

"I've thought about nothing else for the last ten days. I expect we all have except for dummies like Langton and old Fotherguts."

"And yet you've said nothing at any of the meetings?"

"If I've nothing to say I don't say it. You ought to know that by this time, Campbell."

"I am beginning to feel that this is a terribly grave situation."

"Beginning!" snorted Knollys. "Huh!"

"I mean a situation fraught with a very real national danger," said the Prime Minister frigidly.

Spenser Knollys chanted: "And one which must be dealt with rigorously and immediately by all the authorities working smoothly together and stepping in with strong measures, for the properly smooth working of which the whole nation must pull together. . . . Oh, blah, blah, black sheep!"

The Prime Minister was too much distressed to take further notice of breaches of the social code.

"Where is it to stop? Here we have had five deaths in six weeks. Is the power behind the crimes anarchistic or maniac? Where does it intend to stop? How are we to stop it? . . . My heavens, Knollys, apart from the national aspect, this could break *us!*"

"It will break us—and damn quick, too! A couple more rozzers up the spout and off we go to the country. You weren't in the House at question time yesterday. You ought to have heard 'em razzing Langton."

A long silence fell. Once more the Prime Minister looked down with unseeing eyes over the garden which was temporarily his, while his Secretary of State for War lay all asprawl in the big chair, blowing fat smoke rings and watching them break against the ceiling.

Knollys was the first to speak.

"Had Frensham on the mat again?" he said.

"He's seeing me, with Langton, at noon. . . . Perhaps . . . do you think the trouble lies there?"

"No!" said Knollys. "If you can find a better man than Hector Frensham for that thankless job I'll eat my pants. What's more, you couldn't find one half so good."

"I wonder," said the Prime Minister. "Are we right in allowing Frensham not to communicate to the press the steps he's taking? He was very firm about that, you remember. He told Langton that he'd resign if . . ."

"Of course he did! Don't be silly, Campbell! Tell the press what you're going to do and you tell this X guy what you're going to do."

"You and Frensham, I think, are agreed in believing that this X, this unknown quantity, is—ah—one man and not many?"

"Every time! We've been into that before. Mad, if you like. But only mad on one point. Unfortunately, he's making it a very sore one for London. If he only keeps his head I don't see what's ever going to stop him."

"Langton tells me that Frensham has some new measures to discuss."

Spenser Knollys heaved himself to his feet. "Let's hope they're some use." His voice suddenly had lost all trace of mockery. It had become the deep, sonorous, and moving organ which had so often swayed so many men. "I tell you, Campbell, I hate to think of England—because London is England—being wrecked by a bloodthirsty lunatic."

"Wrecked?" said the Prime Minister. "Surely your choice of words . . ."

"I said wrecked," said the Secretary of State for War. "And I meant wrecked. Don't you see, man, where this may lead us? Aren't there enough subversive influences amongst us already without this? Aren't there thousands of men and women, some vicious, some foolish, some lustful, some mad, all of whom have been praying night and day for some such collapse of authority as we're faced with? Don't you realize, man, that it wouldn't be beyond the truth to say that the whole of England's social fabric rests upon her trust in policemen? For trust in policemen is trust in the law, which means the country's trust in herself. Don't you see that if we have to go to Bill Brown (who is the country) and say: 'Look here, Bill, for the last umpty years we've been pulling your leg. That chap in the blue clothes and the helmet and the big boots couldn't *really* stop Jim Smith from pinching your beer; he isn't big enough. Everything's gone all right so far because we've managed to hoodwink Jim Smith into thinking that there was a hell of a great big man inside that uniform. But now the whole gaff's blown because Smith's seen the bobby in his bath and knows he could kill him with one hand.' If we've got to go to Bill Brown (who is the country) and say that, where's Bill Brown? Everything he's based the safety of his existence on is gone. And now comes the rub—although Jim Smith might not want to pinch Bill Brown's beer, there are plenty of Sykeses about who would if they could. If *they* find out—there you are! And they're beginning to find out. The last time I spoke to Frensham I asked him whether any of his regular clients were beginning to take advantage. He said not yet, but he admitted that undoubtedly they would soon. They'll begin at any minute. It's a hell of a mess, Campbell! There's no doubt about it! I'm sorry I pulled

your leg about strong measures, but, by God, we want 'em.
What makes me lose my rag about the phrase is that I'd love
to find out what they ought to be."

He broke off suddenly. He looked at his watch and whistled.

"I'm off," he said. "I've got to get a shave and something to eat and catch that 'plane. By the by, they let young
Barberoni out, I suppose?"

"Of course, of course," said the Prime Minister.

"And he *couldn't* have been X?"

"My dear Knollys!"

"Stow it! Did they look into . . ."

"Of course, of course. As a matter of routine. It tran-
spired—as of course it must—that the boy could not . . ."

"All right, all right. Only we don't know where we are, so
there's no harm in asking. Chippy-chippy."

The Prime Minister was left staring at a closed door.

Chapter XV

KALEIDOSCOPE

Look through!

July.

An Englishman wins the lawn tennis singles championship
at Wimbledon. Lady June Bisham loses the great emerald
which the Maharajah of Kolaba had given to her grand-
father in the days of the zenith of John Company. The
Chancellor of the Exchequer announces that, despite the
budget, it is possible that there will be an important announcement in regard to the reduction of income tax. John
Stuart Wilberforce is released from Holloway Gaol and
immediately starts, under another name, his fiftieth bucket
shop. A taxi driver, Mr. Joseph Palmer, discovers Lady
June Bisham's emerald behind the cushions of the back seat
of his taxi and, returning it to Scotland Yard, is very handsomely rewarded on the usual ten per cent. scale. Mr. Noel
Coward writes and produces and acts the only part in a
musical play which he puts on at a new theatre financed
and designed by himself. Two young aëronauts are drowned
in an attempt to fly the Atlantic the reverse way. Lady
Plaistow dies, leaving five hundred thousand pounds to the

remnants of her husband's political party. Miss Jane Frensham, singing the praises of the Brillon-Meyer car at a dinner
party, learns that a friend of a friend of her host's had once
a Brillon-Meyer but had it stolen upon a continental tour.
Detective Inspector Molyneux of the C.I.D. is retired on half
pay. The craze for vaudeville increases until there is a non-
stop variety programme at the Haymarket Theatre. A policeman collapses upon point duty and is found subsequently to
have been shot. Sir Christopher Vayle is released from
Wandsworth Prison, having served his self-chosen fourteen
days. Mrs. Ferdinand Dunkelbaum, living at 343 Balhamwell
Road, gives birth to quintuplets. A drunken journalist, search-
ing through old files for the name of a confidence trickster,
becomes aware that, many months earlier, two British scien-
tists succeeded in disintegrating the atom: still drunk but
calling upon what remains of a reasonably sound scien-
tific education, he writes an article, which is rejected by his
editor, pointing out that it is hardly worth while to worry
over today's problems when tomorrow will dawn upon a different world. The international disarmament conference
breaks up in despair, and Hobbs and Sutcliffe make a first
wicket stand of six hundred and fifty runs. A sergeant of
the City Police is found dead in a tube tunnel and men
forced to stay out late seek company upon homeward
journeys. The ex-vicar of Fondall recites "Gunga Din" at the
new cinema palace in Lewisham and a Greek waiter, threatening a policeman with a knife which he is too drunk to
use, is shot dead in Soho. An unprecedented scene of
violence occurs at question time in the House of Commons
and twenty-four hours later a special and confidential report
is circulated to certain Members of Parliament; the report
outlines the steps so far taken by the police to deal with the
X murders. The Bishop of Andover contracts bronchitis
and Miss Gloria Mundy marries again, retaining the custody
of her child. Sir Christopher Vayle, bearing a note from the
chief commissioner of police, calls upon Superintendent
Connor of the C.I.D., and fourteen writs for libel are
served upon Chloris Lady Daly following the publication
of her memoirs. Sir Oswald Stoll lays the foundation of a
theatre to be five times in size that of the Coliseum and a
forty-to-one outsider wins the Steward's Cup. Princess Eliza-
beth's doll's house catches fire for the second time and Dick
the Dodger is disqualified at the White City. Sir Hector
Frensham discusses with Superintendent Connor three sheets
of paper covered with the handwriting of Mr. Nicholas Revel.

Nobody is thrown out of a special meeting of the R.S.P.C.A.;
Mr. Victor Gollancz denies that Francis Iles is the pseudonym
of Mr. Martin Porlock and Charlie Smith of Deptford defeats
Carnera in fifteen rounds. A bill is hurried through both
Houses to provide for the enrolment of two thousand extra
special constables in the London area. Mr. Julies Frieberg
writes his thousandth letter to the *Morning Standard*
asking whether this number constitutes a record, and at a
meeting at Scotland Yard four new emergency measures are
decided upon. A plain-clothes detective is found dead on the
towing path near Hurst Park race-course. Mr. Nicholas
Revel discovers that wherever he goes, one of two strangers
is sure to go, and Mr. J. H. Thomas purchases a gent's straw
boater. A mass meeting of protest against the failure of the
authorities to deal with the victimization of the police is held
at the Albert Hall. The Eucharistic Congress is adjourned and
a B.B.C. announcer drops an H.

Shake and look again!
*Lady June Bisham loses the great emerald. . . . Mr.
Joseph Palmer . . . returning it to Scotland Yard, is very
handsomely rewarded. . . .*

Jane Frensham took her father to the Duke of Clarence's
Theatre to see *My Name is Mud*. She had difficulty in getting
him there; but she had made up her mind and he went. She
knew it would do him good. She took a box, feeling that it
would not be well for him to be too much in evidence.
Until, at eleven-fifteen, they stood at the back of the packed
vestibule waiting for the crowd before them to dissolve
through the inadequate doors onto the street, she thought they
were going to see no one whom they knew and was pleased
accordingly. But while they stood and watched, June Bisham
happened upon one whom they knew. In the ordinary way
Jane would have been pleased enough. June Bisham, though
leaning towards flamboyance, is not only good to look at but
amusing to hear. Tonight she looked her best. Her extraordinary blondeness was astonishingly set off by a velvet
gown of so dark a blue as to seem blacker than any black.
Upon a snowy expanse of bosom glittered the one jewel in
London that Jane coveted. For a minute and a half June
Bisham was more amusing even than usual, but then was interrupted. There came up to the group another friend of
Jane's. Mr. Nicholas Revel, very smart and very much at
his ease, was presented to Lady June Bisham and thereafter
shook hands with Sir Hector Frensham. The chief com-

missioner of police eyed Mr. Nicholas Revel with considerable interest.

"Heard a lot about you from my daughter," he said. And then, after polite murmurings from Mr. Revel: "I should be very glad if you'd dine with us one night. Soon. I should like to talk to you."

Mr. Revel having said that he would be delighted, the night was fixed, Jane agreeing, for the following Monday.

June Bisham moved off. Mr. Revel, who said that he was waiting for someone, moved off too. Jane found herself looking, with an interest which surprised herself when she came to analyze it, for the "someone." She did not see him. The press in the vestibule was now being increased by descendants from the dress circle. She slipped her hand through her father's arm, and they began to move towards the street.

"Want more doors," grumbled Hector Frensham. "Gad, old thing, I'll be glad to get home."

In the hall of Fourteen Gordon Place they were met by Porter exhibiting certain signs which, in him, were indicative of agitation. Porter explained that Lady June Bisham had telephoned three times within the past six minutes.

Jane, answering the next call, refused to tell her father what it was about. She was very sorry that June Bisham had lost the stone. She was extremely envious of whoever had it now. She had always thought June a fool to take so little care of it, and now she knew she had been right in thinking so. She told many lies and advised June, in addition to having rung up the fountainhead, to ring up Connor at Scotland Yard. She did not tell her father until the morning.

At eleven a.m. Sir Hector mentioned the matter to Connor. Connor, asked whether he had heard, replied with a grim smile that he hadn't stopped hearing. Unfortunately, Lady June Bisham was vague as to where the emerald must have been taken or dropped. She knew that she had had it on in the vestibule of the theatre just before leaving. She knew that twenty minutes later in her own drawing room she had not got it. . . .

At fifteen minutes before noon Lady June Bisham was consoled. A taxi driver by the name of Joseph Palmer reported to the Lost Property Office at Scotland Yard that on cleaning his cab early that morning he had found a bit o' joollery behind the cushions of the back seat. Asked to remember his fares of the night before, he stated that he had only had three. Of these one only appeared germane—a middle-aged "respectably dressed" woman who stopped him in Shaftesbury Avenue at twenty-five minutes past eleven and was driven to Victoria Station. Lady June Bisham, asking what was the usual scale of reward, was told, albeit apologetically, ten per cent. Her husband being many times a millionaire, she did not mind. Instead she asked that the taxi driver might immediately proceed to Berkeley Square.

At one p.m. Mr. Joseph Palmer parked his cab in the cul-de-sac outside the public bar of the Bull and Trumpet in Notting Dale. Entering the bar, he was delighted to find Captain Phelps. He drank with Captain Phelps, and as usual they took their drinks to the corner table.

Shake and look again!
Miss Jane Frensham . . . learns that a friend of a friend of her host's had once a Brillon-Meyer but had had it stolen. . . .

Jane went to the Fairlies' dinner firstly because she could not very well refuse and secondly because one never knew, with the Fairlies, whether one was going to be bored to within an ace of death or vastly entertained. The chances were fifty-fifty. She was taken in to dinner by a young man she did not know who professed acquaintance with and adoring admiration for Christopher Vayle. This later was, so far as Jane could be bothered to find out, the young man's one redeeming feature. But it was a long dinner, and she had to talk to someone. It was not difficult to guess the only topic, and steadily she talked cars. The young man, it appeared, ran a super-sports, front-wheel-drive Bianca. . . .

"The most comfortable, best-looking, and fastest motorcar that I've ever been in," said Jane, "is a Brillon-Meyer."

The young man opened his eyes. "Seen one," he said. "Never been in one, though. You don't get the chance in England. Don't think there's one in the country."

"I came back from Surrey in one this afternoon," said Jane.

"Good Lord! Did you really? I say, good Lord! Who's got it?"

"Friend of mine."

"Oh! Open?"

"Whichever you like," said Jane. "You turn a handle and in a couple of minutes what you thought was an open car's a coupé."

"Really fast?"

"On one straight stretch we touched eighty-five," said Jane complacently.

"Good Lord! I say, did you really! Good Lord! . . . Know a bloke who used to have one but I never saw it. South American fellah. Argentine. Not such a bad bloke, though. Name of Garcia. He used to swear by it. Got a Rolls now."

"Really?" said Jane. "What did he change it for?"

"Had the Brillon pinched," said the young man. "Most 'strordinary thing! He was on tour in Portugal. It just went—foof, like that!"

"Oh!" said Jane. "What a pity!"

The young man lifted sloping shoulders. "What's it matter to a fellah like Garcia? Got about umpty million dollars a year. If I'd a Brillon no one'd pinch it. I'd live in it, what! Ha-ha! Sleep in it and all that! Good Lord, yes!"

Shake and look again!
Sir Hector Frensham discusses with Superintendent Connor three sheets of paper. . . .

"Why are you so silent?" Sir Hector Frensham's voice was very much the chief commissioner's.

Connor shrugged his shoulders. "Because I'm afraid, sir—with all due respect—that you and I will never agree on this point."

The chief commissioner frowned at his blotting pad.

"I think you've got a bee in your bonnet over this thing, Connor," he said at last. "These are extraordinary times for us, God knows! And here comes along an extraordinary man and you don't want me to use him!"

"Extraordinary's the right word, sir," Connor said. His tone was almost surly.

The chief commissioner opened a drawer at his right hand and took from it three single sheets of paper.

"Do you or do you not admit that it shows extraordinary—what shall I say?—*capability* for a layman to have written these first two sheets? My daughter tells me that he did them in under five minutes. Straight off the bat. And on them he's got a good eighty per cent. of the special measures we've taken."

"Capability's the right word, sir," Connor said.

The chief commissioner picked up the third sheet. "And here . . . well, here's an idea; an idea on fresh lines altogether, and you won't tell me what you think of it."

Connor knew what was written upon those sheets of paper by heart. But he wanted time.

"Might I see it again, sir?" He took it to the window and stood pretending to read. The well-known words danced before his eyes. Nicholas Revel had written:

> The next time a bobby's killed, give out he *isn't* dead. Give out that he's being doctored by all the big bugs, who think they *may* save his life. If possible give out that his condition was so critical that he was not taken to hospital, but that a room in a near-by house has been commandeered. The smaller the house the better. Give out that the authorities have great hopes that if he does live he'll be able to describe X. Then wait. There's the chance, if the job's done properly, that X would try and get at the man to finish his job and keep his own description from coming out.

"Well, Connor?" The chief commissioner's voice had steel in it. "I haven't got all day."

"None of us have, sir." Connor's tone was now rude beyond doubt. He was curiously like a sullen house captain having a difference of opinion with his house master.

Hector Frensham, who has often said that his sense of humour has been against him all his life, wanted to smile. But he did not. He looked at Connor. He said nothing.

Connor shifted his weight uncomfortably from one foot to another. Unprecedented sight, the blood rushed to his square face! He mumbled something in his throat by way of apology.

Hector Frensham sat down. "I can't understand you, Connor. Some men here I know would resent even a suggestion of outside help, but I thought you weren't like that. Dammit, I *know* you aren't like that! What's your trouble? Get it off your chest."

Connor drew a deep breath. "I will, sir. It's this: I don't like this Mr. Revel. I couldn't tell you why. I suppose it's what the Yanks call a hunch."

"I do not like thee, Doctor Fell," said the commissioner to himself. Aloud he said: "You must have some grounds."

"Well, sir . . ." began Connor, and once fairly started was no longer tongue-tied. He did not leave the room for twenty minutes. When he did it was with the chief commissioner's words ringing unpleasantly in his ears.

"Don't be a fool, Connor!" Hector Frensham had said.

Shake and look again!

Sir Christopher Vayle . . . calls upon Superintendent Connor of the C.I.D. . . .

"Won't you sit down, sir?" said Superintendent Connor.

"Thanks." Christopher Vayle dropped into the chair pushed forward for him.

"Cigarette?" Connor held out a box. "Or perhaps you don't smoke these?"

"Smoke nothing else," Christopher said and took one.

Connor sat himself down behind his table. "And now, sir, what can I do for you?"

Christopher produced an envelope which he handed across the table.

"Read that," he said.

Connor read a note in the handwriting of his chief commissioner. Hector Frensham had written:

> I am sending Sir Christopher Vayle to you. He feels very deeply the unfortunate part which he may have played, quite unwittingly, in the death of Constable Beecham. He is extremely anxious to be given work in connection with the capture of the murderer. Please see what you can do.—H.F.

Connor looked at his visitor. "I take it you know what Sir Hector wrote?"

Christopher nodded.

Connor knit his brows. There was silence for several minutes. Connor went on frowning. Christopher continued to smoke.

"I'm going to take a great liberty," said Connor at last.

"Go ahead," said Christopher Vayle.

"I'm going to ask whether I may trust you; not trust you to do any job of work which I might or might not be able to give you, but trust you to respect a confidence."

"You can," said Christopher Vayle.

Connor looked at him. "Yes," he said.

He rose and began to pace the room, coming to a halt at last at the window which looked out over the Embankment and the Thames. He stood with his hands in his pockets and stared out in silence.

Christopher studied him, seeing a tall, broad-shouldered, stiffly built man of middle age, with a plain, blunt-featured face undistinguished save by a certain sharpness in the small blue eyes and a good deal of determination about the underhung lower jaw.

Connor turned to face his visitor fully. "Please let me finish what I've got to say, sir, before you get angry. And I must have your word that anything I say now won't go back to the commissioner. If this business wasn't the deadly serious thing it is, I'd rather cut my tongue out than say what I'm going to say."

"Go on," said Christopher.

"I suppose, sir, that you've seen a good deal of Miss Jane Frensham since you . . ." began Connor, with a curious hesitation about his speech most unusual in the man.

Christopher sat upright. "Since I came out? Yes. Naturally. What's Ja—Miss Frensham got to do with——?"

"Just a minute, sir, just a minute!"

"Sorry!"

"It may or may not have come to your knowledge that Miss Frensham has become acquainted—perhaps I might almost say friendly—with the gentleman who so fortunately provided you with your alibi?"

"Revel, you mean?" said Christopher, his great body twisting uneasily in his chair. "Yes. I know. What are you driving at?"

"Let me go on my own way, sir. . . . I'm going to ask you a question. What's your opinion of Mr. Nicholas Revel?"

Christopher stared. He said slowly: "I don't know that I've got one."

"Ah!" The monosyllable seemed to reflect satisfaction either at Christopher's words or the tone in which the words had been spoken.

Shake and look again!

A Greek waiter . . . is shot dead. . . . Detective Inspector Molyneux . . . is retired on half pay.

Frampton Street runs parallel with Old Compton Street. On Thursday nights its narrow way is almost blocked by barrows whose flaring naphtha lights make bright and smoky magnificence. On the southeastern corner of Frampton Street stands the Café Martinique. It is exactly like a hundred of its Soho brethren, from the curtained shop window of its frontage to the tubbed trees which flank its narrow doorway. To the casual patron, of which it has few, the Café Martinique is not pleasant; its cooking is indifferent its service vile, and its charges disproportionate. But to its regulars the Café Martinique is different. Of its regulars, Richard Molyneux was a favoured member. He never knew whether or no the oily, pot-bellied Luigi Galoni knew him for what he was. But he did not care, for Galoni looked after him and did not overcharge.

Mr. Richard Molyneux came out through the narrow door onto Frampton Street at ten-thirty of a Friday night. As the day was a Friday the street was empty. There were no barrows and no flares and accordingly very little light. Mr. Richard Molyneux paused upon the top of the Café Martinique's two steps, lit himself a cigarette, and strolled leisurely west. He was halfway down the winding length of the street when he saw, immediately beneath the lamp some fifteen yards ahead of him, the figure which leaned against the wall some ten feet behind the policeman but which, as he watched, became galvanized into a jerky and erratic life.

Mr. Richard Molyneux increased his pace. He walked fast for ten strides. . . .

Detective Inspector Richard Molyneux of the C.I.D., tugging at his hip pocket, broke into a run. As he ran he shouted. Just before him the policeman turned. In front of the policeman the jerky marionette of a figure danced, swaying, and waved something in its right hand which glittered in the yellow light of the lamp.

Detective Inspector Molyneux fired three times. The jerky figure jerked once more and then slumped to the pavement like a sack half empty.

Shake and look again!

A plain-clothes detective is found dead . . . near Hurst Park racecourse.

"I told you, sir," said Chief Constable Charlesworth and thumped upon the table with a fist like a leg of lamb.

"You're certain, Charlesworth, that this must have been the Carlotti's?" said the assistant commissioner. "Certain it can't be . . ."

"They want us to think it's X," said Charlesworth. "But X has never done anything on the plain-clothes men, and even if he had I *know* that Carlotti's did this. We'll never get 'em for it, but they've had it in for poor Brent for the last six months—ever since he sent Sam Carlotti up for a stretch. I knew it'd happen. It was bound to happen! And this'll be the first of a lot more . . . and all down to Mr. X's account. . . ."

Shake and look again!

*Mr. Nicholas Revel discovers that wherever he goes . . .
A mass meeting . . . is held at the Albert Hall.*

Mr. ·Nicholas Revel came slowly down the steps of the
Hyde Park Hotel and, turning right, walked towards Knightsbridge. Unusually for the hour, which was near to nine in
the evening, he wore day clothes. Reaching the eastern end
of the Barracks he crossed to the other pavement. Not since
leaving the Hyde Park Hotel had he looked round. Immediately opposite the doorway which leads to Prince's Tennis
Club he halted suddenly and swung sharply round on his
heel. He came face to face with a burly man who neatly
avoided him and walked on. Mr. Revel followed with his
eyes, the beginnings of a smile pulling down one corner of
his mouth. Mr. Revel took a taxi, making parade and considerable noise of so doing; he told the taxi driver in a· loud
voice to take him to the Lyric Theatre, Hammersmith, but
after four hundred yards or so of journeying changed this
direction to the Albert Hall.

At the eastern entrance to the hall Mr. Revel paid off
his cab. He stood on the pavement, just beneath a poster
which announced in letters of scarlet seven feet high that
a mass meeting under the chairmanship of Lord Otterworth
would be held at nine-thirty upon this night.

Already a thin stream of people was trickling along the
pavement and up the steps and into the door. Mr. Revel
waited. He saw that another taxi had pulled up on the
other side of the road. He saw that there descended from
this a burly man—not so large a burly man as had nearly
cannoned into him opposite Prince's Club, but nevertheless
a burly man.

Mr. Revel, whistling to himself, produced from his
pocket a blue ticket of admission to Lord Otterworth's
meeting. He went slowly up the steps.

Shake and look again!

*An unprecedented scene of violence . . . in the House
of Commons . . . confidential report is circulated . . .*

On a morning in July the following appeared, *inter alia,*
in *Hansard* under the heading QUESTIONS:

Member for Kensington: Will the Home Secretary state
whether the names of slaughtered policemen notified to the
public through the medium of the daily press constitute in
fact a complete list?

The Home Secretary: The public have been fully informed through daily press.

Member for Kensington: I submit that that is no answer. Have there been any policemen killed whose names and the occurrences of whose deaths have not been published in the press?

The Home Secretary: No.

Member for Silverton: How much longer is it going to be before something is done?

The Speaker: That question is not in order.

Member for Kensington: May the House be informed of what measures are being taken to deal with the new aspect of the menace—to wit, the murder in broad daylight of Constable Brackley on point duty?

The Home Secretary: I must have notice of that question.

An Hon. Member: You ought to have notice of the sack!

Hon. Members: Sit down!

Member for N. Kensington: Will the Home Secretary state whether a suggestion put forward that the military should be used to augment the police force has been rejected by his department?

Hon. Members: Order!

The Home Secretary: I will answer that question. The whole matter has been under the constant and unremitting attention of my department, working directly with the police, since the beginning of these terrible crimes. Suggestions amounting in number to hundreds have been put forward. Some of these suggestions have been adopted, others have been rejected as impracticable for one reason or another. The suggestion outlined by my gallant friend has been, and still is, under careful survey.

Member for Stepney: Put a sock in it!

Mon. Member: Order! Order! . . . Sit down!

Member for Stepney: I will not sit down!

Member for Bayswater: Will the Home Secretary state whether the decision of his department not to communicate the special steps taken by the police to deal with the menace even to the Members of this House is based upon the supposition that the unknown criminal may be a Member of this House?

Hon. Members: Shame!

Member for Silverton: That's the stuff!

The Home Secretary: The decision upon the point raised by my learned friend was taken in the public interest.

Member for Chelsea: Is the Home Secretary aware that

the failure of his department to deal with this tragic
situation is making Britain the laughing-stock of the world?

Hon. Members: Sit down!

Member for Silverton: Sack the lot!

Further on in the small blue book, under the heading
DEBATES, appeared the following:

The Prime Minister: I have an announcement of considerable import to make to the House. At a Cabinet meeting this afternoon it was decided that a full report of the
steps taken by the police should be privately circulated
to Members. I would remind Members that this report
must be treated as intensely confidential. I earnestly hope
that the circulation of this document will satisfy Members
that every possible measure is being taken and will also
ensure that there shall not be any recurrence of the pain-
ful scene witnessed at the close of question time today.

Upon the day following the uproar in the House of
Commons at question time there was delivered to each
Member of Parliament a long envelope containing many
sheets of foolscap. The first of these sheets was headed
with the address of New Scotland Yard and the last footed
by the reproduced signature of Hector Frensham. To give
the whole of this document in full is unnecessary, but its
important preamble must be referred to. In this, after
stressing the necessity for secrecy and even smoothly
hinting that only unbearable political pressure had brought
the present report about, the chief commissioner of police
made it abundantly clear that the report dealt only with
extraordinary measures taken. The usual measures, which
were, the preamble hinted, perhaps more likely to produce
results in the end than any of the extraordinary measures,
were of course being pursued. So far, however, these had
been hindered by the fact that there had been no ghost of
a clue.

The concluding paragraph of the preamble gave Hector
Frensham's reasons, among which there loomed very large
the absence of clues (*i.e.*, the absence of mistakes upon the
part of the murderer), for assuming that the criminal was
a unit and not a multiple.

The list of extraordinary measures is given below, taken
straight from the report:

PRÉCIS OF NEW MEASURES TAKEN SINCE THE
12TH MAY, 193—

"A"

REMARKS.

1. Wherever possible all extensive and very lonely beats within the Metropolitan and City Police areas have been doubled during the night time.

It has not been possible to carry this out everywhere owing to the obvious reason of shortage of men. It may be possible to double the beats altogether shortly by the use of special constables. See below.

2. Constables and detective officers in plain clothes have been allotted a certain number (varying from one to three) of night-time beats. They patrol these beats regularly throughout the dark hours, visiting each uniformed constable in turn.

3. All constables on night duty and plainclothes men on night and day duty are now furnished with firearms.

4. Additional mounted police from provincial forces have been attached to the Metropolitan Force. The total mounted force now performs more night duty than day duty. Each mounted constable has a certain number of beats to visit during the night.

This inspection is, of course, additional to the plains-clothes inspection referred to in 2 above.

5. New orders have been issued to every member, both uniformed and plain-clothes, of the Metropolitan and City police forces to the effect that great care must be taken in regard to persons who approach any officer with the

If, despite the warning which officers have been instructed to convey to people approaching them, any person does continue to approach beyond the reasonable limit, officers hold such persons for examination.

apparent intention of speaking to him. All ranks have been warned not to let such persons approach within less than six feet.

6. Large rewards have been advertised both in the press and by means of posters, etc., for information leading to the arrest or identification of the criminal. A varying scale of rewards for any information whatsoever in regard to the criminal has also been publicized.

The second sentence opposite may be taken as referring to information which is proved to furnish *any* reasonable clue. The rewards range from £2,000 to £50.

7. A bill has been drafted and has now passed its second reading imposing very severe penalties for the carrying of firearms. The bill also imposes new penalties, *e.g.*, penalty for being found in unlicensed possession of firearms.

All preparations have been made to put these regulations into force as soon as the bill is finally passed.

8. Measures are in process of being taken in regard to hotels, boarding houses, etc., whereby the proprietors of such establishments are being requested to aid the police by lodging information in regard to *any* person or persons whose behaviour may seem suspicious.

This will, of course, entail an enormous amount of headquarters work in sorting and classifying and sometimes investigating reports made by ambitious or foolish or over-imaginative persons. It is considered, however, that the possible end justifies the means.

9. Motor-police patrols have been strengthened by over 50 per cent. Patrols tour the whole town during the night hours.

10. All constables, dismounted and mounted, and plain-clothes officers have been instructed, within the last forty-eight hours, to challenge and examine all solitary

This will also apply to special constables. See below.

walkers between the hours of midnight and dawn.

11. The Reserve of Uniformed Special Constabulary has been drawn upon and (as will be seen in tomorrow's press) further volunteers have been asked for.

When the complement of special constables has reached a certain number it may be possible to double all night beats. The question of having a certain number of picked special constables in plain clothes is under consideration. It will, however, take some considerable time before the special force is in full operation since (as will be readily appreciated) it is very necessary that every applicant's credentials should be most carefully considered in view of the fact that to become a special constable might conceivably suit the criminal's plans.

(This is not considered likely as it would hamper his freedom, but the possibility must not be ignored. See note below.)

12. A system of passwords (the words being changed every night) has been inaugurated in order to prevent any uniformed officer from suspecting any non-uniformed officer.

This system will be elaborated when the special force is in full working order.

Note.—The suggestion has been made from various quarters that the murderer might be a member of the regular police force. After careful analysis it has been found that this is well-nigh impossible, a study of the times and places of the murders making it extremely unlikely that any member of the police force could possibly have been the murderer.

After some explanatory notes upon this table—notes which seemed to suggest that Scotland Yard's opinion of the

intelligence of the House of Commons was far from high
—came the following:

"B"

Précis of Suggestions Given Favourable Consideration but Impracticable for Reasons Shown

Suggestion.	Reason for Rejection.
1. That military forces should be used to augment police forces.	That the undermining of police prestige would be too great at the present juncture. (Cabinet decision.)
2. That protective clothing (*e.g.,* bullet-proof) should be provided to all uniformed police officers.	That the cost would be far too great. The best prices that could be obtained worked out at something like £1 a head. (*Note:* There is under consideration, however, a scheme for obtaining a limited amount of protective clothing and issuing it to officers upon particularly lonely night-time beats.)
3. That a sectional curfew system should be established.	That so great an interference with public liberty would be injudicious at the present juncture. The suggestion is under periodic review.

Shake and look again!

At a meeting at Scotland Yard four new Emergency measures are decided upon.

Sir Hector Frensham drew sea horses upon his blotting pad.

"All that being over," he said, "we'll come to suggestions. I have one to make myself, but I shall not put that forward for discussion until I have heard anything any of you may have to say."

He raised his eyes and sent a glance round the long table of the conference room. Besides him there were nine men present; nine men as different in appearance as any nine men well could be; but nine men who yet bore, each in some indefinable way, the stamp of their calling.

There was a long silence.

"Smoke if you want to," said Hector Frensham.

There was a sudden confused rustling and creaking of chairs as seven large men searched about themselves for tobacco.

It was the grizzled John Goles who spoke first. Often there were concealed smiles from his colleagues and superiors at his manner of speech, which had never altered from his first days in the force as a constable in his native borough of Stepney, but today, after he had begun speaking, were no smiles, only interest.

"Bin finkin', " said John Goles. "Seems ter me as we'd be a sight better off even if we knoo what this 'ere Hex was like to look at. Wot I mean: you'd have *somefink* to get your teeth in. Now this Hex, 'e's not a-goin' to come up 'ere and let's 'ave a dekko at 'im. Nor isn't 'e goin' to send us a nice photo. But why shouldn't we see if we can't take his photo for 'im without 'im known' that we're a-takin' of it? Wot I mean: if there's any road to give all the blokes on duty a sort of 'idden camera to take a snapshot, why don't we do it? . . . It's no good, Mr. Charleswork, lookin' at me like that. If you asks the pleece in Vyenna you'll find as 'ow they've got little cameras no bigger'n a button. You know that, Nicholls. Now why shouldn't we 'quip as many o' the boys as we can with some sort of camera like this wot they've got in Vyenna? I'd 'ave to leave it to some o' you clever ones to work out 'ow, but my idear is: if so be as this e're Hex was to get any o' the boys although this boy might be a gonner there's no knowin' but wot we mightn't be able to develop a photo wot 'e sort of automatikly took of this Hex. Wot I mean . . ."

"An excellent idea, Goles," said Hector Frensham. He made a note on a slip of paper and handed it to the assistant commissioner. "Get a report of the possibilities." He sighed. "The only thing I'm frightened of is the cost. . . . Now, any more suggestions?"

"Sir," said Chief Detective Inspector Bazelgett. He got to his feet, a tall gaunt man with a collar which seemed many sizes too big for him. He spoke toward the head of the table, as if he were a member of the most formal of whist-drive committees. He cleared his throat.

"Sir," he said again, "it has occurred to me—as I am sure it must have occurred to you and to many of us sitting round this table—that one reason why this unknown criminal is able to command such success must be that he is able

to get close to any officer without in any way exciting suspicion."

"Go *hon!*" said John Goles beneath his breath, and
Charlesworth coughed to disguise a snigger.

"It's all very well to mock," continued Bazelgett, unruffled.
"For those that like to mock! But perhaps the mockers have
not realized the point which I am striving to make, and that
point, sir, is this hat the unknown criminal may be in
unlawful possession of a Metropolitan Police uniform. . . ."

A murmur rose upon the tobacco-laden air. Some of its
component sounds were astonished and laudatory; some
weary and disillusioned.

"But however that may be," said Bazelgett, "my suggestion
is that in view of the possibility, past, present, and future,
of such a step being taken by such unknown criminal,
contact should be established with all theatrical costumiers,
etc., in order to ensure that no further uniforms are sold
or hired out, and, perhaps more important, that such par-
ticulars as can be obtained of uniforms which have been
sold or hired out during a past period to be decided upon
should be obtained. That, sir, is my suggestion."

The false teeth of Chief Detective Inspector Bazelgett
clicked together upon his final word, and he resumed his
seat.

"Not bad, Bazelgett," said Hector Frensham. "Not bad."

He made another note upon another slip and passed this,
like the first, to the assistant commissioner.

"Any more suggestions?" he said.

"Yes, sir," boomed the voice of Maull of X.L. Division.
Anticipatory smiles flitted across the faces of one or two
of Maull's colleagues, while everyone at the table, including
Hector Frensham and the assistant commissioner, seemed
to take on suddenly a more alert attitude. This was not
due to the expectation of anything brilliant or out of the
ordinary—although such might be to come—but to the
necessity for paying great attention while Maull was speaking. For Maull did not believe in wasting words any more
than he believed in wasting time. These disbeliefs worked
in him to produce a style of speech which in delivery and
arrangement could sometimes be less easy to understand
than an unknown foreign language.

"Go ahead," said Hector Frensham.

"Like Bazelgett said," spurted Maull. "Whole secret get
up close without suspected. Stop getting up close, stop murders. May not catch 'm but crab his game. Suggest tightening

instructions re halting 'costers and torches. Mean: issue strong flashlights. Extra strong. Men c'nstable halts 'coster, *can* use flash. If 'coster don't halt, c'nstable *must* use flash. Flash in eye disconcertin'. Makes helpless. Give c'nstable time. Not large expense. Good idea."

Maull sat down. There was argument about this suggestion; argument in which Maull, his mouth shut so tight that no vestige of his lips could be seen, did not join. But Hector Frensham put an end to discussion by handing another slip to the assistant commissioner.

"Any more?" said Hector Frensham and once more looked round the faces.

This time he got no answer.

"Now for mine," he said. "As I only thought of it this morning, I haven't had time to have it gone into by experts, but inquiries are being made already. I'll outline it for you. It's this: that as many night-duty constables as possible should be provided, as soon as possible, with some sort of radio device which would automatically give an alarm if a man wearing it were unwittingly to fall. Whether the cost will be prohibitive or not I don't know. If it isn't, well and good. Radio telephony has been suggested, but the cost's against it. This idea, however, might be workable. . . ."

Chapter XVI

EXTRACT FROM A DIARY

31st July, 193—

I've had them all out again tonight, the photographs, the ribbon—with seven knots in it—and the blue envelope. For once I took all the relics out of the envelope. I've often wanted to lately, but the want has not been so strong as the fear of remembering. Tonight the want was a great deal stronger than the fear. I sat at the table in my room with dear sweet little Elsie's photograph facing me and the ribbon underneath it and went through the relics one by one. To remind me of the first, as if the photograph and the ribbon were't enough, is the clipping I got out of an *Overseas Daily Mail* nearly fifteen years old which I remember buying in Winnipeg which stated that the swine had been awarded the Humane Society's medal for fishing some kid or other out of the river. To remind me of the second I've got another cutting from the *Clarion* giving the full details of my "unwarranted" attack upon the King swine, whose hellborn lying gave me my first taste of prison. That "unwarranted" makes me laugh. (Ha! Ha! nth.) I like the last little bit too. I can write it out from memory. "The accused, who refused to give his name (believed to be Schmidt or Smith) gave every indication, to use the words of the magistrate, 'of being already at an early age a hardened and brutal criminal of the worst kind.' "

Then there's four things to remind me of the real horror of five years later. A copy of the lying deposition made by that archdevil Blakeney (and won't they wonder how I got that when they find my things when I'm dead!), several cuttings giving the evidence of those poor swine Lefty Saunders and Jack Flynn (I've never felt too hardly about them; after all, a heaven-sent scapegoat doesn't come the way of that sort any too often), my ticket of leave dated three years later than the deposition, and my final discharge paper. Great God! How I wish I could get back the real flame of hate I used to make in my head during some of those long nights when you couldn't keep warm even by rolling yourself up like a hedgehog and pulling their filthy mingy blankets right round you. God, it was good, that flame! What I've got now is just an echo of it. It was like a lovely white light inside your head that made you feel warm all over for quite a long time.

Then, of course—I must stop to laugh!—there's the coping stone. The great strike nineteen years after the night when I went home and found him with dear sweet little Elsie. Nineteen years! Me now a well-to-do retired man come back to his native land, only to get, within three weeks of landing, such a crack on the head from one of their batons that I was in a nursing home for three solid weeks and convalescent for two months. And all because I just put out my arm to stop that one from splitting a child's head open. I'll never forget the look of that burly beast on his black horse. The Broadway was full of them on horses with their long batons. The kid couldn't have done him any harm—he was pulling at his legs trying to get him off, but he couldn't have succeeded, and just because I put out my arm I must get it. Well, I can laugh now! The one on Hampstead Heath didn't have a black horse, but perhaps a white one was better.

Just knocked off to go and get myself a drink. Funny how tired this writing makes me! I'm as fit as a fiddle, and harder and stronger at forty-two than I've ever been, *except* when I get down to this book, which is the one thing I seem to love. Then that tight feeling comes in my head and my hands begin to shake. Silly, really! Still it's there right enough. Perhaps if I don't write about this I shan't think about it. When I sat down I meant to write pages and pages and pages and pages and pages and pages and pages. Now I'm sure I shan't get anything more off my chest at all tonight. Not that there's really anything now I'm here with my pen in my hand. I thought there was, but it all seems to have gone away somehow.

They're still very much exercised about how that one on point duty was shot. Well, one day I'll put it down in this book. Or perhaps I shan't. Perhaps I'd better leave them something to scratch their thick heads over. What I'll do now, I think, is to get another drink and just get to work quite quietly and calmly, taking as many rests as I need, and write down a full account of how I'm going to do the next one. Oh, I've got him marked! I'd like to write and tell him what's coming to him. But it won't do. Never mind, you can't have jam on both sides of your biscuit. I've had another drink, so here goes. . . .

I can't. Hell, I can't! Too tired. Have to go tomorrow. Cheerio, book! Why the hell d'you make me feel like this?

Chapter XVII

BLIND ALLEYS

Superintendent Conner scratched his head. He glowered down at a bulging, yellow-bound file upon the desk before him. The file was shut, but for more than the past hour it had been open while he had read it through once, twice, and again.

A knock came upon the door. Connor started; remained silent for a moment while he deftly whipped the file into a drawer; growled out admission. A visitor came and went. He had not been gone more than a minute before the file was out again and the frown back upon its reader's brows. For a long time Connor sat and stared at the file, once or twice opening it at specific points. But nothing lessened the look of frustrated bewilderment in his small, sharp eyes. Twice more he was interrupted, and each time, almost guiltily, he hid the file before admitting his visitor. It was plain that not only did the contents of the file worry Superintendent Connor, but also that the existence of the file alarmed Superintendent Connor so soon as there came possibility of it being discovered.

Superintendent Connor was at war with himself in regard to this file and its subject. The yellow-bound bundle had cost money; more, it had cost much time and many men. And for the police at the present was neither a superfluity of money nor men's time. When he looked at it Connor felt guilty, and he was not used to feeling guilty. Neither was he used to acting in a manner directly contrary to the expressed wishes of his chief commissioner. . . .

But he had a conviction. Or had had a conviction. The frown grew deeper, and he pounded gently upon the edge of his desk with a clenched fist.

What was a man to do? If only he could get *something;* something which he could show to the commissioner which would enable him to gloss over his disobedience to the commissioner's wishes. Something which would enable him to say to the commissioner: "Look here, sir, you know I've had my eye on this man Revel? Well, just look at this!"

For the yellow file contained nothing which was not upon the subject of Nicholas Revel. There was much of it— all summing up to nothing!

The frown deepened until its converging lines looked as if they had been cut into Connor's crag-like brow with a sculptor's chisel. All this money, all this time, all this work; all for *nothing!* Paradoxically, this nothingness was the one ray of light—thin but existent—in Connor's gloom. For the very nothingness was in itself something. When all the intricate paths of a man's life turn out to be barred by unscalable walls at the very moment when they should become interesting, there must be—so ran the thoughts of Patrick Connor—something queer behind those walls. The paths could not stop; they must go on and go on into regions about which the very existence of the walls proved their owner suspicously discreet.

Connor sat back and linked his hands behind his head and put his feet upon his desk and looked up at his dull ceiling and pondered. He reviewed the essence of the file for perhaps the fiftieth time.

Who was Nicholas Revel? He lived at Number 4 Barkston Mansions, Knightsbridge, a block of expensive service flats. Who were Nicholas Revel's parents? No answer. Was a copy of Nicholas Revel's birth certificate on the files at Somerset House? No. Where had Nicholas Revel lived before the date, two years earlier than today's, upon which he had taken this flat? Nowhere—out of the everywhere into here! What was Nicholas Revel's calling or profession? Nothing; he lived the life of a gentleman of leisure. Whence came the means for this life? Immediately before they reached him, from three different banks (so far as the makers of the file had been able to ascertain). Where did the money come from before it reached the banks? In one case from a solicitor in Nottingham; in another from a broker's office in New York; in the last from a Parisian attorney. The solicitor in Nottingham was unapproachable; would probably have been so in any case but most definitely was so when, as now, inquiries must tread Agag-like. A colleague of Connor's in New York gave the broker as good a name as any, but could get nothing from him. The Parisian attorney encased himself behind the unsullied and unbreakable glass of virtue. . . .

How did Mr. Revel spend his time? He spent his time in travelling, in motoring, in playing golf at four reputable clubs and lawn tennis at one reputable club. He dined out. He went a great deal to the theatre. He visited regularly three of the smartest dance-cum-supper places. He was known at the Savoy, the Berkeley, and half a dozen of their lesser brethren. Who were Mr. Revel's greatest friends? He had none, or so it seemed—a thousand and one acquaintances; but of what use to the inquirer are acquaintances, never forgetting the necessity for the Agag walk? What were they, such as they were? Exactly the sort of acquaintances which one would expect from a man spending his life in such a way. Where, when he was not travelling in England, did Mr. Revel travel? In France, in Italy, in Portugal, in Austria. So his passports said, and passports are not given to lying. What did he do when he travelled? Only, so far as could be ascertained, what he did when he did not travel. At what rate did Mr. Revel live? At the rate of three to four thousand pounds a year. How dearly would Superintendent Connor have liked to apply to the inland revenue authorities for the tax returns of Mr. Nicholas Revel for the past year or so. But again the delicacy of the situation forbade an approach to the authorities. Did

Mr. Revel owe money? No. Did Mr. Revel borrow money or lend it? Apparently not. Did the payments into Mr. Revel's varying accounts fluctuate? So far as could be ascertained, yes, and largely. But what of this? Nothing. So might any moneyed young man's accounts vary were this young man or his advisers given to even mild speculation. Did Mr. Revel employ a servant? No; he was waited upon by the staff of the service flats. Did the servants in the service flats have anything interesting to say about Mr. Revel? Nothing. They liked Mr. Revel, who seemed to them the very acme of what a service-flat occupier should be. Had Mr. Revel any particular piece of skirt? Who could say? Was there any place, or district even, which Mr. Revel appeared to frequent more than any other? No. Mr. Revel was an ardent motorist, being the possessor of an extremely expensive and unusual car of continental make: when had Mr. Revel first appeared in this car? Two years ago. Had Mr. Revel bought his car in England? No. Where had he got it from? Who could say? Did the appearance of this car tally with the appearance of any missing car? No more than any car of any breed resembles any other car of the same breed. Did the chassis and engine and other odd numbers of Mr. Revel's car tally with any numbers for which any police anywhere might be looking? They did not. Could these numbers, which were seen through the agency of a bribable garage hand, tally with numbers which the Brillon-Meyer Company might have upon their books? Impossible to tell. The Brillon-Meyer Company was now not really the Brillon-Meyer Company but the huge company of the Automobile Generale di Milano, and all the original Brillon-Meyer records had been burned in the great fire at the Turin works three years since. Had Mr. Revel been known to employ more than once the taxicab of Joseph Palmer of 114 Whitler's Rents, W.13? No. Where had Mr. Revel been between certain hours upon seven specific dates? God might know, but (thought Superintendent Connor) probably did not. . . .

In short, Superintendent Connor knew what Mr. Nicholas Revel ate and where he ate it, what he wore and where he bought it, what he looked like, how he spoke, how much money stood to his credit in current accounts at three banks, what were his favourite colours, wines, dance tunes, and brands of golf and tennis ball.

Superintendent Connor knew that he knew nothing about Mr. Nicholas Revel.

2

Mr. Nicholas Revel issued from the front entrance of Barkston Mansions. He was harmonious in brown. He stood a moment on the pavement, looking up at a cloudless and brazen sky. He turned right and strolled leisurely up towards the main road and the shops. From the courtyard entrance of Mauleverer House, which is upon the other side of the road from Barkston Mansions and a little lower down, there issued a tall, thickset man most inappropriately clothed for a day of such heat. His suit was of a thick harsh tweed, his hat a heavy winter felt, his boots large and shining. He wore a green tie pulled through a large gold ring. His eyes were small and quick and his tread, for all his bulk, quite noiseless. He followed Mr. Revel at a distance of about fifteen yards. He saw Mr. Revel, who had turned left in the main road, go into a tobacconist's shop. He withdrew himself into a convenient doorway and waited. Presently he saw Mr. Revel come out of the tobacconist's and come back towards him. He faded with discretion and considerable skill, to come to light again when Mr. Revel had passed.

Mr. Revel did not once look behind him. He walked leisurely back to Barkston Mansions and disappeared through the door whence, only five minutes before, he had emerged.

The rear entrance of Barkston Mansions is rarely used by those who live in the flats, for it gives into the unseemly Weever Street. But through it, barely two minutes after his disappearance into the front entrance, came Mr. Revel. He stood upon the top step and looked cautiously up and down the street. He must have been satisfied with what he saw or did not see, for presently he was walking, with a briskness contrasting strongly with his lassitude of a few minutes before, once more towards the main artery of Knightsbridge. From a doorway in the other side of Weever Street there came, when Mr. Revel had proceeded some twenty yards, a tall thickset man in a bowler hat and blue serge; a smarter-seeming man than the man in tweed; but a man whose boots might have been off the same last.

He had seen Mr. Revel's cautious look up and down Weever Street. He was, accordingly, very cautious himself. He was not to be discerned when, at the corner, Mr. Revel stopped and turned sharply to look behind him. But nevertheless he was still within fifteen yards of Mr. Revel by the time St. George's Hospital was reached, and when Mr. Revel took a taxi from the rank beside the coffee stall which is known as the Junior Turf, blue serge and bowler hat disappeared into the second cab on the rank.

In due time Mr. Revel's taxi drew up at the Jermyn Street entrance to Piccadilly Circus Tube Station. Mr. Revel paid his fare quickly and disappeared into the station. A moment later the second taxi drove up and blue serge and bowler hat came out of it like a shot from a gun. A coin sailed through the air to fall upon the driver's lap. The taxi driver looked after his fare with weary wonder.

The man beneath the bowler, whose name was Hallows, was worried. Had his quarry gone through and out into the Circus again, or down the steps to the circular booking hall? Hallows took a chance. He went quickly down to the booking hall; so quickly that many indignant glares went after him. In the booking hall he sighed relief. His quarry was at the change kiosk. His quarry, change in hand, went to the three-penny ticket machine. . . .

Presently both of them, Mr. Revel some ten treads lower down, were on the descending escalator. Cautiously Hallows moved slightly nearer. He was confident that he had not been seen since he had come on this job the day before yesterday, and by all accounts this was a slippery customer. Faucett had had to call himself beat twice before the Super took him off the job, but Hallows swore to himself that Hallows would not be taken off the job if it were one possible to humanity.

At the foot of the escalator Mr. Revel turned right and went down the centre corridor. Hallows followed. Mr. Revel went on and so to the platform. A train came in with a roaring rattle. It pulled up. Its doors yawned. It looked like the caravan of a nightmare. Mr. Revel made for the doors to his left. Hallows, cautious as ever, made for the other door to the same carriage. He was through it and standing when he saw his quarry once more upon the platform and moving with every appearance of haste towards the tunnel mouth marked "Way Out."

The closing doors missed Hallows by a bare half-inch. He stumbled on the platform and nearly fell. When he got to the mouth of the exit tunnel, with his lungs heaving and the sweat on his forehead making his hat totter precariously, he saw the brown-clad back disappearing at the other end. He thanked his stars. He was sure he had not been spotted: his quarry was merely being careful. He doubled his pace, the soles of his big boots making no noise even upon the mica flooring. Up again at booking-hall level he once more congratulated himself. He still had his teeth in the job, though just now the metaphorical tail had very nearly been pulled from between them.

Mr. Revel went up the stairs to Shaftesbury Avenue. At the top he took a taxi. Hallows, by great good fortune, secured another at once. In it he leaned well back and took off the bowler hat and mopped. This time he had a good driver and better luck. Never for a moment did the first taxi look like escaping from their sight. They drove down Haymarket, round Trafalgar Square, up Whitehall, over Westminster Bridge, down alongside the river to Vauxhall and thence by streets behind the Oval to Kennington.

At the corner of Willowdale Avenue, South Kennington, stands a shop whose display window is full of steel. Over the shop gilt letters say S. WIDGEON, CUTLER.

Hallows made a sound halfway between a coo of astonishment and a whistle. He tucked himself into the doorway of a news agent opposite to S. Widgeon. He only got himself off the empty pavement just in time. Luck was certainly with him today, for, having given every appearance of being about to enter the shop of S. Widgeon without looking behind him, Mr. Revel suddenly halted, turned, came back to the pavement again, and looked this way and that along Willowdale Avenue.

"*Phoo!*" said Hallows and took off his bowler and ran his handkerchief round its leather band.

He then waited. His quarry was inside Widgeon's for so long a time—ten minutes by the clock—that Hallows began suddenly, with a sick feeling, to wonder if S. Widgeon had allowed this customer the eccentricity of departing by the back door.

But no. Here came Mr. Revel again and not empty-handed. He was carrying a rectangular brown paper parcel about ten inches long, an inch high and two inches across. Hallows's eyes opened widely as he peered from his shadowed retreat. Once more Mr. Revel paused upon the pavement and sent a glance this way and that along Willowdale Avenue; then, apparently satisfied, turned to his right and walked leisurely along the righthand pavement of the busy thoroughfare of the High Street. More discreetly than ever, Hallows followed. After some two hundred yards of progress Mr. Revel halted before the saloon-bar entrance of the Leopard and Keys. He turned and entered without a glance behind him.

It chanced that Hallows knew the Leopard and Keys for one of those public houses which have a circular bar divided at intervals of varying size into many bars—Saloon, Private, Jug and Bottle, Public. Hallows took himself into the narrow segment of the private bar. Leaning cautiously upon the counter and ordering a pint of bitter, he could see into the saloon bar through one of the glass-and-wooden shutters. Quarry was seated at a small table, a newspaper in his hands and a glass containing ginger beer and possibly gin in front of him.

Hallows took off his hat, glad of respite. He was very hot but much pleased with himself. The contents of the tankard reached only half an inch from the bottom when the door behind him opened. He did not turn. Not having glanced through the partition for perhaps a minute and a half, he did so now—to see, with a wild pang of horrow and surprise, that quarry had gone! . . .

It was with another pang, whose component parts were impossible of analysis, that Hallows became aware that the person who had entered the private bar and who now stood shoulder to shoulder with him was Mr. Revel himself.

"Morning," said Mr. Revel pleasantly.

Hallows, making stern effort to pull himself together, produced a grunting sound which would serve.

"Marvellous weather!" said Mr. Revel and rapped upon the counter with a florin.

A young woman came to the sound. She expressed surprise with eyes and voice at this new customer of the private bar.

Mr. Revel smiled at her. "Forgot cigarettes," he said and ordered twenty.

"Aow!" said the young woman, "I see." She put a packet and a shilling down upon the counter.

"Not sure that I won't have another drink after all," said Mr. Revel. He turned affably to the shaken Hallows. "Will you join me, sir?"

It is to Hallows's credit that he got himself in hand. "Don't mind if I do," he said. "Thank you, sir. Pint o' bitter, please."

The young woman made play with good brown eyes. "You're a One!" she said to Mr. Revel. "See you in the Public in a few minutes, I s'pose."

"As soon as I got out of that saloon bar," Mr. Revel said, "I thought I *must* see you again."

The young woman giggled. "You quite well? Hope so in

case not!" She produced a pint tankard and a gin and ginger beer with deft and refined speed.

Mr. Revel paid and turned to the sweating Hallows and lifted his glass.

"Cheeroh!" said Mr. Revel.

"Your good health!" said Hallows placidly. Almost was he satisfied that here was no trick.

Mr. Revel drained his glass and set it down upon the counter. He smiled at the young woman; a smile which seemed to prophesy a speedy return to the Leopard and Keys.

"Morning," he said. "Got to hurry off."

He had the swing door half opened when Hallows stopped him. "Left something," said Hallows, and pointed to the counter where, beside Mr. Revel's empty glass, was the parcel from S. Widgeon, Cutler.

"Oh, that!" said Mr. Revel. "Be a good chap and deliver it for me, will you? It's addressed."

He passed through the door. It swung to behind him. Wildly Hallows checked a rush to the door, wildly he turned to the bar and snatched from it the parcel. Upon the side which had been next to the mahogany it was addressed, in bold letters, to Superintendent Connor, Criminal Investigation Department, New Scotland Yard.

Hallows stared. After a long moment four words came from his mouth.

"Per-*lease!*" said the young woman.

3

It was twenty minutes past noon when Detective Officer Hallows was reprimanded for his language by the barmaid of the Leopard and Keys. At that time Sir Christopher Vayle had been with Superintendent Connor for nearly half an hour.

"So that's all you've got to tell me, sir," said Connor, breaking the silence. "Doesn't amount to much, does it?"

Christopher lifted great shoulders. "Amounts to nothing," he said. "Sorry, but there it is. Just when I think I'm going to get something I come up against a blank wall."

Connor smashed his fist down upon the table with such force that the lids of his inkpots rattled and a startled pen rolled to the floor.

"You've said it, sir! *Blank wall.* That's what I get wherever I go with Mister Nicholas Revel. And blank walls aren't right—not so many. The fact that they're there means that there's something behind 'em. What is it? By God, I've been trying hard enough to find out and find out I will! I don't suppose there's any man in England that I'd take all this trouble about without getting any further than I have!"

"I'm going to ask you a question, Connor," said Christopher Vayle. "A question I haven't had the nerve to put to you before. Do you think that Revel equals X?"

Connor was silent for a long moment. "I don't know, sir," he said at last. "But I do know this: that he's the only man that I can put an identity to that I've got any grounds for suspecting. And in a case like this that's enough cause for doing something. I don't care what the com—what *anyone* says!"

Christopher Vayle looked at him. Christopher Vayle's face was thinner than it had been and had new lines upon it, and there was the ghost of a permanent frown between his eyes which had not been there before. Beneath the blond brows his blue eyes looked keenly at Connor.

"You've got me to help you tab the man all this time," said Christopher, "but you haven't told me your grounds for suspecting him."

"Grounds is it you're wanting!" Connor cried, and the trace of Irish in his speech showed him to be strongly moved. "Grounds is it! Now look you here! Here's my grounds: You got yourself in the way of being suspected of being X. Nearly twenty-four hours after you've been arrested along comes Mister Nicholas Revel and tells his story. It all seems reliable enough and we let you off. You may say that we'd 've had to annyways, because the next day there's another killing which yourself couldn't have had the doing of, but 'tis beyond doubt that Mister Nicholas Revel and this taxi driver, Joe Palmer, got you clear at the time. If that had been the end of Mister Nicholas Revel, if that had been the last I'd seen or heard of him, maybe"—Connor shrugged—"maybe I'd have thought no more about him, although there was something about the fellow. . . ." Again he lifted his shoulders. "But it *isn't* the last I hear of Mister Nicholas Revel—not by anny means! Very soon I hear so much about him that I get sick of the sound of his name. Mister Nicholas Revel, it seems, is a friend of Miss Frensham's. Mister Nicholas Revel has a bet with Miss Fresham over the lunch table that he can tell what we're doing in the matter of X and he guesses right. Challenged by Miss Frensham, he also produces his idea of what we ought to do to get X. And it's not so bad an idea. The commissioner talks Revel, Revel, Revel at me until I can't help thinking about the man. And when I start thinking about anyone I start doing something about that someone, as a matter of what you might call routine. It strikes me to wonder first of all how long Mr. Revel has known the Frenshams. I put a man on the job and make a few careful inquiries and what do I find? I find that we've every reason to suppose that Miss Frensham had never set eyes on Mister Nicholas Revel until lunchtime on the day you were arrested. I've every reason to suppose, also, that Mister Nicholas Revel was not introduced to Miss Frensham except by himself, and that he introduced himself in the lounge of the Restaurant Savarin. . . ."

Connor broke off. From under his overhanging brows his small eyes looked shrewdly at his visitor.

"Yes," said Christopher. "Go on!" His face was devoid of expression—too much so, Connor thought. The voice was flat and emotionless.

Connor went on: "I understand that Miss Frensham was looking very much—what shall I say?—distressed before Mr. Revel spoke to her. I also understand that they lunched together and that they went away together after lunch, Miss Frensham looking the reverse of distressed. Putting all this together, sir, I think it's myself is entitled to my theory— unless, of course, you are able to contradict it—that what happened was this: Miss Frensham did not know Mister Nicholas Revel. Mister Nicholas Revel, seeing her in the Restaurant Savarin, knows who she is and knows why she seems distressed. He tells her that he can remove the cause of her distress by having you freed. He does so. But what I'd like to know is: did Mister Nicholas Revel drive in Mister Joseph Palmer's taxi and did Mister Nicholas Revel and Mister Joseph Palmer see what they said they saw?"

Connor stopped abruptly. Across the desk the two men stared steadily at each other.

"What's your point?" Christopher said. "Suppose he did lie? Suppose he could bribe the taxi driver to lie too, what could his object have been?" He paused a moment and then added, speaking more slowly and not once removing his eyes from Connor's: "Apart, of course, from the obvious object which one might consider if it had been any other woman than Miss Frensham."

"H'm!" said Connor, and then: "Easy enough, sir, isn't it? 'Tis him wants to be in with the chief commissioner. He does the chief commissioner's daughter a great service and the rest's easy. If he couldn't meet Sir Hector then he'd never be able."

"Quite!" said Christopher. "Quite!" Still his eyes searched Connor's. "But even then what's his point? Here! Let's take it farther. Let's assume that he's X for the purpose of this branch of the argument. If he's X, what's his point in getting to know the commissioner?"

"The oldest in the world. You'll be knowing the theory, Sir Christopher, as well as myself: if it's hiding yourself you're after, don't go to the country, go to the city. If it's hiding a thing you're after, leave it in full view. If you want to throw suspicion off yourself, put yourself in such a place that there's never a man would ever think of suspecting you."

"H'm!" said Christopher in his turn. "Well, then, what's his idea in this clever stuff about guessing what the police have done?"

Connor stared. "Isn't it clear as water—to lead up to telling the police what *to do?* If he knows that, he'll be knowing how to dodge it."

"You *do* think Revel's X!" said Christopher Vayle.

Connor shook his head. "'Tis yourself saying that!" His voice was angry. "But you asked me, Sir Christopher, the why I was thinking Mister Nicholas Revel worthy of attention. Maybe I've said too much annyway." He cut off speech abruptly, his mouth closing into a thin hard line. He no longer looked at Christopher but glared past him at the window.

Christopher got to his feet. Even in the big bare room he bulked enormous, seeming, as he did everywhere he went, to throw his surroundings out of scale. For the first time during this interview—for the first time upon this day, in fact—he smiled. The unearned years which seemed lately to have settled upon him rolled away with the smile. He came up to the table and sat sideways upon it, swinging one leg and looking down at Connor.

"There's no use in being cross with me," he said. "Not a bit of use! When I said that you did think Revel was X, it wasn't a statement so much as a reiterated question. Anyhow, whatever it was, I take it back."

He looked at Connor until the steady stare of his eyes brought Connor's round to meet it.

"I'd be very much obliged," said Christopher Vayle, "if you'd go on."

There was a small silence. Connor smiled and broke it.

"I'm sorry, Sir Christopher," he said. "We're all on a bit of a strain these days. There was no call for me to . . ."

"Forget it!" Christopher said, and once more smiled. "And go on."

Connor picked a pencil from the table before him and began to twist it this way and that between his fingers. His eyes no longer met Christopher's. He began to speak, hesitated, began again, and once more cut himself short.

"There's one thing," he said at last. "It's really the thing that I've been leading up to. . . ." His words no longer came fast. They were slow in themselves, seeming to be each one weighed before utterance, and between them were long pauses. And all trace of Hibernia was gone from both idiom and inflection. He said:

"There's no doubt, I take it, sir, that Miss Frensham is seeing Mister Nicholas Revel at times?"

"None at all," said Christopher Vayle.

"Alone?" said Connor. And now he did look up to meet the gaze of his visitor.

Christopher Vayle looked long and hard before he spoke. And, before he spoke, he lifted his shoulders in a gesture so slight as to be less than a shrug and rose and walked over to the window and stood gazing out over the sunlit Embankment.

"Yes," he said, without turning. "Occasionally."

Connor stood up. He, too, went to the window. A big man by ordinary standards, beside Christopher Vayle he seemed both insignificant and clumsy.

"Occasionally is too often," said Connor in a low voice of different tone to any which he had used throughout the interview. "I'm speaking as a friend now. Or perhaps it would be stronger if I said I was speaking just as one normal, right-thinking man to someone in possible danger. Occasionally is too often, Sir Christopher. *Once* might be too often. . . ."

Christopher turned sharply. His right hand came up and brushed the inner side of its fingers across his forehead. Once more the frown was back between his eyes. He opened his mouth to speak but checked himself as Connor raised a hand.

"Listen to me!" Connor said. "When I've told you what I'm going to tell you now it'll be in your mind to say again that I know that Mister Nicholas Revel is X. Don't say it. Don't even think it. I *know* nothing. But this is the thing I'm going to tell you—not in my official capacity, but, as I've said, as one human being to another in possible danger. We cannot account, after the strictest investigations, for Mister Nicholas Revel. . . ." For a moment he paused, only to add, just as Christopher was again about to speak: "We cannot account for the movements of Mister Nicholas Revel during the times when the murders must have been committed." He was speaking more slowly now than ever, each word a separate and somehow deadly entity.

"You understand what I'm saying," he said. "Each of the seven men who have been killed must have been killed within certain times. We have been unable to find out even where Mister Nicholas Revel was supposed to have been during any of these times."

"I see," said Christopher, and was silent.

A telephone bell pealed shrill. Connor went back to the table and took from it one of the three instruments and spoke. He put the receiver back upon its hook and turned to his visitor again.

"I'm sorry," he said. "The assistant commissioner wants me."

Christopher came away from the window and took his hat from a chair by the door. He turned to find Connor at his elbow. He hesitated a moment, then held out his hand. Connor took it.

"I'll remember what you've told me," Christopher said. "It goes without saying that I'm grateful. I suppose that you still want me to keep you posted?"

"If there's anything to post," said Connor, with a grim twist of his mouth which was no smile.

4

Having seen the assistant commissioner, Superintendent Connor came back to his room. He took his hat from its peg and was going out when his eye was caught by a note upon his blotting pad which had not been there when he left.

In less than three minutes there stood before him, paler than was is wont, Detective Officer Albert Hallows. In Hallows's none too steady right hand was an oblong, brown paper parcel.

Hallows told his story, nervously at first, more surely as time went on. Throughout the recital Connor said no word. At the end of it he pointed to the parcel, holding out his hand. Hallows passed the thing over. Connor, with a deliberation which his subordinate found nearly unbearable, undid the careful knots of S. Widgeon's assistant, folded the white string neatly, deliberately unwrapped brown paper to reveal a box of green cardboard, lifted the lid of the box, and began to take out wrappings. The last of these neatly in the waste-paper basket, there lay exposed, at the bottom of the box, a long, fat whetstone. Connor lifted this, looked at it, looked at Hallows, and set the thing down upon his table.

He looked again into the box. There, at the bottom, lay a visiting card, staring impudently up at him. It bore upon its upper side neat copperplate which announced the name of Nicholas Revel and the address of 4 Barkston Mansions, Knightsbridge. Upon the other side of the card were two lines in neat small script.

"Read that," said Connor, having himself read.

Hallows read:

With compliments. Why not get your men to give their heads a rub on this every now and then?—N.R.

5

Mr. Nicholas Revel took luncheon at Number Fourteen Gordon Place. Unusually, sir Hector Frensham lunched at home. At the long table were four places, but only three persons.

"Christopher's late," Jane had said. "We'll start."

And now they had nearly finished and Porter had closed the door behind him with finality, and Sir Hector Frensham was looking fixedly at his guest.

"Might interest you to know, Revel," he said, "that you're the reason of my lunching at home."

Nicholas looked polite inquiry, but Jane glanced sharply at her father, for there had been in his voice a note which she knew at least to presage annoyance.

"The last time I saw you, Revel," Hector Frensham said, "I not only complimented you upon the manner in which you had won a bet from my daughter but suggested to you that you should really put your brains to work and then come and see me again, either here or at the Yard. Remember?"

"Yes," said the guest mildly. "I remember."

"That was getting on for a fortnight ago," said Hector Frensham. "I haven't heard of you since. I believe Jane's seen you, but I'm sure you mentioned nothing on this subject or she would have told me."

"Daddy!" said Jane. She infused into the word a subtle mixture of reproof and warning and apprehension.

Hector Frensham did not so much as glance at her. It is doubtful, indeed, whether he heard her. All his mind nowadays was upon his problem, and at the moment his guest was part and parcel of this problem. Or should have been.

"Sorry," said Nicholas Revel. "Very sorry. Tell you the truth, sir, I'm afraid I haven't had time to think any more about it. And even if I had . . ." A lift of wide shoulders, today covered with a pleasantly striped blue flannel, completed the sentence.

Hector Frensham brought his hand down upon the table with a little sharp crash. "Not had time! Rubbish!"

"*Daddy!*" said Jane.

Again her father paid no heed. He gazed stonily at his guest with eyes behind whose coldness smouldered small flames of resentment. His guest looked back at him with a nicely modulated blankness; a look which struck exactly the right note, Jane saw with some admiration, of puzzled and tolerant but polite concern.

"You're an Englishman," said Hector Frensham. "You are also a citizen of this town. Just as it is your duty to give physical assistance to a Crown servant in difficulties, so it is your duty to give any other sort of assistance to Crown servants when asked to do so."

"Yes," said Nicholas. "Yes."

Jane, looking at her father, saw with distress that today, like its precursors, had brought its added tinge of pallor to her father's face and its signs of stress to his carriage. She strove to catch the guest's eye but failed.

"Why the devil haven't you been to see me?" said Hector Frensham. "I'd have been more explicit in my request if I hadn't known—as I know now—that you knew perfectly well what I meant. It's an unusual course"—his mouth twisted in a bitter little smile—"for a commissioner to take. But unusual things are happening, and unusual things need unusual measures. Why haven't you been to see me?"

"I'm afraid, you know, that we're a bit at cross purposes." The voice of Nicholas was tuned to just the right pitch of blandness; it was soothing without being enragingly so, polite without being sycophantic and firm without aggressiveness.

"Cross purposes?" said Hector Frensham.

"Yes. I thought I'd explained just now that I hadn't been to see you because I hadn't——"

"I heard you say that you 'hadn't had time to think'—if that's what you mean!"

"It is," said Nicholas and once more lifted his shoulders.

"I heard you say that," said Hector Frensham icily. "And I should like to point out to you that even if you were a man of many business affairs—which on your own showing you are not—that's no excuse."

Poor Jane strangled another remonstrative sound. She knew her father. She knew just when she could control him; and this, patently, was not one of the times. She shut her mouth and suffered in silence. The extra colour in her face made the blue eyes, so charmingly at variance with the black brows and hair above them, sparkle with a lovely brilliance.

"That's no excuse!" said Hector Frensham again but was prevented from further speech by the opening of the door.

Jane sighed relief as Porter came to her side. "Sir Christopher is here, madam. He instructed me to ask whether you would prefer him to wait in the library until you had finished luncheon, or whether——"

"Oh, no!" said Jane. "Please ask him to come in." She did not look at her father.

Christopher Vayle came. He bent over Jane's chair and kissed her. He shook hands with Hector Frensham and nodded to Nicholas Revel. He sat down at the place which would have been his.

"I ought to be angry with you," Jane said. "I'm not. Had lunch?"

"Yes," said Christopher, without truth.

"Ought to have told me," Jane said.

"Sorry," said Christopher and was silent.

Porter came to his elbow and gave him whisky and soda. There was silence. Jane sought desperately in her head for some topic which, started, might be sufficient to carry them through coffee and out into the library. She could not, as is the way with most of us upon such occasions, think of anything at all.

The silence continued, to be broken by the host. He looked at the stranger of his guests and made apology of some sort.

"Please don't," said Nicholas Revel. "I suppose you're right, anyhow. But I always was lazy."

Christopher set down his glass. "About what?"

"Everything," said Nicholas, looking at him.

The smile upon Hector Frensham's face which Jane had hoped might change from the evidently forced to the natural vanished altogether. He turned to Christopher.

"This man," he said, "happens to have the sort of mind I think we could do with borrowing at the moment. I told him so a couple of weeks ago and asked him to work it and bring the results to me. He hasn't been. He says he's been too busy. I've just told him, although he's my guest, a little of what I think."

Jane slipped down in her chair a little. Beneath the table she raked about with her right foot for Christopher's legs. She found that she could not reach them.

"Oh!" said Christopher, noncommittal. "Ah, yes."

"I should like to say," said Nicholas Revel, "that I've a perfect obsession for my own business."

"Which is?" said Christopher.

"My own business," said Nicholas and smiled.

"But look here——" began Hector Frensham.

Nicholas interrupted him smoothly. "Just a minute, sir. In an idle moment not so long ago I had a bet with your daughter. My laziness doesn't go so far as to stop me from trying to win bets. I won that one all right. But I contend that anybody with any imagination could have done what I did and done it better."

Momentarily Hector Frensham's face relaxed. A real smile lit up its gaunt thinness, and very white teeth flashed against his tanned skin.

"If it'd be any good, I'd be willing to bet you two to one in, say, thousands, that you couldn't give me a selection of ideas one of which would lead to our getting our man."

Nicholas smiled and shook his head. "I should have added just now, sir, that not only have I got this passion for my own business but that I'm also the laziest man—except where my own interests are concerned—in the whole world."

The smile went from Hector Frensham's face. His eyes narrowed and became very cold.

"I suppose I'm to take that as definite?" he said. "You don't propose even to try and help?"

"I'm very clumsy at expressing myself," said Nicholas. "I didn't mean that at all. If I get an idea, Sir Hector, you shall have it. But I'm afraid I can't think to order."

"Or won't try," said Hector Frensham.

He rose, pushing back his chair. He looked down the long

table at his daughter. "I'm sorry, dear, I must get back.
. . . See you tonight, Christopher. Afternoon, Revel."

He walked with his long cavalryman's stride to the door.
With his fingers on its handle he turned.

"Revel!" he said, and Nicholas turned in his chair.

"It strikes me," said Hector Frensham, "that I've made a
very poor host. Worse, a rude one. You'll have to forgive
me. You may understand the effect that the strain of this
business is having. If I had anything to say to you of the
sort that I've said, I should have said it in my office."

He opened the door and was gone. To the ears of the
three he had left in the room came the muffled sound of his
voice as he spoke to Porter in the hall.

"Poor Daddy!" said Jane then. She looked at Nick. "I hope
you understand?"

"Of course. I'm afraid, anyhow, that I'm an annoying person."

A snort-like sound came, stifled as soon as it was born,
from the lips of Christopher Vayle.

"I wish that you——" began Jane and stopped herself.
"Shall we go upstairs?"

6

Mr. Nicholas Revel left Number Fourteen Gordon Place at
half-past three. From the windows of the drawing room
Jane and Christopher Vayle watched the big grey car glide
soft and swift up Gordon Place and turn left and lose itself in the traffic stream of the main road.

Christopher sat a little heavily upon the window seat.
Jane, on her knees beside him, dropped a kiss upon his temple. Christopher turned and took her shoulders in his two
hands and held her away from him and looked at her.

"The boy friend upset the old man," he said.

Jane stiffened. "It was very nice of the boy friend not to
let the old man upset *him!*"

"Bunk!"

"What d'you mean, bunk?"

"Bunk!"

"You've got to admit he behaved well," said Jane, her
voice rising.

"The old man?"

"Don't be silly, Kit! Boy friend, of course."

"Who asked him here, anyway?"

"Yours very truly, sir, she said. But I can't understand why Daddy——"

"Why shouldn't he? If the fellow's got this plus brain it's his duty, as the old man pointed out, to give Scotland Yard the benefit of it. If he hasn't he shouldn't, at any rate, give the excuse of laziness, which is just uncivil and most decidedly pose. Your father was perfectly justified in losing his temper."

"Don't be a fool!" said Jane. Her eye flashed disconcerting blue fire. "And I must say I think it's pretty bad taste on your part to vent a sort of general cattiness on a man that got you out of . . ." Her voice faltered and died away.

"If he saw me," said Christopher slowly, "the only thing he could do, whatever he is, was to come forward and say so. It cost nothing——"

Jane interrupted. *"If* he saw you? What d'you mean?"

"Exactly what I say. But if he *didn't* see me . . ."

Jane stared, wriggling her shoulder free of the hands which held them. Blue eyes met blue eyes. Jane was very pink. Christopher was very white.

"Look here!" Christopher said, and the voice he used was a new one to Jane's ear. "Do you *know* whether Revel saw me or not?"

"I . . ." said Jane. "I . . ." She paused, then said quickly: "How could I *know?* I wasn't there."

"D'you think he saw me?"

Jane, for a moment supporting the weight of her lithe body upon her hands, wriggled her legs from underneath her. She stood over her lover. Only by a few small inches did she top him even then.

"I don't know what's got into you," she said. "I . . ."

Christopher lost his temper. "I'll tell you. A first-class number-one mystery-cum-counter jumper who upsets Hector Frensham and turns the head of Hector Frensham's daughter."

"You fool!" said Jane. "You *damn* fool! I love you, but you're worse than a damn fool!"

"I wonder—twice!" said Christopher between his teeth.

7

It was half-past four when Mr. Nicholas Revel parked his car in the courtyard of Barkston Mansions. It was an hour and forty-minutes later when Captain Phelps pushed open the door of the Bull and Trumpet in Notting Dale.

The brown suit of Captain Phelps was neat and well-hanging still, but it was showing wear more definitely with each time that he came. Its seams were threadbare and its elbows pouched, while its cuffs showed signs, to one so sharp-eyed as Bessie, of having had certain frayings attended to by scissors.

Captain Phelps had no sooner taken one swig out of his half-pint of bitter than he saw, signalling to him jovially from their usual table in the far corner, Mr. Joseph Palmer. Today Mr. Joseph Palmer was not alone. He had a young woman with him. It appeared that she, too, knew Captain Phelps, for to Joe's hail and gesticulation she added a smile and a wave which was more than half a beckoning.

Captain Phelps smiled at Bessie, picked up his tankard, and walked over to join his friends. Presently he sat between them at the little table.

Today Mr. Joseph Palmer, by reason of the fact that this was his day off, was clothed not in any collection of oddments but in a suit of unsubdued checks which made it seem that at any moment he might produce from one of his pockets a book and pencil and from his mouth the offer of, say, 100 to 7 bar 2. The girl, on the other hand, was smart with a severe and simple smartness which might have been either of the west or of certain places east. She wore a small black hat and a coat and a skirt of light grey which fitted her. Under the small black hat there showed a face of dark beauty, perhaps a little heavy until she smiled, which seemed often now that Captain Phelps was here. She was beautifully stockinged, neatly shod, and admirably gloved. From her ears hung two small drops which danced and sparkled. She smoked Mr. Palmer's cigarettes through a green holder of length.

The three old friends had a round upon Mr. Palmer and a second upon Captain Phelps. Mr. Palmer and Captain Phelps drank beer from tankards, Miss Crabtree gin and tonic water. It was not until they were in the middle of the second round that they left idle badinage for business. No one sat near them, but even if he had it is doubtful whether he would have noticed any change in their demeanour. And, as for overhearing words, it was soon patent that Miss Crabtree was as adept as were Captain Phelps and Mr. Joseph Palmer themselves in the art of not being overheard and not appearing to be trying to avoid being overheard.

"What's the earliest date?" asked Captain Phelps.

Mr. Palmer shook his head. "I dunno. Ask Doris."

"Ripe now," said Doris, looking first at Mr. Palmer with a friendly smile and then at Captain Phelps with a smile which had in it a good deal more than friendliness. "To-night, if you like."

Captain Phelps beat a tattoo upon the table top with his fingers. He seemed to be thinking.

Miss Crabtree looked at Mr. Palmer. "What's eating you, Joe?" she said.

Captain Phelps looked up sharply. "Thought you were down in the mouth, Joe. What's up?"

"Nothin's up," said Mr. Palmer in the back of his throat. " 'Cept that it's all off."

"All what?" said Doris.

"Meaning?" said Captain Phelps.

"All off. Hay-double hell-off. *And* Haitch-hay-double hell-off!" said Mr. Palmer. "Whichever way you like to take it."

Miss Crabtree's full-lipped but beautifully shaped mouth opened as if she were about to speak. But she cast a side-ways glance at Captain Phelps and was silent.

"Why?" said Captain Phelps.

Mr. Palmer leaned forward. From the beam which was now back upon his round red face one might have gathered that he was doing what was known in the Bull and Trumpet as "coughing up one of his yarns."

"Bulls!" said Mr. Palmer. "Millions and millions of bulls."

"But you told me——" began Captain Phelps.

"I knows what I told you; but that don't alter the fact there's bulls there by the score. And there all day, every day. All night, every night!"

"Damn and blast and hell!" said Miss Crabtree.

"But why, man, why?" Captain Phelps seemed to have taken the news hard.

Mr. Palmer lifted his shoulders, and the outer corners of his eyes and the tip of such nose as he had and the corners of his mouth all went up.

" 'Ow the 'ell should I know?" said Mr. Palmer. "*But* I can guess. Hex! There was a cop got it in the neighbour'ood, you remember. And it's a lonesome sort of a place. It strikes me that the bulls've got the breeze."

A silence fell. Captain Phelps stared at his fingernails. Mr. Palmer went through the motions of whistling a dolorous tune without producing from his mouth so much as a note. And Miss Crabtree, resting her pretty chin upon crossed hands, looked at Captain Phelps. Captain Phelps suddenly looked at her.

"How long will it stay ripe?" he said.

"Ripe now," said Miss Crabtree. "Prime fruit a week to-day. Last gasp of the fruit—before going rotten, I mean—tomorrow fortnight at latest."

"But it's all no use. Nottabitta use," put in Mr. Palmer. "Bulls and bulls and bulls and bulls! You can't 'ear yourself think for the thuddin' of their feet!"

Another long silence. Miss Crabtree sighed.

"I suppose that's that," she said at last. "Nothing doing after all. All I can say is, it's a crying shame!"

"Wait!" said Captain Phelps suddenly. "Now listen here!"

The three heads once more came close together. It seemed to Bessie, eyeing them across the room from behind the bar, that Miss Crabtree was a thought too interested in the sort of story that so obviously was being told. "What it is, dear," said Bessie afterwards to her colleagues of the public bar, "she couldn't of been no lady."

Chapter XVIII

EXTRACT FROM A DIARY

10th August, 193–

Didn't mean to write anything today, but a conversation I just heard—and took part in—made me change my mind. It is not that I wanted to write, it's that I've got to get this off my chest or burst. I asked Charlie just now what the big fellow's name was, and found that he was a newspaper man by the name of Ward. "Always in the know," Charlie said. "If Mr. Ward tells you the latest rumour, it's in the Stop Press News as a fact about a month later." I managed to keep my face straight over that. It's been more and more borne in upon me that I can't afford to take the risk of even appearing to have an unusual point of view over the business. I joined with Charlie in admiration of Mr. B. Ward and expressed a pious hope that he was right again. Charlie leaned over the bar, looking just like Satan in a white coat. He tapped on the counter impressively and said: "If he says that's what, that's what it is." I had to go away then. If I'd stayed another minute I should have roared with laughter.

D'you know what the idiot had said? He said that the reason why there hadn't been any deaths among them for the past ten days was this: that they had got X.

Can you beat that? Can you beat it, I say! I wanted to chuck my drink in the swine's great red face and tell him what a God-forsaken liar he was. Really, for a moment or two I thought I should. But mercifully I managed to keep hold of myself. I began to act and, I flatter myself, act damn well. I was an earnest seeker after information. I asked how it was that if they'd got X they hadn't told the world? The answer, I must say, was ingenious. Still the man Ward is a successful journalist, so I suppose one might have expected it. He said that their case against him wasn't complete. They were holding him all right and they'd have him. Naturally, until they got enough stuff to bring him up for trial, they couldn't or wouldn't publish the information. . . .

If I know anything about the sort of man this Ward is, and I think I can say that I do, that silly schoolboy lie will be all over London by tomorrow lunchtime at the latest. D'you know, it made me so damned angry that after I'd finished talking to Charlie I had to come straight back here and lie down. I found I was shaking all over like a young horse with colic, and sweating rather like that too. I've got to take care of myself—I've been going in for this sort of thing too much lately. Too many—what shall I call them? —nerve storms, I suppose. After all, I've taken on a stiffish job, and a job I think I can safely say that no other man in the world could have got through even so far as successfully as I have.

But that fat, red-faced fool with his silly lies got my goat. It's such impertinence for one thing to go about saying that they've got X. X is me, isn't he? And they haven't got me, and never will!

By God, I'll show him! I'll show the whole lot of 'em! I had meant to leave another fortnight, but, by God, I won't have this sort of thing! I'll show 'em!

Now what shall I do? Wait while I think. . . . Listen, I'm thinking! You know, if I wasn't so damned angry I should have to laugh. I'll put you away, book, for half an hour while I lie on the bed and think.

Got it!

I'll show 'em! I'll do two tomorrow, two. I'll hang about and see if I can see that red-faced fool again.

Chapter XIX

RIDE AND DRIVE

THE skies were lead grey, and for the first time in weeks rain threatened. London was full enough—not of her slaves but of guests and holiday-makers.

In this August, as for the past two, Mrs. Keble-Thrupp and her daughter, Mrs. James Headley, came up from Devonshire for two weeks' shopping. They stayed as usual at the Alsace Court Hotel, this combining well the virtues of inexpensiveness, comfort, and sonorous title. Also, unlike the real Alsace, it was not upon the Embankment but tucked away between Manchester Square and Selfridge's and so much nearer to the shopping centres.

This day, the 11th of August, was Mesdames Keble-Thrupp's and Headley's third in London. Untired yet, they still shopped. They breakfasted at nine. They were accoutred by nine-forty-five. At ten they were entering the doors of their first strategic point of attack. They went, indefatigable, from store to store. Here they bought, there they rejected. Sometimes they walked, sometimes they bussed. Once—because its way would take them through Hanover Square where lived the wealthy cousin of Mrs. Keble-Thrupp—they took a taxi. At eleven-thirty they drank coffee in the blue-and-gilt lower chamber of Watershed's tearooms in Piccadilly. They paused for a moment upon the pavement while Mrs. Keble-Thrupp looked with disfavour upon the lowering skies.

"I believe, Hilda, that it is going to pour," said Mrs. Keble-Thrupp.

"It's going to do nothing of the sort," said Mrs. Headley. "And anyway, we've got brollies. Come on, Mother!"

"Where next?" said Mrs. Keble-Thrupp, her nostrils already slightly dilated.

"Freedoms," said Mrs. Headley, who was a larger and younger and positive edition of her mother. "We'll walk along to Bond Street and take a bus."

"Yes, dear," said Mrs. Keble-Thrupp.

They strode purposefully, side by side, down the lightly crowded pavement. By the mouth of the Academy courtyard stood a newsboy from whose yellow placard black print blared:

only dispersed with difficulty by mounted policemen, and an angry crowd, not allowed within the street itself, gathered at the entrance to Downing Street to hoot and jeer at ministers coming to a suddenly convened Cabinet meeting.

And at half-past five Captain Phelps spoke upon the telephone to Miss Crabtree.

"Can you make it any later than the 25th?" said Captain Phelps.

"No," said Miss Crabtree.

"The 25th it is, then," said Captain Phelps.

"What'll we do in the meantime?" Miss Crabtree's voice had grown suddenly plaintive.

"Hold everything," said Captain Phelps and rang off.

At a quarter to six o'clock the grey Brillon-Meyer of Mr. Nicholas Revel, its owner driving, was halted at the Embankment gate of New Scotland Yard. At five minutes to six Mr. Nicholas Revel was looking out of the window of an ante-room to the chief commissioner's suite. He wondered how long he would have to kick his heels. He leaned one shoulder against the wall and gazed pensively out over the river. The threatened rain had not come, and grey morning had turned into a golden eve. It was not so hot as it had been, but hot enough. Mr. Revel looked at the reflection of the sun upon the water. He seemed happy enough to be where he was.

Hector Frensham saw him at a quarter past six. He gave him a chair and tobacco. He grunted at him and waited.

Mr. Revel burst, albeit smoothly, *in medias res*. "First of all," he said, "I've got to apologize."

"Ah!" said Hector Frensham.

"Secondly, I've got to explain that I had no intention of being unpleasant yesterday; the fact of the matter is, I suppose, that I hadn't given the thing enough thought. It seems to me that it was only this afternoon, when I heard about this latest affair, that I really saw how serious . . ."

"That's all right," said Hector Frensham. "Glad you've come to your senses. Now that you're here, got anything to say? We'd have tried that notion of yours about pretending the fellah wasn't dead, only the blasted press was too quick for us—as much too quick for us as . . ." He broke off and muttered something in his throat which his audience could not catch.

Audience smoothly took up the story. ". . . As the murderer was too quick for you."

Hector Frensham glared. In his white, seamed face the

tired eyes of faded blue suddenly glowed with the fire of anger.

"There aren't enough men in the force," said Hector Frensham, "to post at intervals of ten yards down every thoroughfare in this city. I wish there were. If there were enough even to double every beat I should not be talking to you now."

Mr. Revel remained unperturbed. "I wasn't trying to be rude," he said. "But I did want to emphaisze the fact that, as I see it, there aren't any—what shall I say?—*concrete* measures you can take against this—against X. Aren't any, I mean, which will be the slightest use, providing he keeps his head, and he certainly looks like doing that."

There came a tap upon the door and, following it in answer to Hector Frensham's bidding, the burly person of Superintendent Patrick Connor.

It says much for Connor's self-control that, although he had had no idea that Mr. Nicholas Revel was within a mile of Scotland Yard, let alone closeted with the commissioner, he did no more than check in his walk—and that almost imperceptibly—at the sight of Mr. Nicholas Revel.

Hector Frensham looked up. "Ah, Connor. This is Mr. Revel. Revel, this is Superintendent Connor."

"We've met," said Connor with a briskness unusual from him in such circumstances. He did not smile. He was thinking, doubtless, of a certain brown paper parcel.

Mr. Revel did smile—a bland and sociable smile.

"Superintendent Connor and I have met before," he said.

"Yes," said Hector Frensham. "Yes, of course. I was forgetting." He turned to Connor. "Anything special?"

Connor crossed to the table and set down upon its blotting pad some typewritten sheets. "You asked for this précis, sir, as soon as it was ready," he said and added bitterly: "Not that it will do you any good. It's just what we knew before. Nothing."

Hector Frensham frowned down at the thin pile of paper. After a moment he set it upon one side. He looked up at Connor and then across at the seated Nicholas.

"Mr. Revel is here at my invitation," he said—and both his listeners were struck by the weariness of his voice despite the quickness of its words. "I've spoken about Mr. Revel to you before, you remember."

"Yes, sir." Connor's voice was without tone as his face was expressionless. He stood immovable at something very much like the position of attention. It was as if the man had schooled every inch of himself against the exhibition of any emotion whatsoever.

"Yesterday," continued Hector Frensham, "Mr. Revel lunched with me. I reminded him that I should be glad of any suggestions which he cared to make, since he had already shown, as I have told you, a remarkable ingenuity in regard to our—problem. Yesterday he had nothing to put forward. Today—" here he glanced away from Connor to his other visitor—"I assume that he has, otherwise I can't imagine that he would be here. Take a chair, Connor." He turned his gaze upon Nicholas and waited.

Nicholas was unperturbed. He sat there, one leg crossed over the other, one hand holding a silk-clad ankle, and was cool and completely master of himself. In the unspoken words of Sir Hector Frensham's butler, a well-dressed gentleman and very easy in his manner.

"I really came," he said, "as I was explaining just now, to tell you that I was sorry for my attitude of yesterday directly I heard the news this afternoon. It wasn't so much that I had any definite *new* idea."

A short silence fell. It was Connor who broke it. When he spoke, his voice revealed itself as even more strictly schooled than his blank face and rigidly held body.

"If Mr. Revel was thinking of that scheme of his which you showed me, sir," he said, "I'm afraid there's nothing doing in this case. It's all over the town that the man's dead."

"Yes," said Hector Frensham. "I've pointed that out." He glanced for a moment at the typewritten sheets which Connor had given him and tapped them with a finger. "Anything here about the distance the shot must have been fired from? Anything new, I mean?"

Connor shook his head. "No, sir. Jarvis got Sir Bertram Matchdale to have a look at the body. Sir Bertram puts the distance even lower than the others, and, to make it worse, sir, Sir Bertram is of the opinion that the shot couldn't possibly have been fired from any ordinary make of car. None of them would be near enough to the ground to get the right angle for the wound."

Hector Frensham turned his head sharply to look at the speaker. The bushy grey brows over the tired eyes were raised.

"A lot of these open sports cars are as near the ground as you can get without touching it," he said.

Connor nodded. "Yes, sir, But it's not likely a man would fire from one of these. Too likely to be seen. If the shot was fired from a car it's my view—and Jarvis and the others agree—that it must have been from a closed car. And, as Sir Bertram says that in nothing but a car right on the ground would fit the angle of the wound, we think it wasn't fired from a car at all."

"Must have been a car," said Hector Frensham, his voice almost an octave higher than usual. "Must have been! Are you trying to tell me that this—this X, who's been so careful up to now, would be such a damned idiot as to pull a gun while he was walking? The risk's far too great, man. He can't be as insolent as that. . . ."

"Don't forget, sir," said Connor, "that the odds are a hundred to one on his being mad, and a madman will get away with things that no sane man would ever attempt."

"And a madman," said Hector Frensham, "is also a great deal more careful than a sane man. A madman on his hobby-horse, that is. I maintain, Connor, that the probability of his madness only increases the certainty that he wouldn't be so reckless as to fire a gun when he was walking in a crowded street; I see your point about the open car, though. Whichever way you look at the thing it's impossible! I thought we'd touched the rock bottom of incredibility with the poor devil on point duty, but this is worse!"

"There's such a thing as a man carrying a coat over his arm," said Connor slowly. But his tone carried no conviction.

Hector Frensham made a harsh sound in his throat. He turned on Nicholas Revel a face from which, now, every trace of colour had gone; a face lined and tired past belief; a face which many of Hector Frensham's friends who had not seen him during the past three months would barely have recognized. He laughed, and the sound was not pleasant, having nothing in it of mirth.

"Now's your chance, Revel," he said. "Tell us how the thing was done and you'll have us eating out of your hand."

For a moment Connor's face and pose lost their rigidity. He turned quickly on Hector Frensham and opened his mouth as if remonstrance, and perhaps more, were coming from him. But with an effort he held his peace and once more barricaded himself behind rigid walls of a greater blankness than before.

"Well, you know," said Mr. Revel easily, "I've always thought I knew how the point-duty man might have been killed. Now this other daylight one's happened I'm more sure of it than ever. . . ."

"Just a minute," said Hector Frensham harshly. "I don't

want you to make a fool of yourself. I'm sure Connor
would like you to, but if I'm to get him and any of the
other men to take any notice of what you may say, I've got
to convince them to start with that your cleverness over that
bet with Jane wasn't just a fluke. Before you say anything
you'd better know at least what we know. The shot that
killed this man this afternoon was fired, according to four
doctors, including Sir Bertram Matchdale, from a distance
of less than five feet. Mark that, because the shot that killed
the man on point duty in the City was fired from a distance of over twenty. A bit different, you see. If you still want
to show us what fools we are, carry on."

"Thank you," said Nicholas Revel mildly. "But the distance
really doesn't matter. I think I'll begin by saying that I agree
with Superintendent Connor that the shot this afternoon
didn't come from a motorcar, but from a pedestrian. I don't
agree with you that that is impossible, any more than I agree
with Superintendent Connor when he talks about coats over
arms. Did you ever read a story by Chesterton called *The
Invisible Man?*"

Of his two listeners there was one who made a sound of
"Tcha!" and one who showed signs of great interest at this
mention of perhaps one of the greatest of imaginative detective stories. And, strangely, it was Connor who showed
the interest and Hector Frensham who showed disgust.

"In *The Invisible Man,*" Mr. Revel continued, "Father
Brown pointed out that a man wearing the uniform of a
postman was as good as invisible because 'nobody ever no-
tices postmen somehow! They are mentally invisible.' "

"You're not suggesting . . ." said Hector Frensham angrily.

"No," said Mr. Revel and shook his head. "But I would
like to point out that, while Chesterton may have destroyed
the invisibility of postmen, there *is* a sort of man who walks
about London, sometimes alone and sometimes with as
many as a dozen others of his own kidney, who is far more
strikingly clad than any postman and, I submit, twice as invisible. He is a man who not only carries with him a complete
cover for a gun—even while it's being used—but also a man
whose very conspicuousness makes him inconspicuous to
the point of nonexistence in the minds of even those people
immediately surrounding him."

Connor coughed an artificial cough. He stood up. "You'll
excuse me, sir," he said as Hector Frensham looked at him
inquiringly; "but I'm busy. I'm afraid I haven't time to listen
to drawing-room theorizings." For a moment his tone gave

some indication of the bitter wrath that burned within him. "I've got work to do," he said.

"Sit down!" said Hector Frensham. His voice was quiet, but Connor abruptly resumed his chair. "Go on, Mr. Revel," said Hector Frensham. "Who is your—ah—invisible man who is so conspicuously clad?"

"Perhaps I wasn't right to use the word clad," said Mr. Revel musingly. "No, I see that I wasn't. The conspicuous things this man wears aren't clothes. I'm sorry. I shouldn't have said clad." Mr. Revel shook his head slowly in condemnation of himself.

"I think you should remember, Mr. Revel, that we are even more than usually busy here." Hector Frensham's voice was cold and dangerous.

"Eh?" said Mr. Revel. "Of course. Sorry. I didn't mean to waste your time. But you did ask me, you know."

"But I have not yet received an answer," said Hector Frensham. "Who, or what, is this man or class of man?"

Mr. Revel smiled apologetically. "Oh, I see! I thought you'd understood." He leaned back in his armchair and uncrossed his legs. "A sandwichman," he said easily.

"Eh? . . ." began Hector Frensham and then shut off speech as abruptly as if a hand had been clapped over his mouth. He turned slowly in his chair to look at Connor and found that Connor was already looking at him. There was a curious expression in Connor's eyes—one that Hector Frensham did not remember to have seen there before. They looked bewildered, with the bewilderment of a child who cannot believe what he sees.

For a moment or two they stared in silence while in his armchair Mr. Revel lay much at his ease and regarded them. Connor began to get to his feet.

"Yes, do," said Hector Frensham.

The door closed softly behind Connor.

Hector Frensham looked directly at his visitor. "You're an extraordinary fellow," he said. "Mind you, I don't say that we admit you're right. But I do say that it's an idea. And what we want now, God knows, are ideas." His mouth twisted into a wry imitation of a smile. "Until Connor comes back you might oblige me by giving me *all* your ideas on the subject of this man we are forced by the press to call X. Or perhaps you don't think it's a single man?"

"I am absolutely certain it's a single man," said Nicholas Revel.

Hector Frensham nodded. "So am I. Come on now! Tell

me all you think about him. I don't mean just what you think
of the steps we're taking, I mean all you think about the
whole business. Care to do that?"

Mr. Revel smiled and lifted his shoulders as one who
would say, "Anything to oblige."

"I think," he began, speaking slowly, "that X is a madman
who is mad on one subject only. Unfortunately for you that
subject happens to be policemen. I think this—which must
be obvious—because there can be no question of personal
gain for X. Nor can there be any question of personal re-
venge or personal hate. It's just possible that this might be
so if all the murders had been in one division. But they
haven't been. They've been, except for the first one, over
the whole of London. And it's my view that very soon, if
you don't catch him, Mr. X will get tired of London and
the same thing will happen all over again in another big town
—Glasgow, for instance. The advantages of London, of
course, are obvious—from X's point of view I mean. It's so
big and really, when you come to think of it, so inadequately
policed. You said yourself a few minutes ago that it's quite
unthinkable to double your beats all over. . . . But to come
back to the point: X is a man, as I see it, whose madness
lies in the fact that he hates policemen—not as John Brown,
Tom Smith, and Harry Robinson, but as policemen. He would
kill John Brown in uniform but would be quite unmoved by
John Brown as the most obvious of plain-clothes detectives."

"Wait a minute," said Hector Frensham. "Wait a minute.
You're saying nearly all of what I've said myself. But are
you sure in your own mind that X isn't a madman who is
mad on the subject of law and order and, generally, Things
as They Are; in short, a mad anarchist—a fanatic who's seen
a very subtle way of undermining government by destroying
the faith of the public in the power of government to protect
its servants? When I was first faced with this business—it
seems more like years ago than weeks—I held the view that
you've just expounded. Latterly, though, I've come round
to the anarchist view."

Mr. Revel leaned back in his chair and once more crossed
his legs. "I think my view is right. The other crossed my
mind but I got rid of it. Like this: The man's mad whether a
uniform hater or a law-and-order hater. He's only killing
uniformed policemen and, further, he's killing them singly.
If his madness was anarchistic it's very unlikely that he'd be
satisfied with this wearing-away process. I think I'd be safe
in saying that all cases of anarchy have turned into cases of

smashing on a big scale. Have you ever heard of anarchy—especially really insane anarchy—being satisfied to wear away the stone by the repeated-drop-of-water process? You haven't; neither have I and neither has anyone else. What a mad anarchist does with the stone is to pick up a hammer and smash it into a dozen pieces. If X were an anarchist he wouldn't be using sandbags and knives and single bullets. He'd be using T.N.T."

"Y—es," said Hector Frensham hesitantly. "Yes, I'm inclined to think you're right." His tone was now very different from any he had used to his visitor at any time during this afternoon. And it was to be noticed that when he addressed his visitor by name he no longer gave him title. "You've gone so far, Revel," he said. "Go a bit further. Tell me what sort of a man you think this madman is. Or is that asking too much?"

Nicholas Revel shook his head. "Not a bit. I think Mr. X is in early middle age; is in very good physical health; is powerful and quick; is undistinguished in appearance and quiet in address; is very comfortably off, with money which he has made or has recently had left to him; has probably been in prison in England, and some time before the war lived in Surrey. I also think that he lives now in a large and expensive hotel. Or possibly hotels."

On the last words there came a tap at the door and then Connor. He crossed the room and stood to face Hector Frensham.

"So far as I can find out, sir," he said, "there were three or four about in the City and one this afternoon. Men have just gone round to all the agencies. We may know a bit more later."

"H'm!" said Hector Frensham. "Well, Revel, Connor's found that there were sandwichmen both times. That proves nothing, of course. But still . . ." His voice trailed away into silence. He frowned and stared at the ceiling. He looked like a man worried by failure to remember something which would still worry him when he remembered it.

Mr. Nicholas Revel smiled blandly at Superintendent Patrick Connor. His smile was not returned. But it was noticeable that there was a difference in the way in which Superintendent Connor looked at him. Not that there was friendliness in the superintendent's stare; but there was, in place of controlled but apparent hostility, a worried and bewildered wonder.

With an effort Hector Frensham brought his gaze back to

the men before him. "Sit down, Connor," he said. "Mr. Revel and I have just agreed that in our opinion this—ah—X is a man who is mad on one point—his hatred of policemen. Or perhaps I should say his hatred of the uniform of the police. . . ." Again his voice died away. Again the troubled frown drew his brows together; then, suddenly, was smoothed away. "Got it!" he said and brought his fist down upon the table. "Revel! What makes you say that X only kills *uniformed* policemen? You read your papers, I take it?"

Nicholas nodded.

"Aren't you aware, then, that three weeks ago a plain-clothes man was killed?"

"The one at Hurst Park, you mean?" said Mr. Revel and smiled. "I didn't think you'd try and catch me like that."

"Catch you? What d'you mean?"

"Merely that what I know by guess you must know by fact: that the plain-clothes man was the work of everyday common or garden crooks—I should think a race gang. Quite possibly the what-d'you-call-'ems—the Carlottis."

Hector Frensham stared. He became conscious that his lower jaw had dropped and closed his mouth with a snap. He looked at Connor with a half-admiring, half-rueful lift of the eyebrows.

Connor looked hard at Nicholas Revel, to meet, as usual, the blond and quite unmeaning smile.

"What does Mr. Revel know about the Carlottis?" Connor said and looked at Hector Frensham as he spoke.

"Ask him."

"That's easy," said Mr. Revel. "I go racing a lot. If you can find me a race-goer who doesn't know about the Carlottis I'll have him put in a museum. Why the excitement? It's easy enough, surely. If one thinks, one sees that X must be giving heavensent chances to all the regular crooks who would like to get rid of their pet aversion in the policeman line. The Carlottis made a bad mistake—they didn't work out that X wasn't interested in plain clothes."

"They made a mistake all right," said Connor grimly. "We'll have the man next week. It was Victor Carlotti."

Hector Frensham still stared at Nicholas Revel. He said: "We'll leave that. Connor, Mr. Revel was telling me before you came in that his idea of X is a powerful quick-moving man of early middle age who is comfortably off with money he has either made himself or had left to him recently, and who lives now in expensive hotels but who used to live some time before the war in Surrey. That right, Revel?"

Nicholas nodded.

"Reasons?" said Hector Frensham.

"Right," said Mr. Revel easily. "Mr. X's type of madness indicates that his going mad has been a gradual process, because it must take a considerable time to acquire a hatred so strong that it turns into madness. It *could* be a sudden thing, but that's so unlikely that I rule it out. Hence the middle age. To go about killing policemen in the carefully plotted ways that Mr. X has used implies a life otherwise leisurely. Hence money. But to acquire a hatred of policemen through apparent ill usage by policemen infers an originally humble position. Hence the deduction that X is a man who has either made his pile and retired, or a man who has just had money left to him. The ill usage, real or fancied, probably includes a sentence. Hence prison, which, by the way, is a first-class forcing house for grievance. Money and leisure combined with the absolute necessity for comings and goings at any hour to pass unnoticed implies not only a hotel but a big hotel. Finally, every murder except the first has been in London. The first was in Farnley. Why should this very careful madman choose to start his career as a policeman-exterminator in a town of only fourteen thousand inhabitants? The inference may seem a bit wild, but I maintain that it's more likely that X had some definite reason for visiting the first signs of his wrath on Farnley than that Farnley was just haphazard chance. I think that this one murder, which was the first, mark you, shows Farnley to have some connection with the cause of X's madness. D'you mind if I smoke?" Mr. Revel leaned forward in his chair and pulled a slim gold case from his hip pocket.

"Eh?" said Hector Frensham a little wildly. "Smoke? No, of course I don't mind." He looked at Connor. "What do you think? About Farnley, I mean?"

"You'll remember, sir," said Connor stiffly, "that at one of the meetings early on Bazelgett put forward that it would be a good thing not to forget Farnley."

"I know, I know!" said Hector Frensham impatiently. "But what was done at Farnley?"

Connor shrugged. "Everything that could be. We went back over all the old ground. All the visitors to the town during the period were checked up. No result. You couldn't expect it. Sergeant Guilfoil's record was checked up. Nothing there. Further inquiries were made about the fake call that took the men out to Sir John Morton's house. Nothing there. It may be some good to look for a needle in a haystack, sir, but what's the good of pulling the haystack to pieces to look for something which for all we know may be a bit of hay itself? Perhaps, as Mr. Revel's being so good as to tell us all this, he'd also be kind enough to tell us what sort of inquiry we could make in Farnley to get us any forrader. Should we make a house-to-house call and ask every one of the fourteen thousand people whether they know anybody who used to live in Farnley before the war who might have had a grudge against policemen? We'd get so many answers that we'd be arresting twenty-five per cent. of the population. Perhaps Mr. Revel would care to borrow a couple of clerks and start the job himself."

Hector Frensham frowned. "That will do, Connor," he said. "Have you any idea what inquiries could be made at Farnely, Revel?"

"I think the superintendent's right," said Mr. Revel surprisingly. "We may know that Farnley's got something to do with Mr. X and his madness, but it's a different matter altogether to find out what it is. Might be worth while to go over the police-court records for, say, ten years up to 1914 to see whether there was any case in which the defendant seemed to think he'd been maltreated or cheated or otherwise badly used by the police. But that sounds pretty hopeless. The usefulness of Farnley, Sir Hector, will come in later when we've got our man. Then you can check up on him and get what might turn out to be the missing link in your case."

Mr. Revel stopped speaking. For a moment there was silence, but it was broken by Superintendent Connor who, astonishingly, put back his head and laughed long and loud—a harsh and discordant sound.

Mr. Revel smiled.

"Connor!" barked Hector Frensham.

There was that in his voice which cut short the angry mirthless laughter. Connor, red in the face, sat upright and silent while his chief commissioner stared at him with cold and wrathful eyes.

"Beg pardon, sir," mumbled Connor in his throat.

Hector Frensham turned upon his other visitor. "You sounded as if you seemed certain that we should get him."

"I don't see any reason why we shouldn't," Mr. Revel said placidly. "You know, Sir Hector, this can't go on!"

A choking sound, strangled at birth, came from Connor's throat.

Sir Hector Frensham stared, not at Connor but at Nicholas

Revel. Mr. Revel, apparently as unaware of scrutiny as he was of the strange noise which had come from the superintendent, placidly continued.

"I don't see any reason at all," he said. "It's a question of how we go about it. I think I may say that up to date nothing but elaborations of the existing police system have been tried. Am I right?"

For a moment Hector Frensham pondered. When he spoke, it was to Connor. "You answer that," he said.

"I can't," said Connor. "I don't know what it means." He was almost childish in his gruffness.

"H'm!" grunted Hector Frensham. To Nicholas Revel he said: "You're right. At least you are if I take what you say in the fullest sense of the word. To use a phrase of your own, nothing that isn't concrete has been done. I'm still to be satisfied, though, that any other sort of measures *could* be taken. I remember your suggestion that we should pretend one of the murdered men was not dead, but the more I think about that the more difficult it appears and the more it depends upon circumstance."

"We're agreed," said Mr. Revel, "that X is mad. Being a monomaniac he has, upon the subject of his mania, all the brain power of a dozen sane men. By using concrete—I don't think I'm using that word right, but it'll have to do— by using concrete measures you're only giving him more hurdles to jump. But he likes jumping hurdles. He'll go on jumping hurdles from now till doomsday. By giving him more hurdles you're simply pandering to his madness. What you've got to do, therefore, is to use his madness to catch him. That first suggestion of mine *wasn't* a good one. It was hurriedly thought of and, as you say, depended too much on circumstances being favourable. But it *was* on the right lines." Mr. Revel stopped talking to rise and extinguish neatly the end of a cigarette in a tray upon the commissioner's table.

Hector Frensham watched his visitor back to his seat. "Any more?" he said. "Ideas, I mean."

"A bushel," said Mr. Revel. "I've been thinking. For instance, suppose we reverse my original scheme. I don't know whether you've yet supplied men on night duty with any weapon-proof clothing; the idea must have occurred, but I should think the cost's probably been prohibitive."

Again Mr. Revel paused, this time to light a fresh cigarette. In the small silence the eyes of the chief commissioner and his superintendent met.

"The reverse of my first scheme would be this," said Mr.

Revel: "Give as many isolated night duty men as you can weapon-proof clothing. Tempt X by making it known through the press, or, better still, by judiciously projected rumour that apprehension was felt in certain quarters regarding the safety of certain isolated beats. Instruct your armoured men that whether they are shot at or struck at or stabbed they must pretend immediately to be dead. If X chose the right sort of murder for us we should then be this much better off—that we should at last know what we looked like. It wouldn't be much, but it might be a good deal more than it seemed at first. We should have, of course, to carry out the pretense of the man's death down to the very last detail—even to a funeral. There's one idea for you."

"Again it depends so much on favourable circumstances," said Hector Frensham after a pause. "I don't . . ."

"Think much of it," agreed Mr. Revel. "Neither do I. It's simply another step in thinking out how we can attack. *Attack:* that's really what I should have said instead of that business about concrete and abstract methods and all the stuff about making use of X's mania. It all comes down to the old saw that attack is the best method of defense. Everyone knows that, and from personal experience I'm convinced that it's true." Mr. Revel looked for a moment at Superintendent Connor. "You see," he went on, "all this elaboration of existing methods, this doubling of beats where possible, this enrolling of special constables, this tightening up of the regulations about firearms—all these things which I guessed at and got paid by your daughter for guessing at, Sir Hector —all these things and the many others which you've doubtless done, they're all *defense*. Think of it: the whole of the best police force in the world defending itself against one lunatic. It won't do, for more reasons than one. What the best police force in the world has got to do is to *attack*. The reason they haven't attacked before is that they haven't known what to attack, and they thought that, because they didn't know what to attack, they couldn't attack. I say that they can. To come to a third and, I think, better idea which I had this afternoon, I think we'd better start on the assumption that, like all monomaniacs, X is extraordinarily vain—at least on the subject of his mania. We must get at him through his vanity. Suppose we write a letter to the papers tonight—to every paper in London—purporting to be from X himself, making the thing a triumphal crow about his progress to date, threatening what he'll do in the future, claiming to be a sort of man which we know very well that X is not, giving a motive which can't be X's. That might have the effect of decoying him into the open at least enough to write a contradictory letter. We might, of course, get dozens of contradictory letters, all of which might be from the curious type of unbalanced person who confesses to a crime which he has not done. But we might also get one, either surrounded by those crazy letters or by itself, which was from the real X, and even if we had two hundred letters, which we wouldn't, we'll have narrowed down our field a lot. It's possible to inquire into the source of two hundred letters. It isn't possible to inquire into the movements of eight million people."

Mr. Revel's voice died away. He sat and placidly smoked and looked with a certain benevolence at the scowling face of Superintendent Connor.

"Yes," said Hector Frensham slowly. "Yes. What d'you think, Connor? There's a good deal in what Mr. Revel says."

"I can't say much for it, sir," said Connor, his tone more obviously than ever disguising his real emotions.

"Why not?" Hector Frensham snapped.

"Too much up in the air," Connor growled. And then, because he was an honest man: "It's a new line, certainly."

There fell another silence which was not broken until, two long minutes later, Hector Frensham spoke.

"Any *more*, Revel?" he said.

"None worked out," said Mr. Revel. "Lots in embryo. For instance, I've just had the rather beautiful thought of an Anti-Police Union. We get a figurehead—he would be easy enough to find—who reviles the police, wants on specific grounds to do away with the police. . . . Trump up something —a couple of minutes' thinking would do it. We might then get our man X into the open. Then there's a better idea. . . . Wait a minute. . . . How about a faked or friendly foreign policeman who comes to England, much heralded by the press in not too obvious a way, to help Scotland Yard out of their difficulty? Couldn't we get X through vanity or fear or a bit of both to have a go at him? Couldn't we put the foreigner in the way of X, so to speak? Tempt him again?"

"H'm!" said Hector Frensham. "Any more?"

Mr. Revel smiled and said: "Embryo, embryo."

Hector Frensham smiled. It seemed to Connor, looking keenly at him for a moment, that some of the fatigue had gone from his face, that there was back in it something of the old keenness and desire for fight. Connor's eyes came slowly round to rest upon the face of Nicholas Revel. Connor's eyes were puzzled now beyond all doubt.

Hector Frensham looked at his watch and stood up. Mr. Revel, taking his cue, rose as well. Hector Frensham came from behind his table and held out his hand to Mr. Revel, who took it.

"Go away and think," said Hector Frensham. "And come and see me. In the morning, anyhow. At any time tonight, here or at my house, if you hatch one of your eggs."

"You know," said Mr. Revel, "I was thinking of writing that letter."

"Yes," said Hector Frensham slowly. And then with sudden decision: "When could you let me see a draft?"

"Half an hour," said Mr. Revel.

"Dine," said Hector Frensham. "And bring it with you."

Mr. George Scott, private secretary to the chief commissioner of police and slave to the daughter of the commissioner, was astonished to see, for the first time in his experience, the commissioner personally escort a visitor out through Mr. Scott's room to the passage.

In the commissioner's room Superintendent Patrick Connor stood and scratched his head. His thoughts were in turmoil, his mind a house divided against itself.

Chapter XX
"KAMERAD"

THERE were three tall men at one end of the cocktail bar of Stagg's Club. There entered the bar a man who dwarfed them. The barman beamed.

"Evening," said Christopher Vayle. "Dry Martini. Very dry. Double."

"Yes, Sir Christopher," said the barman at seven-fifteen.

"Quite like old times, Sir Christopher," said the barman at eight-fifteen.

At eight-twenty Jane Frensham entered the library of Number Fourteen Gordon Place. Her father and Nicholas Revel, dinner-jacketed, were seated side by side at the big writing table in the west window. Her father was saying:

"It's good. We'll make up a dozen and get 'em posted, eh? You do it? Or shall I get someone?"

"You get someone," said Nicholas Revel and smiled.

"Lazy young devil!" said Hector Frensham, and the un heard Jane behind them marvelled at the friendliness of his voice. She marvelled also at the capacities of Mr. Revel, for Hector Frensham was not wont to change his moods so rapidly between a luncheon and a dinner.

She walked towards them across the long room. Nicholas heard her and got to his feet. Jane hoped desperately that the redness of her eyes had been sufficiently disguised, for, most unusually, she had been weeping. Christopher Vayle had left Fourteen Gordon Place at a quarter past four, and the front door had slammed behind him with unprecedented violence. Christopher had said things. Jane had said more things. Now Christopher's capacity was recalling "old times" to the barman of Stagg's, while Jane, with a hard brightness of manner most foreign to her, was shaking hands with Mr. Revel.

At a quarter to ten Porter entered the drawing room to announce to his master that Mr. Scott was below.

"Hell!" said Hector Frensham and got to his feet and stretched. "Work," he said and shook hands with Nicholas and dropped a kiss on his daughter's head and was gone.

Mr. Revel took the cigar from his mouth and regarded his hostess with the beginnings of a smile twitching at his mouth. Jane was not looking at him. She was looking at the door which had closed behind her father.

"Poor Daddy!" Jane said. She looked at Nicholas Revel. "It is ghastly the way he's aged! But I must say he looks better tonight."

"All my work!" said Mr. Revel. He looked at her keenly. "Looks as if I'd better get busy on the family, too."

Jane froze. "What d'you mean?"

"What *you* need," said Mr. Revel, "is a nice evening to take away the taste of a nasty afternoon."

"I suppose you know what you're talking about. *I* have no idea." Jane's voice was more glacial than her face.

"Fancy!" said Mr. Revel. "Did Vayle tell you I was X?"

Astonishment and indignation strove within Miss Frensham. "What on *earth* do you mean?" said astonishment.

"Oh, he didn't?" said Mr. Revel and got to his feet. He looked down at Miss Frensham. "Well, what about it?"

"What about what?"

"Cardinal?" said Mr. Revel. "Or Café Madrid?"

"Oh!" said Jane. "I—I'm not going out. I don't feel like it."

"Obligation!" said Nicholas Revel.

At ten-thirty Miss Frensham and the car's owner drove

westwards away from Gordon Place in the Brillon-Meyer.

An open Bentley, which had been parked upon the other side of the wide street, followed the Brillon-Meyer.

2

Nicholas Revel, his dinner jacket replaced by a dressing gown of vivid silk, his dress shoes by slippers, sat in an arm-chair in the small but pleasant sitting room of his flat in Barkston Mansions. Upon his knee was a pad of paper, in his right hand a pencil with which he tapped reflectively at his teeth.

The clock upon his writing table showed the time as a quarter to three when, cutting through his reverie, came the loud peal of his front-door bell.

He sat up, very quickly. He frowned. He waited motionless; a minute went by. The bell rang again, this time with an angry persistence which told of a thumb held upon it. He raised his eyebrows, got to his feet, put the pencil and paper down upon the writing table, and went out into the passage. He switched on the light. Through the ground-glass of the upper half of the door he saw a large and dark and looming shape. He went noiseless to the door and opened it in a sudden jerk.

Facing him, seeming to fill the whole of the small landing space, was the vast person of Christopher Vayle.

Nicholas looked at him.

"Well, well!" said Nicholas.

"And that is two holes in the ground," said Christopher Vayle, with a gracious wave of the hand. "May I be per-mitted to enter?"

Nicholas stared, with narrowing eyes. This was a man of whom he knew nothing. He nodded and held the door wider and Vayle entered; in the passage he seemed larger than ever.

The light here was bright. Nicholas scrutinized his visitor with no pretense of doing anything else. He saw that the whites of the blue eyes were bloodshot, and he saw that, im-perceptibly and without any suggestion of having his body out of control, the whole man swayed with an almost invisi-ble rhythmic movement.

"Shall we go on standing here?" said Christopher Vayle. "Or shall we find a room?"

Nicholas opened the door of the sitting room. "Come in," he said and stood aside while his visitor passed.

Christopher stood in the middle of the room and looked about him with blatantly appraising eye.

"Ve-ry nice!" he said. "Ve-ry nice! Quite the gentleman's apartment!"

"Sit down," said Nicholas and sat himself upon the edge of his writing table, thrusting his hands into the pockets of the vivid dressing gown.

"Thank you, no!" said Christopher Vayle and bowed. His eyes still roved the room. "I should like a drink," he said softly.

"Help yourself," said Nicholas. He nodded towards a small table upon which stood decanter, siphon and glasses.

But Christopher Vayle shook his head. "I should like a drink," he repeated. "But I cannot drink with you."

"Dear me!" said Nicholas Revel. "Perhaps you are right, though!"

His visitor came a step toward him. Now, as he stood, the rhythmic sway was more pronounced; from the ball of the foot to the heel and back. Had Henry Beecham been alive and present he would have recognized the movement as he would have recognized the careful speech, the hint of mockery in the voice, and the curious smile in the slightly bloodshot eye. But he would not have recognized the look which was both behind and round the smile in the eyes, because against Henry Beecham, Christopher Vayle had borne no malice.

"Do you insinuate that I am drunk?" said the guest.

"I never insinuate," said the host.

"Good!" said Christopher on an approving note. "Quite the gentlemanly riposte. In fact, the whole behaviour is perfectly refined and nice."

"Time two-fifty," said Nicholas. "You won't drink here. You don't want to sit down. Shall I telephone for a cab?"

"I pray you do not bother. When I have finished here I will drive myself home."

"About what time will that be?"

Christopher cocked his head and half closed his eyes and calculated aloud. "Let me see. . . . If I start at once and am very careful I might make it last ten minutes . . . a minute or so for clearing up. . . . Shall we say a quarter of an hour?"

"Yes," said Nicholas. "Do let's."

"Fresh!" said Christopher Vayle to himself, very sorrowfully. "Very fresh! Are you ready?"

"For what?"

The swaying movement of the giant seemed to increase, and when he spoke it was in a different voice—a voice suddenly choked and harsh with rage too long pent up.

"For a damned good hiding," said Christopher Vayle.

"Not quite," said Nicholas Revel. "I'm entitled, I suppose —as from one gentleman to another—to ask what it's for?"

"Your ground for assuming yourself entitled to explanation seems weak," said Christopher Vayle, his voice once more cool and deliberate and mocking. "But explanation you shall have. First, I feel in regard to you as the unknown poet felt in regard to Doctor Fell; second, this afternoon you did wilfully and deliberately irritate my prospective father-in-law, who is a man for whom I have the greatest affection and respect; third, you have thrust yourself, unsolicited, many times into the company of my betrothed; fourth, you make my skin creep by reason of your dreadfully apparent ability to leap over counters; and fifth and most important . . . But we will let that pass. It must remain veiled in mystery. Unless, of course, with your great detective ability you are able to tell me what it is."

"Easily," said Nicholas. "Your fifth reason is that you hold one belief at least in common with Superintendent Connor of Scotland Yard."

"Eh?" said Christopher Vayle, startled, and then, between his teeth: "You're damned clever, aren't you?"

Nicholas, watching with careful eyes, saw that the hands of his visitor had become fists.

"Wait!" he cried sharply and with a new strange note in his voice. "You are right!"

"Eh?" said Christopher Vayle and stared.

The hands of Nicholas came from the pockets of the bright dressing gown and waved themselves, claw-fingered, in the air. "You are right!" he gabbled. "Right, right, right! You thought I was X. You're clever! I am. I thought I was clever but you are cleverer!" His voice was a whispered shriek.

"Good God!" said Christopher Vayle beneath his breath and went on staring.

Nicholas stood, from his mouth came incoherent noises, and at the corners of his lips a white, thin line of foam gathered. His arms waved wildly, and one of them went behind him for a moment.

"Good . . ." began Christopher Vayle but did not finish. In one spring Nicholas had come away from the table. As he landed on his left foot his right leg swung, and the instep of its foot caught the outer side of Christopher Vayle's right knee.

Christopher fell as a tower falls. As he fell, face downwards with his hands already thrust out to save himself, the right hand of Nicholas came from behind his back. In it was the small bronze statue of a nude girl that graced his writing table. The round base of this clicked neatly against the back of the skull of his visitor.

3

The hands of the big clock over the sergeant's desk in Beddoes Road police station in the royal borough of Kensington pointed to three o'clock. On a bench, helmetless and in a condition of camouflaged doze, sat Constable Ernest Wanborough. At his high desk, poring over a report, sat Sergeant Brayton. The night was quiet and still. A heavy peace enwrapped the station, broken every now and then by distant muffled sounds from one of the cells.

Constable Wanborough dozed. Sergeant Brayton puffed and wrote. And then commotion. From the passage leading from the street entrance to the swing doors which enclosed the charge room came a scuffling and a hoarse exultant shout. Sergeant Brayton dropped his pen. Constable Wanborough jumped to his feet.

The swing doors shot open. There entered to the astonished gaze of his comrades Constable Tait.

But Constable Tait was not alone. He dragged with him, one hand on its collar, the other about its right wrist which he had twisted behind its back, a small and squarely built man who kicked and squirmed and struggled in a silence more violent than any noise.

" 'Ullo!" said Sergeant Brayton. " 'Ullo-'ullo."

"And you may well say 'ullo!" said Constable Tait. And there was that in his voice which made the sergeant and Wanborough stare at him with eyes wide and faces suddenly pale.

Still clutching his prisoner, Tait stood squarely in the middle of the big bare room. He was a large man, but tonight he seemed to have grown larger. His head was erect and his eyes shone, and his face was pale with a pallor born of anything but fear.

Through the silence came Sergeant Brayton's voice. "You don't mean . . . ?" he whispered and began to clamber down from his high stool.

Slowly and with great impressiveness Tait nodded his helmeted head.

"Cor!" said Wanborough.

"On the corner of Hill Street and Foster Lane it was," said Tait. "Not ten minutes gone. I was walking down towards Brackley Street. I thought I 'eard something be'ind me. I turned round like a flash. There 'e was. When I looked at 'im he shoved one of his 'ands be'ind his back. That was enough for *me!* I made one dive for 'im *and* I got 'im. Here's wot 'e 'ad in his 'and." From a capacious pocket Tait produced a sharp knife of the type known as Norwegian.

Suddenly the bent and huddled figure in his grasp burst into speech. Owing to the grip upon his arm he could not straighten himself, but at the end of a long neck his head reared up, showing a white ravaged face with a straggling moustache and bushy black brows from beneath which glared eyes as mad as a trapped animal's. From the loose mouth came a string of shouted words and with them drooling of saliva.

"Can't stand it!" said the voice in a muffled shout. "Can't stand it any longer! You've got me. Hang me! Hang me, I tell you! I've done you all in. Hang me, I say! Hang me, hang me!"

Articulate words became lost in a confused and rattling shout, and then, as suddenly as it had begun, the voice ceased and the man slumped forward in his captor's grasp.

4

An oil factory on the bank of the river had caught fire, and the surface of the water was a moving sheet of flame. Whenever you came up to try to breathe, your head was scorched by fire. Whenever you ducked down to avoid the fire, the water choked you. You knew that soon your head would either burst from lack of breath or be scorched to a charred skeleton.

The water ebbed away and the flames died down. Guns were firing somewhere in the distance. You were no longer drowning or burning, but the noise was bad; and all the Very lights in the world were being sent up at once. . . .

Christopher Vayle opened his eyes, to shut them immediately with a groan. The light hurt them.

"Take a swig of this," said a voice in his ear.

Very cautiously he tried again. By screwing up his eyelids until there were only the smallest of slits to see through, he managed to bear the light. He found himself huddled in an armchair upon the arm of which sat Mr. Nicholas Revel, unmoved and unperturbed, holding a glass in one hand and a cigarette in the other.

Christopher put up gentle and tenderly inquiring fingers to the back of his head. They found a lump like a small apple.

"Take a swig of this," said the voice again. "Sorry if your head's bad. But you did ask for it."

Christopher put out a hand whose fingers shook and took the glass held out to him and drained it. A flood of new life went through him. His legs no longer felt cold. His body was no longer an untidy, uncomfortable mess of ill-joined units. He could open his eyes, too, but his head still hurt most damnably. He gave the glass back and closed his eyes and thought while memory came back to him.

He opened his eyes suddenly. He twisted round in his chair with a movement which sent a red-hot stab through his head from temple to temple.

"But y-you . . ." he said stammering. "But you—you —said you were . . ."

Nicholas Revel smiled. "Forget it! I'm not. I gave you that stuff to keep you quiet for a minute while I got hold of Nellie there and decided just how I was going to crown you before you got rough." He looked down at his visitor and shook his head sorrowfully. "I'm surprised at you, Vayle! You shouldn't try and fight out of your weight."

5

At one corner of Howard's Rise, that monotonous short cut from Pedlar's Road to the Aldgate High Street, there stands one of those grey zinc bins which in winter hold gravel for strewing the roads and so making the way easier for horses.

Master Morris Rosenklotz went up Howard's Rise every morning upon his way to school. He was a small and punily built boy of thirteen years with a head a size too large for his body and upon either side of a colossus of a nose two small and black and very shiny buttons which never omitted to see anything worth seeing.

Master Rosenklotz whistled his way up Howard's Rise, the black buttons, restless and ever-moving, darting glances this way and that. Master Rosenklotz topped the Rise and came abreast of the gravel bin. He was one pace past the gravel bin before something which the black buttons had noticed as unusual was telegraphed to the brain behind them.

Master Rosenklotz halted and turned and went back to the bin. The lid of the bin, he saw, was not flush with the body of the bin as it should have been. Something dark— cloth maybe—showed a minute piece of itself projecting between the lip of the lid and the body of the bin.

Master Rosenklotz put his hands to the lid and lifted. He looked down into the bin, which should have been empty, and gave a shriek of abject terror and dropped the lid and fled.

Ten minutes later a group of his comrades were transferring from the bin to an ambulance the dead and blood-drained body of Constable 5482 Frederick Arthur Silcox.

Chapter XXI
EXTRACT FROM A DIARY

10th to 11th August.

That'll show 'em!

I feel much too tired to put the full details of both the jobs down tonight. May do it tomorrow if I feel like it. I certainly have earned a week's rest. What a day! It makes me giggle how that sandwichman trick works. I feel almost inclined to work it again, although I swore to myself after the one in the City that I wouldn't. Still, I think that today I was justified. I'd got no time to make any other arrangement. The night job was neat, though. Wait till you hear about it.

I wonder how Mr. B. Ward feels about things now. I only hope he's told all his pals and that they'll all make him feel a bigger fool than he is—if that's possible—for a very long time to come.

Now for some bed—and sleep if I can get it. I'm afraid I may be a bit too excited waiting for the papers in the morning, but still, here goes.

Just got out of bed to take one of my sleeping pills. Got you out, Book, to note that I'm putting Elsie's picture under the pillow. Somehow, I feel I can sleep better with it there.

Poor dear sweet little Elsie—may her soul rot in a very cold sort of hell for ever and a week-end.

Chapter XXII
T AND O

THE afternoon and evening press of the 10th had been, in all conscience, shocking enough. But their roaring was as nothing to that of the morning papers of the 11th, in which was the news of the discovery of the body of Silcox. In unison for once, they hurled execration at the Cabinet, Commons, Home Office, and police. The *Echo* found magnificent lever for yet another attack upon the Prime Minister. The editor of the *Daily Messenger* laid the foundations of the biggest libel case of the decade, and Crosby Cussen of the *Daily Banner* got himself discharged with ignominy from a post worth £5,000 a year, the owners of the paper holding that his was the responsibility for theirs being the only journal not to have the news of Silcox's death in their morning editions, but to carry instead shrieking headlines—borne upon a fortuitous breeze from Beddoes Street station—to the effect that at last X had been captured.

A special cabinet meeting was called at eleven in the morning. At this there attended, besides Members, the three highest officials in the Home Office, Hector Frensham, and two of his assistant commissioners. Before the meeting broke up there was added to it no less a person than Field Marshal Lord Barraclough.

Early in the afternoon there was another "scene in the House," but this time a scene which had in it no element of knockabout farce, but rather a sustained dramatic note of political and national crisis.

In houses and trains and offices, on pavements and at street corners, everywhere and anywhere that men and women gathered together, there was talk upon only one topic. The faces of each and every member of the Metropolitan and City police forces, uniformed and ununiformed, active and clerical, from the commissioner down to the newest recruit, were strained and set, with mouths tightdrawn and brows strained together by permanent, seaming frowns.

Throughout the day came a stream of callers to Scotland Yard, each and every caller the bearer of his own or a friend's or a brotherhood's suggestion as to how the menace could be dealt with. Ten thousand pens scratched ten thousand letters to the commissioner of police, Members of Parliament, the Prime Minister, the Home Secretary, and the editors of morning and evening journals. The interior telephone exchanges of Scotland Yard and the Home Office had to be hurriedly reorganized so that blocking should not ensue through the calls of would-be saviours of the City.

In the early afternoon came another shock for London. For in the first editions of the evening papers there appeared, in all cases upon the front page and in a position of extraordinary prominence, the facsimile of a letter signed merely with a large X.

London gaped. And London read:

DEAR SIR:

I feel that it is time that I broke my silence. At the foot of this letter you will see the symbol by which I have, through no act of my own, become known to the world. You will, therefore, deduce that I am the man responsible for the removal of the various police officers who have recently died in violent and mysterious circumstances. Your deduction will be correct.

This letter is for one express purpose: to contradict certain theories regarding my motive in removing these unfortunate men. It has come to my knowledge that there are three main theories, namely—(a) that I am insane and inspired purely by blood lust; (b) that I am insane and inspired by an anarchistic desire to undermine constitutional enforcement of the law; and (c) that I am not, in fact, a man but an organization of what are commonly called Bolsheviks.

All these theories are equally fallacious. I am certainly not mad, but coldly sane. I am not one of those who desire the overthrow of constitutional government, and most certainly I am not a body of men, nor even the chosen representative of such a body.

I am a man who has a flaming and inspired conviction. What I have done I have done purely and simply in order that, when the time is ripe, I shall be in a position to dictate my own terms and thus enforce the adoption of my method.

The time has not yet come to divulge more of my plans, but you must believe me, sir, when I solemnly

and before God make the assertion that I am working
for the betterment of my fellow men. I cannot reiterate
too strongly that I bear no malice towards any man—
least of all towards any of these excellent types of
British manhood, the police. What I have done, I have
been forced to do. What I shall do in the future, I
shall have been forced to do. Later, I will write to you
again and I pray that you will give my explanation and
terms the publicity which I now ask of you for this
epistle.

X.

There was also reproduced, upon the front page of four
out of six papers, the envelope in which the letter had come.
It was in the same backward-sloping and obviously disguised
script, and it bore a postmark showing it to have been des-
patched in southern Camberwell.

2

At 4 p.m. Sir Hector Frensham brought to a conclusion
a meeting which he had called of all the members of the
higher ranks of the force under his control. He said:

"So that is the position. We have three days—seventy-
two hours—in which to get our man, or, if some of you
still prefer it, our *men*. If we do not succeed within seventy-
two hours, control of the police forces in the administrative
county of London will be taken over by the military. Already we are—unjustly, as I think, and I am sure most of
you will think—the laughing-stock of the country, perhaps
of the world. Our cup of humiliation will only be completed by our becoming an unsatisfactory addition to the
army. You can imagine for yourselves what it will be like
if we are taken over lock, stock, and barrel and reorganized
and turned inside out and run by soldiers. As you know, I
have myself been, until I came to you, a soldier. I therefore
speak with all the more certain knowledge. I do not want
any of you to think that this decision, which was given to
me by the Prime Minister earlier today, is anything but ir-
revocable. I spent a considerable time with the Prime Minister and the Home Secretary. I tried, by ever means in my
power, to impress upon them the, to my mind, fatal stupidity
of such a step. But I failed. The best I could do was to get

for myself, for you, for the rest of the force, and, I think I may say, for the country, this respite of three days.

"My hands were tied. To all of my arguments there was a very simple answer. It was this: 'It is twelve weeks and more since the start of this series of murders. The murderer is not only still at large but, as is shown by the happenings of yesterday, is more active and insolent than ever. If the existing organization cannot deal with its own enemy, something else must take the place of the existing organization.'

"I will not detain you any longer. You know the position, and for what it is worth I will merely add that for seventy-two hours from now I shall not only be here, but available to any of you who wish for any reason to get into personal touch with me. Good-afternoon."

3

The Prime Minister let tea, untasted, grow cold. His Secretary of State for War drank whisky and soda whose depth of colour betrayed its strength.

"I suppose . . ." began the Prime Minister.

"Suppose," said Spenser Knollys. "You *know!* General Election inside a couple of months. If you want my special wire from the course you can have it now. We're out, Campbell, and for once the great electorate are damn well right. Why, there isn't a single member of your Cabinet except me who's fit to run the Woodpecker Patrol of Wolfcubs! You'd be all right, only you haven't got the right men. . . . I know what *I'll* do, of course."

The Prime Minister raised his head sharply. He stared, with a look in which incredulous amazement and something very much like horror were curiously blent, at his War Secretary.

"My dear fellow!" he said. "You don't mean . . ."

Spenser Knollys's face cracked into a wide smile. The smile became a chuckle; the chuckle a roar of laughter.

"And your considered opinion is," said the Prime Minister, when the laughter had died, "that it is inevitable we should go to the country?"

"Don't be a fathead, Campbell! If we don't go to the country, the country'll damned well come to us! But why worry? We were due for it, anyhow. Look what a completely spherical mess we made of the Milan Conference! Look how popular Barstowe is over the Beer Tax! Look at the Sweepstake muddle! Look at the service pay cuts! Look at every damned thing we've done in the last four years! And now, to crown it all, there's Master X! And if *he* goes on, it won't matter whether there's an election or not. . . . God! It's queer, Campbell, but if Frensham's right—and I believe he is—there's one man heading the old firm of G. and B. Ltd. straight for the *burgoo*. . . ."

"Straight for the *what?*" said the Prime Minister.

"Burgoo—Cockney—Hindustani. Anglice, porridge. If you prefer it—Bouillon—that's French, Campbell—very difficult! Soup!"

"Oh!" said the Prime Minister. His head dropped again onto his hands, and his long white fingers ruffled his grey locks.

"If only . . ." he said, "if only we could get this X . . ."

4

"All I can say is, it's *dreadful!*"

Thus Mrs. Rawle of 14 Laburnum Road, Upper Sydenham, to her friend Mrs. Billiter, the licensee of the Dog and Fox.

"R!" said Mrs. Billiter. "You're right! . . . Try another, dear?"

"Well, it's a bit past my ration as you know, Jane . . . still, I think tonight I will. What with two boys in the force, I'm just a bag of nerves these days. . . . It beats me why the gov'ment don't *do* something. You know—step in! Pack of idle useless good-for-nothings!"

"R!" said Mrs. Billiter. "You're right. Tell you what, dear, you ought to see the letter my Harry's sendin' to the papers tomorrow! Got his head screwed on the right way, that lad!"

"Step in," said Mrs. Rawle. "That's what the gov'ment ought to do!"

"This letter," said Mrs. Billiter, "you ought to have a-read of it, Ruby!"

"Good boy is Harry!" said Mrs. Rawle. "But they oughter *do* something. That's what the gov'ment ought ter do."

"I wonder . . ." began Mrs. Billiter and groped under the counter. "Yes, here it is—I'll read it out. This is what Harry's writin' to the papers. 'Dear Sir,—Is it not time that drastic measures were taken by those responsible for the government of this country to deal with the Menace to those up-holders of British constitootional law, the p'lice. As a 'umble member of the elec—elec—electorate, may I put forward the suggestion that immediate steps should be taken to have the p'lice *all* dressed in plain clothes. I venture . . .' "

"R! Ve-ry good!" said Mrs. Rawle. "Joo know, dear, I'm such a twitching bundle of nerves. . . . Why don't you join me? . . ."

5

At the War Office, in a room resplendent of its kind, Lieut. General Sir Harcourt Rhind-Fortescue spoke with Brigadier-General Sir Herbert Collison, his chief of staff.

"You really think we'll get the job?" asked Collison.

"*Think!* I know we shall. I saw Barraclough an hour ago. The bobbies have got three days. Ha! It's a damn nuisance, Collison, but for all that, it may be interestin'. Now cut off and get busy!"

6

At a corner table in the saloon bar of the Bull and Trumpet, Mr. Joseph Palmer sat with Miss Crabtree.

Mr. Palmer looked at his watch.

Miss Crabtree shook her head. "He won't come now," she said.

" 'S'pose not," said Mr. Palmer and looked suddenly like a battered and crestfallen child.

"Wonder what he's up to?" said Miss Crabtree, half to herself.

"What did 'e say?" asked Mr. Palmer. "Did 'e seem as if 'e *reely* thought it'd be O.K.?"

Miss Crabtree lifted her shoulders. The drops of her earrings sparkled in the lamplight.

"Personally," said Miss Crabtree, "I think that for once he's bitten off more than he can chew! Look at yesterday, and then see if you think there's the least chance of 'em catching this X! She shivered and made a wry mouth. "And if they don't, they'll never pull off those extra flatties. And while *they're* about . . ."

Again Miss Crabtree shrugged. "Bazonk!" said Miss Crabtree.

Mr. Joseph Palmer leaned across the table, thumping upon it with a square-tipped, banana-like forefinger. "When 'e says there's something doing," said Mr. Palmer, "there *is* something doing."

7

Superintendent Connor looked with astonishment at two visitors. He had little expected that either Christopher Vayle or Nicholas Revel would call upon him today. He had expected even less that they would call upon him together. That they should not only call upon him together, but do so with bearings and in a manner so beyond doubt indicative that they bore towards each other the friendliest of feelings, was to Connor well-nigh unbelievable.

He strove, by no means with complete success, to mask his astonishment. He greeted them and waited.

It was Christopher Vayle who opened fire.

"We've been making a mistake, Connor," he said.

"Yes?" said Connor.

"Yes. Don't think I'm being indiscreet." Christopher Vayle jerked his head at his companion. "He knows all about it."

"Yes?" said Connor.

"And last night," said Christopher slowly, "I was with him myself from a quarter to three until daylight. And I'd been on his tail from half-past ten until a quarter to three. During *that* time, he was with Miss Frensham."

"Yes?" said Connor.

"And that puts him out of it."

"Yes?" said Connor.

"Yes!" said Mr. Revel, speaking for the first time.

"H'm!" said Connor and rubbed at his chin.

There was silence. Mr. Revel dropped himself into one of the two armchairs. Sir Christopher Vayle perched upon the corner of the writing table and swung one leg and whistled a dolorous little tune between his teeth and looked through eyes quizzically narrowed at the silent Connor.

Connor sat with a hand shading his face. The silence continued. Mr. Revel lit himself a cigarette. Christopher Vayle ceased whistling.

Connor thrust back his chair and stood. He looked first at the giant upon his desk and then at Mr. Revel. Connor's face was inscrutable. Four eyes searched it for some indication of the thoughts behind it, but found none. Four ears waited for what he should say. When he said it, it was brief, but it served to show the man for what he was.

"I'm sorry," he said. He looked, now, full at Nicholas

Revel. "We all make mistakes, and I've made a bad one about you, sir!"

Nicholas smiled—a wide and friendly smile.

Connor did not smile.

"I've made a mistake," he said, "in thinking that you might be X. I'd like to make this quite clear to you, Mr. Revel: that is the only mistake I've made in regard to you."

Nicholas smiled again—a wider and even more friendly smile. He did not speak. Christopher Vayle looked from the smiling face to the impassive one. His look was not without signs of bewilderment.

Connor said: "I imagine, Mr. Revel, that you would not have wasted your time coming here with Sir Christopher just to let me know I needn't go on making a fool of myself."

"No," said Mr. Revel. "I shouldn't."

"I suppose, then," Connor said, "you want to see the commissioner?"

8

Four men had finished an afternoon hand of bridge. On the baize table lay two scattered packs of cards. At each corner of the baize table were an empty glass and a full ash tray. Money changed hands. Three of the men knew one another well; none of them had before played with the fourth or even spoken with him. The largest of the three—largest in height and girth and general impressiveness—spoke to this fourth:

"Much obliged to you, sir," he said. "And, if I may say so, I think you are wrong in decrying your bridge; you play a very sound game indeed!"

"Rusty, I'm afraid," said the fourth man. "*Very* rusty!"

"Rusty, eh?" said the second of the three. "Damn good job for us you weren't in practice, then? Eh, George?"

The three laughed heartily. The largest walked to the window and stood for a moment gazing down at the street below.

"The paper boys have gone mad again," he said, turning back.

"Something new about X?" said the first of the three.

The large man made a disgusted noise in his throat. "Makes me sick!" he said. "Why the hell don't they sack all those soldiers at the head of the police and put some business men there? . . . X indeed!"

"Rum letter, that," said the first of the three.

"Letter?" said the second. "Oh—ah. You mean that thing in the afternoon papers? Fellow must be as mad as a hatter!"

"I wonder," said the stranger. "I wonder. Do you know, it occurred to me to doubt whether that letter they reproduced in the paper this afternoon was genuine."

"Couldn't be anything else, could it?" said the first of the three.

The stranger lifted his shoulders. "I think it might. Just as I believe they have in every murder case a lot of confessions from weak-minded people who are entirely innocent, so some such weak-minded person might want to take on the character of X. . . ."

"I'm sick of X," said the large man. . . . "Coming my way, George? Good-afternoon, sir, and many thanks. Hope to have the pleasure of another rubber some time."

The stranger stayed where he was and watched the three depart. He looked after them, and a strange fire came for a moment into his eyes. Slowly he went out of the smoking room, crosséd the big main lobby of the hotel, and made his way to the lifts. Within moments he was in his own room, the key turned upon the inside of the door.

He sat at a writing table by the window. Before him lay a thick black book with a clasp and lock. He looked out of the window and across to the more squalid side of the Thames. While he stared thus, the fingers of both his hands caressed the book, stroking the smooth surface of its cover.

9

There were three constables in the off-duty room of the Beddoes Street station. To them entered Police Constable Tait. There was, this afetrnoon, nothing triumphal about the bearing of Police Constable Tait, and in his eyes no Olympian sparkle. He appeared, in fact, at once bovine and embarrassed; he looked like an animal who expects unpleasantness but knows itself incapable of the mental or physical agility necessary to save itself.

Tait closed the door behind him. The three regarded him solemnly, and then wide smiles uniformly divided three faces. With a movement so concerted that it might have been rehearsed, the owners of the smiles, smiling no longer, sprang to their feet and to attention.

"All 'ail!" said a spokesman. "All 'ail to the saviour of

'is country! . . . What's it feel like to be famous, Sugar?"

"Shurrup!" said Tait and added three words that need not be set down here.

"Naughty!" said the spokesman. "They had you in one paper, Sugar, all right, and I bet the editor of that rag got it in the neck! Pity they didn't have your picture!"

"Shurrup, shurrup!" The face of poor Tait was now the most discomfortable colour. "I 'eard 'im be'ind me, I see a knife in 'is 'and, I grabs 'im and 'e sez 'e's X and keeps on a-sayin' of it! 'Ow the 'ell is a poor something to know the something else wasn't wot 'e said 'e was? And, anyway, old Muggerlugs got took in, too, and so did the inspector! 'Ow the 'ell was a chap to know 'e'd got 'old of a looney?"

10

"All right," said Hector Frensham. "Have a go at it! It's the craziest idea I've ever struck, and you're the oddest customer, but have a go at it—and good luck to you!"

Mr. Nicholas Revel and Sir Christopher Vayle came out into the yard together, drove away in Mr. Revel's Brillon-Meyer together, and, ten minutes later, entered together the cocktail bar of Stagg's.

"The old man's right," said Christopher Vayle. "You *are* an odd cuss!"

"Oh! Sir!"

"You are, and it *is* a crazy idea!"

"We're dealing with a crazy man!"

"I know," said Christopher Vayle. "And I'm not saying it couldn't come off. Anyhow, whether it does or not, you've done good with it."

Mr. Revel raised his eyebrows. "As how? . . ."

"Put some pep into poor old Frensham. I know he's got guts, but I never thought to hear him, on a day like this—when in a few hours he's going to be sacked and have to stand by and watch the soldiers make a muck of his job—I never expected to see him making bets with a queer lot like you!"

Mr. Revel set down an empty glass. "Have a bit on yourself?" he said. "I'll take a thousand to thirty from you!"

"Will you, indeed!"

"On?"

"Damn it, yes!" said Christopher Vayle.

Mr. Revel wrote once more in his little book.

Christopher Vayle looked at him with curiosity.

"What exactly is your idea in not having any help on the job?"

Mr. Revel shrugged. "I get longer odds, and anyhow a lot of beetle crushers flapping about might ruin it." He looked up at the face of his companion. "And you don't mind?"

"Mind!" said Christopher Vayle.

Chapter XXIII
EXTRACT FROM A DIARY

11th August.

That damned letter! Who is this swine that wrote it? By God, if I knew, I'd kill him! I never thought that except for them I should want to kill anyone. But if I ever find out who this idiot is, I won't just kill him—I'll make him writhe before he dies. Of course, he's mad—must be as mad as a million hatters—but I can't feel any less violently about him for that. I suppose I ought to, really; any sane man ought to feel sorry for a poor, crazy fool who's not responsible for his own actions. In the ordinary way I am sorry for lunatics; but I can't do anything but hate this one!

The first thing I did when I saw it in the *Comet,* after lunch, was to come straight up here and sit down at this table and draft out a letter to send to the press myself. I worked out exactly how I'd send it: go out and buy some cheap paper in one shop, some cheap envelopes in another, a cheap fountain pen, with a fine nib (which I hate) in another. Put all the stuff in my pockets and then come back here and lock myself in and copy the draft out, one copy for each paper. Then go out, about six o'clock, and get the car and drive all round the outer suburbs, posting each copy from a different place.

That's neat and tidy enough, isn't it? And the draft was a damn good draft, though I say it as shouldn't. And if that lunatic can disguise his writing, I, a sane man if ever there was one, ought to be able to. And I can't bear the thought of this fool taking it to himself, and I flatter myself that there would be no doubt whatsoever in anyone's mind, after

comparing my letter with the other, that mine was the genuine claim. . . .

But I didn't send it! I didn't send it! I didn't send it!
I took hold of myself and didn't send it. And I shan't send it.
Careful, I am. Extra, double-plated cautious, I am.

Chapter XXIV
GETTING A GOAT

AT NOON upon the 12th of August, Miss Jane Frensham
came in from a walk across Regent's Park.

It was a sultry, oppressive day, with no sun, but a leaden
sky which seemed far too close to earth.

Jane went into the library and dropped into a chair and
fanned herself. She was very hot. Porter came to her with a
long tumbler which tinkled. Jane drank and was grateful.
She lit a cigarette and lay back at ease and reached out an
idle arm for the newspaper which lay upon a table just
within her reach.

At the front page she made a wry face. It was X, X, X
and nothing but X.

The paper was the *Banner*, and on its centre page was
sometimes to be found the work of a young and journalisti-
cally successful cousin. Jane turned to the centre page, but
this morning there was nothing of Humphrey's there. Jane
began to read, instead, the current article of the series called
"Salute!" She was, when she began to read, only giving half
her mind to what she read, else she would doubtless have
turned from No. 6 in the "Salute" series, before getting halfway through it, with the same disgust that she had shown at
sight of the front page. For today the person selected for
tribute by the author of the series was one Ernest Biggleswade. And Mr. Biggleswade, it seemed, was by calling a police
constable somewhere in the southwest of London.

Under the subheading of "The Man They Could Not
Frighten," the author of the column told the story of Mr.
Biggleswade as he had had it from the lips of Mr. Biggleswade. No fewer than three times, it appeared, had Mr.
Biggleswade been in danger of his life from the unknown
and terrible figure of X. Once Mr. Biggleswade had actually
laid hands upon X! But the unknown—according to Mr.

Biggleswade a man very nearly as powerful as Mr. Biggleswade himself—had managed to tear himself away. On that night Mr. Biggleswade had sworn that if another such chance came his way—and he believed that it would, for he believed the unknown to be determined to right his one failure—he would not again be caught napping. And yet, according to Mr. Biggleswade, another and another chance had come his way, first when a powerfully built man in dark clothes, with hat drawn down over his eyes, had approached Mr. Biggleswade late at night. Mr. Biggleswade, pretending innocence, had recognized the quick, short-stepped walk of the person he knew to be X. He had waited, ready. But something—some inner animal instinct to which Mr. Biggleswade attributed the criminal's terrible success—had warned X of his impending doom. Before reaching Mr. Biggleswade, he had suddenly turned and taken to his heels. Mr. Biggleswade had pursued, but to no purpose. That giant of a man, Mr. Biggleswade, had laughingly admitted to the *Banner* representative that "running was not his strong point," but that running did indeed seem to be one of the strongest points of the unknown.

The third occasion upon which Mr. Biggleswade had come within an ace of capturing the man who for so long now had held London at bay had come only a very few nights before the interview. Mr. Biggleswade, off duty, had been walking along King's Road, Chelsea, when he had seen coming out of a shop some distance ahead of him a back which he thought to himself to recognize. Cautious at first, Mr. Biggleswade had pursued. With every step he had become more and more certain of his man. He had frankly given chase. But, yet again, the unknown had given him the slip.

It appeared that Mr. Biggleswade had laughingly admitted to the *Banner* representative that he was quite certain that X had marked him down. Asked whether this was not a most unpleasant state of affairs for him, to say the least, Mr. Biggleswade had replied, still laughingly, but with "an undercurrent of intrepid sincerity in the bass voice that so well fitted his gigantic frame," that so far from being unpleasant, the state of affairs was vastly exciting. He knew, did Mr. Biggleswade, that X would come for him again. He knew, too, that this next time X would find his match.

After a hymn of praise dedicated to the looks, stature, courage, and record of Constable Ernest Biggleswade and an exhortation to see picture on back page, the article ended.

Jane, having been decoyed by the flowery vigour of the writer's style, finished the column. Having finished the column, she found herself turning to back page. There, slap in the middle, was a huge circle containing a photograph of the helmeted head and vast uniformed shoulders of the subject of today's "Salute." It was a poor photograph—one of those very bad examples of the newspaper enlarger's art which blur their subject by pocked marking of the "screen." It is doubtful whether his own mother would have recognized Mr. Biggleswade. Beyond collar and helmet and long spiked waxed moustache, there was very little in the picture to suggest even humanity.

Below the blurred libel upon Mr. Biggleswade was another and smaller picture. It showed a corner of a London street of the most dismal kind, and underneath it were the words "Gatesend Road, Fulham. It was at this corner that Police Constable Biggleswade (see article on Page 12) came actually to grips with X, the Unknown Murderer."

2

Jane Frensham went to the telephone. She asked for a Mayfair number. As she waited for it to answer there was in her mind's eye a blotched and bleared picture of the head and shoulders of a helmeted man. Nothing of the man's face was recognizable, but there was an indefinable something about the tilt of the head which against her better sense had convinced her, despite the appearance of a well-spiked moustache where no moustache should have been.

The Mayfair number answered her. The Mayfair number said that it was extremely sorry, but Sir Christopher Vayle was not in. No, the Mayfair number did not know where Sir Christopher Vayle could be found. Should the Mayfair number leave a message for Sir Christopher Vayle that he should ring up Miss Frensham? Jane replaced the receiver, left it for a moment in *statu quo*, and then, lifting it for a moment, asked for a Knightsbridge number.

In due course, the Knightsbridge number replied. No, the Knightsbridge number was regretful, but Mr. Revel was not in the flats. No, the Knightsbridge number was not aware at what time Mr. Nicholas Revel would be back in the flats. No, the Knightsbridge number was exceedingly regretful, but it had no knowledge of Mr. Nicholas Revel's present whereabouts.

Jane hung up the receiver. As she turned away from the

instrument to go back to the library, there came the sound
of a key in the front door, and Hector Frensham came in.
Jane, kissing him, felt a sharp stab of pain. It was true that,
inasmuch as his eyes were bright and his jaw was set at the
old fighting angle, he was the Hector Frensham she had always known. But it was also true that he looked an old and
very sick man.

Chapter XXV
TETHERING SAME

JANE FRENSHAM stood with her back to the great fireplace
in the library of Fourteen Gordon Place.

Jane was flushed, and her blue eyes were full of dangerous
fire. She stood very erect, making the most of her five feet
and two inches. The beauty of her and the colour and grace
of her gown lent added impressiveness to her wrath. She
looked from the face of Christopher Vayle, which was hang-
dog in expression, to the face of Nicholas Revel, which wore
a bland and untranslatable smile.

Jane actually stamped her foot.

"*Will* one of you answer me!" said Jane, between white
teeth which did not open.

"Of course!" The voice of Nicholas Revel was soothing.

Jane turned upon him—a small fury. "*Will* you be quiet!"
said Jane and looked at her betrothed.

"Christopher!" said Jane. "Is that ridiculous picture in the
Banner you or is it *not?*"

Sir Christopher Vayle looked at Mr. Nicholas Revel, who
went on smiling.

"And what's happened to you two?" Jane cried. "Daggers
one day—brothers the next!"

Christopher Vayle drew a deep breath. He squared his
great shoulders and suddenly seemed to tower even higher
than was his abnormal wont. He took a long stride and was
close to Jane. He looked down at her and said:

"You're a little nuisance! I love you, and I'm going to
marry you. But you've got to learn that occasionally small
women should be seen but not heard."

Jane's eyes blazed. "If that ridiculous photograph is you—
if this ludicrous Biggleswade business is some fantastic
scheme of yours and this other lunatic's—if this whole fake

means that *you're* going to pretend to be a policeman in
order to try and get killed, and very probably succeed, I'll
—I'll—never speak to you again!"

Mr. Revel nodded sagely. "Quite logical!"

"Will you be quiet!" Jane cried. . . . "Christopher, if what
I am guessing is right, and you do it . . . I'll . . . damn
you, you great big fool! I happen to love you, and I don't
see why . . ."

"You be quiet," said Christopher Vayle.

He took a half-step forward and put out long arms,
whose hands caught Jane upon either side her waist and
lifted her three feet and more from the ground.

"You shut up," said Christopher Vayle, "and keep shut
up!"

"Oh!" said Jane, once more upon her feet.

With round eyes, in which anger and resentment strove
unsuccessfully for the upper hand over fear and love, she
watched while Christopher crossed the room, turned at the
door to say to Nicholas Revel: "Come on!" and was gone.

Jane found that her eyes were smarting. She became en-
raged with herself. She forgot the presence of Mr. Revel.

She became aware of the presence of Mr. Revel when an
arm came about her shoulders. She looked up, startled. She
was kissed squarely upon the mouth.

"Oh!" said Jane and was at a loss for adequate words.

Mr. Revel smiled.

"Obligation!" said Mr. Revel.

Jane was left alone, staring at a twice-closed door.

2

Gatesend Road lies between the Fulham Road and the
King's Road at the Putney end. It seems, like so many of its
dreary neighbours, to serve no useful purpose. It starts nowhere, it ends nowhere. It does not even serve as a junction
between two thoroughfares of importance, but merely joins
Cattering Road to Boswell Gardens, both of which are fully as
dreary and useless as is Gatesend Road itself.

Down one side—the northern—of Gatesend Road are the
blank, decaying backs of gaunt buildings which used once to
be warehouses. Along the other side of Gatesend Road are
clumps of grey and hopeless and much be-stuccoed villas.
There are, to judge by the numbers, forty-nine of these ex-
crescences; but, to judge from curtains and other signs of
usage, only twenty-eight of these are occupied. It tells much

of Gatesend Road that even the inhabitants of that end of Fulham appear unwilling to live in it. In the daytime a few rickety and despairing children play in Gatesend Road, and by night many cats sport there. Throughout the day Gatesend Road does not, in normal times, see a policeman. During the night, however, the constable of B.J. Division, whose beat includes its dreariness, passes usually down its length twice and up its length once.

Since the first of July, Police Constable B.J. H 143 Edgar Roberts, had patrolled the night beat, which included Gatesend Road. Until upon this night of the 12th of August, Police Constable Roberts had received certain orders. He did not understand them. He was pleased, nevertheless, for they were to the effect that upon no account was he to make his usual three or four rounds of Gatesend Road, Cattering Road, and Boswell Gardens. By a curious coincidence, genuine enough, not one of the officers who operated from the two police stations in the Fulham Road had seen the edition of the *Daily Banner,* which included the salute to that "King of Coppers," P.C. Biggleswade. Had Constable Roberts done so, he would have been even more puzzled by his orders than he actually was. For there was not, and never had been, a constable in Fulham of the name of Ernest Biggleswade.

The grey, sultry day turned to a starless, stifling night. Along the drab length of Gatesend Road, four dusty street lamps made pathetic effort to dispel darkness. In some of the twenty-eight occupied houses lights appeared. Upon the other side of the road the blank walls of the warehouse backs loomed uncouth.

A black-and-white half-Persian cat, of feminine persuasion, walked slowly down the middle of the narrow roadway. A virile acquaintance came in hot pursuit, only to find, embarrassingly, that he was not first upon the field. The night was assaulted with sound. A window in No. 3 was flung open, and from it came, in rapid succession, two lumps of coal and a round gallon of water. Gatesend Road was silent once more.

The chimes of the clock of St. Barnabas's Church sounded ten. Only two windows in Gatesend Road remained lighted. The clock chimed eleven and Gatesend Road, save for those ineffectual lamps, was dark.

At the southwest corner of Boswell Gardens a taxi pulled up. There descended from it not only two strangely assorted passengers, but also the driver himself.

The driver was a burly person with battered face and oily, bedraggled dustcoat. The passengers were a policeman of truly giant proportions, who carried his helmet under his arm and exhibited, by nervous fingerings, a certain apprehension regarding a beautiful, spiked moustache, and a man of middle height but distinctive breadth of shoulder clad in trousers of dark grey flannel, an ancient coat of dark blue flannel, and a cap pulled down over his right eye.

The policeman helmeted himself. The man in the cap walked round him as an orderly officer round a sentry suspect of slovenliness.

The man in the cap spoke to the driver.

"Pass him?"

The driver made circular inspection. He nodded solemnly. "Anywheres," he said.

The man in the cap spoke to the policeman.

"First on the right," he said. "Second left."

"I know," said the policeman. "Well, cheeroh!"

"We'll be about," said the man in the cap.

"Ah," said the driver.

3

Hector Frensham had told his men that he would not leave the Yard for the seventy-two hours of the grace. He did not leave the Yard, and so a small mountain came to Mahomet and Jane sat in one of the big leather chairs in the high room looking out over the river.

Father and daughter were silent. Hector Frensham, huddled at his table, looked a man ten years older than the sixty-five he was. Jane, her frock a splash of vivid colour in the sombre room, was unwontedly pale. There was a deep frown drawing together the fine, high-arched, black brows above the blue eyes. And there were lines about her mouth which had no business to be there. Every now and then the abstracted look would leave her eyes, and these would send a glance of compassion and solicitude towards the bent figure of her father.

Once Hector Frensham looked up from the papers which his eyes were apparently studying, but which he was not reading, to catch sight of his daughter at a moment when small white teeth were savagely biting at her upper lip as she strove to force back to their source the tears which stung her eyes.

Hector Frensham rose. He came out from behind his table

and crossed the room and stood beside his daughter's chair and laid a hand upon her shoulder.

"He'll be all right," he said.

Jane did not look up. She said, in a voice so studiously without feeling as to show the extent of the strain which she was bearing:

"Why did you let him and . . . the other . . . why ever did you let them try this on their own?"

Her father's hand tightened its clasp on her shoulder.

"They wouldn't tell me—or, rather, Revel wouldn't—until I'd given my word. Christopher backed him up. Don't worry, old thing. If ever I saw a couple able to look after themselves . . ."

"Don't worry!" said Jane. "Don't worry! How *can* you talk like that; it's—*silly!*"

Hector Frensham went back to the chair behind his writing table. He sat heavily. His eyes stared at the small clock beside his inkstand.

That clock haunted him. Its hour hand went inexorably round and round. Of his seventy-two hours, how many were left?

4

The clock of St. Barnabas's Church tolled a tale of midnight. There were no lights except the street lamps in Gatesend Road. Down the southern pavement came, walking with a pontific deliberation if anything slightly overdone, a giant in the uniform of the Metropolitan Constabulary. Readers of the *Daily Banner,* catching sight of this figure as it passed through one of the dingy islands of light cast by the street lamps, would have had small difficulty, despite the badness of his photograph, in recognizing Constable Ernest Biggleswade.

Having paced the length of the northern pavement, through the shadows of the frowning, derelict warehouses, Constable Biggleswade, instead of passing out into Cattering Road, crossed to the other side of Gatesend Road itself, stood a moment under the first of the lamps, looked about him this way and that with a challenging tilt to his head and a proud hand at his mustachios, and then, still pontific, went back along Gatesend Road, this time along the southern and inhabited side.

In what its designers had presumably intended for the garden of No. 27 Gatesend Road crouched the man in a cap and the taxi driver. A low wall hid them from anyone passing along the pavement. Beneath their rubber-soled shoes was dingy, weed-sprouting gravel; behind them the front of No. 27, drear and uninhabited, with scarce a square inch of glass unbroken in any of its panes, leered like a blousy drab who apes respectability.

Past them, upon the other side of the wall, slow and stately, went the giant helmeted figure. It did not show by so much as a twitch of the head that it knew they were there.

"Good boy!" said the taxi driver beneath his breath.

"Quiet!" said the man in the cap.

Utter silence, not even broken now by occasional far-off traffic in the Fulham and King's roads, reigned in Gatesend Road.

The taxi driver muttered to himself. He did not like Gatesend Road. He did not particularly like the work they were on, for already he had conceived for the man who paraded as Constable Biggleswade a personal admiration to add to that impersonal liking which all the world had for the man it called, foolishly enough, Sudden Vayle.

The uniformed figure reached the far end of Gatesend Road. Once more it stood beneath a lamp and preened itself. Soon it began to retrace its steps, this time upon the northern side once more.

Opposite No. 27 was the third of the street lamps. Behind the wall of No. 27 the man in the cap rose silent and cautious. He looked this way and that along Gatesend Road. His friends often said of him that he had eyes like a cat's. Now they strained themselves to the utmost of their capability for penetrating darkness.

The soles of the uniformed boots were shod with rubber and made no sound, so that the man in the cap saw the great figure of his colleague before he heard it. It came slow and majestic into the dim pool of lamplight opposite No. 27. It was upon the pavement which ran, a bare four feet wide, beneath the frowning walls of the warehouses.

To the ears of the man in the cap came the hoarse whisper of his companion the driver.

"Nothing doing tonight!" said the whisper.

The man in the cap did not speak. He kicked outwards and backwards, and a squeaking, stifled grunt came from the recipient of the kick.

Opposite, the giant blue-clad figure was nearly out of the pool of dusty yellow light. It moved silently.

Then came a sound in Gatesend Road. A small sound

which would in daytime have been no sound at all but which, cracking the hot stillness of the night, magnified itself tenfold. A clanging metallic sound, as of iron being drawn across stone.

The man in the cap started and thrust forward his neck in endeavour to see.

He knew what the sound was: the sound was that of a slight moving of the iron cover of one of the manholes which studded the northern pavement.

For an infinitesimal moment of time the man in the cap smiled at his own nervousness, telling himself that a foot in a uniformed boot had trodden on a loose plate.

And then, as a thought came to him, the smile went. In a flash he was erect and had vaulted the low wall and was halfway across the road. As he ran he shouted.

"Look out, man!" he shouted. "Jump!"

The big, blue-clad figure, only just within the outermost edge of the pool of light, seemed to stumble, pulled itself erect with a curious kicking gesture of its left leg, and leaped sideways and outwards into the roadway.

For an instant the man in the cap saw something which any with lesser powers of vision could not have seen. On the pavement just beyond the spot from which the uniformed figure had leaped, and just beyond the edge of the pool of light, was a hole. A round hole in the surface of the paving. A hole which should have had over it an iron plate almost as dark as itself. A hole coming out through which the man in the cap had seen for a flash of time a hand and part of an arm.

5

There was a small wooden door recessed in the wall of the warehouse close by the uncovered manhole. At this door there was discharged the combined weight—some twenty-six stone —of Christopher Vayle, now helmetless and moustacheless, and Mr. Joseph Palmer. The quiet of Gatesend Road was shattered by the sound of cracking, tearing wood, followed by a clap like stage thunder as the door fell inwards, its assaulters atop of it.

"Come on!" came the voice of Christopher Vayle, made echoing and hollow by the barn-like place in which he was now scrambling to his feet.

But in the roadway stood Nicholas Revel. To his ears

came, following the shout, the sound of heavy feet thudding upon boards as his two comrades began their search.

Nicholas Revel looked this way and that, with quick darting movements of his head, along Gatesend Road. He seemed to be calculating. His calculation was quick. He turned to his right and ran, at a pace which would have put to shame many an avowed sprinter, towards Boswell Gardens. He did not once look behind him.

A tall man in dark clothes turned into the top end of Boswell Gardens. He was walking fast. Anyone close enough to him could have told by his breathing that here was a man in fear or haste or both, but could have seen from his bearing that here was a man most desperately anxious to appear placid. At the southwest corner of Boswell Gardens he was met by a taxi which slacked at the sight of him, its driver, a cap pulled down over his his right eye, leaning from his seat in silent solicitation.

With a jerky gesture the man in dark clothes hailed the cab. He came up to it as it halted and opened its door. The driver, without turning his head, inclined an ear. A husky voice, curiously high-pitched, gave directions.

"Alsace Hotel," said the voice.

The cab door slammed. The taxi chugged away. Boswell Gardens was quiet.

Gatesend Road was not quiet.

Chapter XXVI
FELO DE SE

Two limousines, a taxi of age sandwiched between them, held up the scattered late traffic of the Strand while they turned in a thin stream into the covered courtyard of the Alsace. The first limousine, having halted arrogant before the swing doors of the hotel and discharged a cargo of platinum blondes, swooped magnificent away. The old taxi chugged itself to a standstill. A tall man in dark clothes got out of it, slipped three half-crowns into the driver's hand, and was m'lled into bright warmth by the whirling door of glittering glass and bronze.

The taxi driver craned out of his cab to look after his vanished passenger. With a sudden jerk he straightened himself in his seat, drove the taxi in a semicircle, stopped it, vaulted over its door, and went himself to the whirling doors.

2

Mons. Polidor was bothered. He kept looking at the card which this persistent man, who the porters had told him was undeniably a taxi driver, had thrust beneath his nose.

It was not that Mons. Polidor was ignorant of such cards, for he had, on his private files, a facsimile supplied to him by Scotland Yard itself; it was that Mons. Polidor was cautious.

Nicholas Revel still smiled, but there was something behind the smile which made Mons. Polidor feel that he must not waste time in making up his mind and making it up in the way required by the smiler. Mons. Polidor raised narrow shoulders almost to a level with his ears.

"Number 248," said Mons. Polidor. "Name—John Summerlees. Fourth floor suite. . . . I hope. . . . I hope there will be no trouble."

"Trouble!" said Nicholas Revel. "Of course not!"

A lift boy, spurred into speedy but nevertheless astonished celerity by personal orders to convey what seemed like a cab-door-holder to Number 248 without delay, lost no time.

Outside the door of No. 248, Nicholas Revel halted. He rolled up the cap which he had in his hand and thrust it into a jacket pocket. For a moment his hand went behind him and patted at a hip pocket. The lift boy stood his ground. Mr. Revel smiled at him.

"That'll do;" said Mr. Revel, and the lift boy went, albeit upon reluctant feet.

Mr. Revel tapped upon the door of Number 248.

There was no answer.

Mr. Revel knocked again, louder.

Still no answer.

Mr. Revel tried the door. It was locked.

Mr. Revel knocked very loudly and immediately put his ear to a panel. After a moment he straightened and waited.

The door opened a bare half-inch. Before it opened Mr. Revel, imperceptibly in detail yet most patently in general effect, became changed from the equal of anyone to a servant of many. The expression upon his face, the carriage of his body, the very set of his hair—through which he had momentarily brushed his fingers—all seemed to shout aloud that here was nothing more than a respectable working man of the class known as "skilled."

He spoke to an eye which looked round the corner of the barely opened door. He touched his forelock.

"Beggin' y'r pardon, sir," he said. "They've sent me up to look at the fuse box."

"Fuse box! There's no fuse box here." The voice was harsh and curiously high-pitched.

"Beggin' y'r pardon, sir," said the new Nicholas Revel, respectful but firm. "Beggin' y'r pardon, sir, but there is. You wouldn't know it, maybe, but the box for this floor and half Number Three is in a cupboard just behind your bath."

The door was pulled wide with a sudden jerking movement.

"Come in," said the high-pitched voice. There was a petulant ring to the tone.

Nicholas Revel put a finger to his forehead. He crossed the threshold and softly closed the door behind him. He turned to see the man that Mons. Polidor had called Summerlees walking away from him and into the sitting room which opened off the little entrance hall of the suite.

Noiseless, Nicholas followed. The sitting-room door, like the outer door, he pulled to behind him, but this door he did not shut quietly. The tall figure of the man called Summerlees, who had had his back to the door, whipped round on the instant.

"What the devil——" began the odd voice, this time with a new note in it—a note of fear.

Nicholas Revel was no longer the artisan. That subtle but infinite change had passed over him again, this time in the reversed way. He leant back against the door and looked across the efficiently charming room at the man who was the present occupant.

"Game's up," said Nicholas laconically. "Coming quietly?"

The man called Summerlees crouched like an animal at bay waiting to turn the cringing of defeat into the spring of attack.

Nicholas studied him. He saw a lean and tall and well-nough shaped man of perhaps forty-five years with, atop of an excellent body, a head which was curiously small. The face was dark with a permanent tan and pleasant enough save for over-sharp features and close-set eyes. The mouth was long-lipped and mobile—in ordinary circumstance, no doubt, a comfortable and ordinary and unnotable face; but now, with its eyes wide, a mask of rage and terror. The mouth distorted with the lips drawn back from irregular teeth, and the skin of the whole face twitching with some nervous reaction—a sight as far from pleasing as it was from the ordinary.

Nicholas Revel stood in silence, while the man mouthed. Before coherent words came there were many unpleasing sounds.

"Who are you?" came words at last; and now the voice was no longer high-pitched, but guttural and thick and animal.

"C.I.D.," said Nicholas Revel, with a brisk and altogether convincing mendacity.

The man straightened. It seemed as if his body were jerked upright by a hidden spring. He put back his head, suddenly wolf-like in the soft light, and bayed with a sound which might have been meant for laughter.

The noise went on. Nicholas Revel came away from the door across the room and stood close to his man.

"Ready?" he said.

The baying ceased. With another sudden movement, more inhumanly jerky than the first had been, the man once more crouched. His mouth worked silently. His wide, crazed eyes asked a question.

His visitor was laconic. "Murder of several policemen," he said.

Speech came back to the other man. His mouth opened and words poured from him.

"You've got nothing! . . . You've got nothing! . . . You're guessing . . . making a shot in the dark! . . . You can't know . . . you *don't* knoⱱ . I say you can't know. . . . I say you can't know. There is nothing against me, nothing . . . nothing. . . . Nothing against me, I say."

His visitor yawned. "Coming along?" he said.

"Damn you! No!" The voice was a weird bubbling scream. "Where's your warrant? Where's your warrant? You may guess, but you don't know, you can't know. I'm not mad! I'm not mad! I know you can't know, there's nothing for you to know by. Get out of here. Get out of here, I say!"

"Enough of that," said Nicholas Revel in the same flat, disinterested voice. "We don't want any trouble here!"

With a backward leap, incredible in its neatness and agility, the other increased his distance. His right hand fumbled for a moment inside his dark coat of impeccable cut.

It came away holding something which gleamed with the dull blue gleam of gunmetal.

"Get out of here!" he screamed. "Get out of here. Or, by God, clothes or no clothes, I'll kill you!"

Nicholas Revel, his hands palms forward raised to a level with his shoulders, backed slowly. He backed, not directly towards the door, but diagonally. He bumped with considerable awkwardness against the low bookcase which ran along the wall from door to window.

But with this bump any awkwardness in his movements ceased. Upon the top of the bookcase stood a pair of heavy-wrought brass candlesticks. The fingers of his right hand closed about the first of these. It sailed in a swift, terrific arc through the air. Its loaded base struck the crouching man just below the juncture of the breast bone. He gave a curious choking cough and pitched forward. The pistol flew from his hand.

With a spring like a giant cat's, Nicholas Revel was upon the pistol.

The man on the floor gasped and choked and began to raise himself. He found himself face to face with this visitor who was no electrician.

In the visitor's hand was something which was jammed against his left breast. He coughed again and tried to twist away from the thing which hurt him. Nicholas Revel's forefinger tightened on the trigger. There was a dull crack like the sound of a giant whip, and the heavy acrid smell. On the floor, something which had just now been a man gave one convulsive shudder, twisted, and lay still.

Nicholas Revel straightened. For a moment he stood looking down at the body. His mouth twisted, and once he shook his head.

"Quicker," he said to himself. "He was right. No proof."

He took a handkerchief and put into it the little gun and rubbed it briskly all over. Holding the muzzle in the handkerchief, he pressed the butt into the fingers of the dead right hand. He stood up and, his head on one side, surveyed his handiwork. He stiffened suddenly and cocked his head as if listening. From somewhere, muffled by the two closed doors behind him, there came a sound of agitated voices and a hum of movement. He stood in the middle of the room and looked about him with quick darting glances. His eye was caught by something upon the writing table.

He was at the table in a stride and holding in his hands

a black-bound book with a clasp and a lock from which protruded the tiny haft of a silver key.

Groping out behind him with his right foot, Nicholas Revel found a chair and hitched it towards him and sat in it. He opened the book. He had not read more than a half of one of its centre pages before he reached for the telephone. From the outer door of the suite came a thunderous knocking and excited cries.

"Number, please?" said the telephone.

"Get me Scotland Yard!" said Nicholas Revel.

Epilogue
POSTSCRIPT IN A POSTBAG

EXTRACT FROM REPORT BY INSPECTOR D. JARVIS OF X.L. DIVISION METROPOLITAN POLICE

Burglary at Magersfontein House, Brale Street.

A call was received at No. 2 Station at 10:30 p.m. from Mr. Julius Lagerstrom, the owner of the above house. Sergeant Denny proceeded there at once, accompanied by plain-clothes constables 8746 J. Parsons and 8349 T. Woolscombe. Mr. Lagerstrom had returned from the country at 10:15 p.m. bringing with him a manservant and two maidservants. Magersfontein House had been in the hands of the usual caretakers—old and trusted employees of Mr. Lagerstrom—while the family had been away. On his return, Mr. Lagerstrom discovered that his study on the second floor (see plan) had been rifled. Two extremely valuable pictures had been taken, together with money and documents from his safe, which had been cut open with an oxy-acetylene outfit. (A list of the things stolen is appended at A. It will be noticed that Mr. Lagerstrom has not given a very clear description of the documents up to the present stage.) The caretakers had been in the house, they stated, the whole time. They occupy rooms in the basement. They had heard nothing, although once or twice during the evening they had been up to the ground floor. Further report from Sergeant Denny is attached. It will be seen from this that up to the present nothing tangible has been found to work on. (*Note:* Brale Street has been under double patrol day and night during the recent crisis. The double patrols, however, were removed after the death of Summerlees and Brale Street once more put back as part of the ordinary sectional beat.)

2

MEMO. FROM SUPERINTENDENT CONNOR TO CHIEF COMMISSIONER OF POLICE

21st October, 193—

Strictly private and confidential.

Further to our discussion yesterday *re* Revel, I send you herewith the file I have compiled. You will see that although there is a lot of material, you were correct in saying that no conclusion whatsoever could be drawn from it. As you know I at one time entertained the idea that Revel might be X and that was what first induced me to have the work done which resulted in the file. Although it soon became clear that Revel was not X, the inquiries tended to my mind to point to the fact that *if* we could find anything out about Revel we should be glad to know it. I repeat what I said to you: namely, that no one could be so *negative* as Revel if he were genuine. I hope that these remarks together with the study of the file will convince you that I was not acting beyond my duty. The principal heads of my suspicions of Revel—not as X but as a person in whom we might be interested—were: (1) the way in which the sources of his money are concealed; (2) the fact that he would seem—although it is impossible to prove this—to be associated in some way with the taxi driver Palmer (against whom I must admit we have nothing concrete); (3) the mysterious origin of his unusual car; *and* (4) his interest in the catching of X. I cannot help thinking that, in some way or other, the extra policing of London militated against Revel and that this was the reason for his undoubtedly brilliant work in the matter of X. I would call your attention, in this respect, to this morning's report, in which you will find an account of the clean-up at Lagerstrom's. I have Battle and four of his best men on this and should not be surprised if we found at least some confirmation of my theory.

If it is considered that I have in any way exceeded my duties in the matter of Revel I should be glad to tender my resignation forthwith.

(Signed) P. CONNOR, Superintendent.

P.S.—Word has just come in which I have communicated to your secretary on the phone that Lagerstrom has stated to Battle that should an arrest be made in connection wih the burglary he will not prosecute. He gives no reason. Battle tells me, privately, that he has heard from Craddock of the *Morning Herald* that Lagerstrom has received a letter stating that his property can be returned to him if he is willing to pay. That is all Craddock knows and our men are powerless. We cannot force Lagerstrom's hand. It looks as if we should have to drop work on this.

3

MEMO. FROM THE CHIEF COMMISSIONER OF POLICE TO SUPERINTENDENT CONNOR

21st October, 193—

Strictly private and confidential.

I have your memo for today enclosing the file of Nicholas Revel. I note your remarks. I do not consider that you exceeded your duty, but I feel that you have allowed a natural enough suspicion, bred in extraordinary circumstances, to become an *idée fixe*. In view of your postscript in regard to the Lagerstrom affair I hope that you will now cease to see Revel in every job that comes along. Please close the file and do not waste time. If, in any eventuality, there should prove to be any basis for your suspicions it will surely come up in the ordinary way.

(Signed) HECTOR FRENSHAM.
Commissioner of Police

4

LETTER FROM SIR HECTOR FRENSHAM TO NICHOLAS REVEL

23rd October, 193—

MY DEAR REVEL:

I am sending you, with this, an official letter from the Home Secretary thanking you for the immense service you have done to the police in particular and the country in general. If you have seen the papers you will notice that your request not to have any mention of yourself made to the public has been acceded to. You will also see, from the Home Secretary's letter that there is some wonder in official circles as to what form of recognition, if any, you would like. I have told the Home Secretary that you require none, but I suppose he wishes to hear it from your own lips or pen.

I also enclose a copy of a document which I think may prove of extreme interest to you: namely, the diary of the man we knew as X but whose name was John Summerlees. It explains itself. Of course, he was mad, and I suppose that I should feel sorry for him. For a mentality never very stable to have such a series of unfortunate clashes with the police, beginning at a very early age with the seduction by a police sergeant of what the press have insisted on calling a "girl-wife," was, I suppose, too much. By the way, you will notice that the seduction occurred in Farnley in Surrey. You were right all along the line, even about this. You will doubtless remember saying, in my room at Scotland House, that you thought Farnley might be the origin of the trouble and that this was why the first murder and that only was committed there.

I am exceedingly sorry that you have had to go away at this juncture. I should very much like to have seen you again and hope to do so on your return. I am addressing this to your solicitors who, I understand, will see that it gets to you at some point of your tour.

You must know what I personally feel about this matter. It is impossible to put those feelings into writing, and I will therefore wait until such time as I see you, which I hope will be soon.

> Yours very sincerely,
> HECTOR FRENSHAM.

P.S.—Don't fail to let me know immediately on your return.

5

LETTER FROM MR NICHOLAS REVEL TO LADY VAYLE

15th November, 193—

MY DEAR JANE:

By the time you get this you will no longer be Miss Frensham. May I offer my congratulations? In spite of what I may have said in the past, before I got to know your husband, these congratulations are perfectly sincere. I can only hope that when I return to England you will have settled down sufficiently to be at least aware of your obligations.

I am having sent to you a small gift. It is a statuette. *It is real bronze* throughout. Your husband has already made its acquaintance, and I can only hope that he will like it as much as I feel that you will.

As I told Sir Hector when I wrote to him, it will, I'm afraid, be some time before I am back in London. I am in excellent health here, but have a feeling that London air might not prove healthy for me just for a while. It is wiser anyhow, I feel, to stay away a little longer.

With all affection and respect,
  I remain, my dear Lady Vayle,
    Yours very sincerely,
      NICHOLAS REVEL.